KC Mills Presents

The Young and the Reckless

2:

A Baltimore Love Story

By: Hershé Wrights

THE WRIGHT LIFE

PRESENTS AUTHORESS

Hershé Wright

Text SUPREMEWORKS to 22828 to join our mailing list.

Interested in joining our team? Email submissions

to: supremeworkspublications@gmail.com

Previously in The Young and The

Reckless: A Baltimore Love Story

Tiran

"I thought you said that you got off at 7 p.m. today," I quizzed as I glanced at my clock.

"I was supposed to but some guy named Seven promised to pay me extra cash if I stayed here until closing so that he could pick up his car," Khia explained through the phone.

"Hold up. Did you just say Seven?" I emphasized as I turned the volume up on my phone. There weren't a lot of Seven's floating around in Baltimore City with enough money to purchase a Mercedes-Benz, so it had to be pure luck that the Seven I was referring to chose to do business with Khia's dealership of all places.

"Yeah. Why?" she answered as she switched the phone over to her other ear.

"How do you know him?" I fussed.

"I don't! I just know his brother Omari," she clarified.

"What exact time did he say he was coming to pick up his car?" I interrogated as I made a mental note of all the information she was sharing.

"9 p.m.," she replied into the receiver.

"You say that you love me right?" I coaxed as the wheels in my head began to turn. "Yeah, why?"

"I need you to do me a favor."

"Is it going to cause me to lose my job?" she whined.

"No. I wouldn't ask you to do anything to jeopardize your job," I lied.

"Well what do you need me to do then?" she asked with uncertainty.

"I need you to text my phone as soon as he gets there and stall him until I give you the green light that it is okay for him to leave," I instructed as I simultaneously sent Maycen a text letting him know that I had a plan on how to get Seven.

"Tiran, is something going on between you two?" she asked, fishing for information. "I don't want to be caught up in anyone's beef if there is," she declared.

"Babe, why would I put you in harm's way? I love you too much to let anything happen to you. I just want to talk to the dude. I've been trying to catch up with him about some money that he owes me from a business deal, and he's been ducking me out. I was going to use that money to pay off our trip. You do want to go to Jamaica, don't you?" I cajoled with a sinister grin spread across my face.

"I do, but not if it's going to cost me my life," she voiced.

"Khia are you going to help me out or not?" I huffed through the phone.

"I...I want to but—"

"You know what? Don't worry about it," I sneered, cutting her off. "Whenever you need extra money to handle your business I don't ask you nine million questions, so I don't see what the problem is. This is why I'd rather be by myself because bitches are always one-sided."

"Fine! I'll do it," she yelled through the phone. Khia's ass was so green that she didn't even realize that she was going to help me set Seven up.

"Good! Now that's what I like to hear," I coached. "I have to run and go take care of something before he gets there, but make sure you don't forget to text me. I promise that as soon as I get the money we are going to hop on the next thing smoking for a mini vacation in the islands."

"I hope so because I definitely need it!"

"I have to go; that's my aunt on the other line. Don't forget what I said," I stated before ending the call. Seven had no idea what Maycen and I had in store for him in the next few hours. I just hoped that everything went according to plan.

<u>Harlow</u>

"Good morning beautiful," Seven greeted as soon as I walked into the kitchen.

"Good morning baby," I cooed as I shuffled over to where he stood and kissed him with my morning breath.

"Pewww! Your breath is jamming," he joked as he fanned his nose.

"My breath does not stink," I defended as I blew into my hands to test it.

"Lies!"

"Okay! Okay! I'm going to go brush my teeth," I stated as I backpedaled out of the kitchen and proceeded into the bathroom.

Seven minutes later, I returned into the kitchen to find Seven rummaging through the refrigerator. "Honey, what are you looking for?"

"Something to eat; I'm starving," he responded as he

shifted the Tupperware containers around on the shelves.

"What do you have a taste for Big Daddy?" I purred as I washed my hands, preparing to cook him a hot meal.

"I want breakfast, but we don't have any eggs or bacon," he informed.

"How don't we? I just went to the market three days ago and brought two cartons," I commented confused.

"You know Omari was over here yesterday. That boy will always eat you out of a house and home," he reminded as he closed the refrigerator.

"Unbelievable," I stated while shaking my head. "Well I'm going to run to the store real quick to grab some eggs and bacon. Can you keep an eye on Charli? She's still sleep in her room.

"Of course I will. You going to the store like that?" he quizzed as he observed me grabbing my car keys off the hook and sliding my Adidas flip-flops on.

"Yeah. I'm only going to the store."

"Well make sure you hurry your ass back because a nigga is hungry," he instructed.

Walking out the door, I frowned when I saw an unknown car blocking my path out of the driveway.

"Seven!" I yelled, frustrated that there was no way to maneuver around the car without hitting it. When Seven didn't respond, I blew out a hot breath and returned back inside of the house, pissed.

"Back so soon," he stated as a mischievous grin formed on his face.

"You didn't hear me calling you?"

"No. What was wrong?"

"It's a car blocking me in, preventing me from going to the store," I complained.

"Well move it then."

"How smart ass?" I hissed as I picked up my flip-flop and threw it at him.

"Duh! With these," he said as he presented me with a set of keys.

"Seven whose car is that?" I questioned, wide-eyed.

"Do you remember the bet we had a couple of years ago?" he asked, ignoring my question.

"Which bet? We've had so many," I joked as I took a seat on the ottoman.

"The bet we made at the football game."

"I remember the bet, but I don't remember what the prize was."

"I bet you that if my team won you had to be my girlfriend and if your sorry ass team won, I had to put up half the cost for your daycare," he recited as he reached in his pocket and pulled out a folded up piece of paper.

"Oh yeah! I remember," I recounted.

"Here," he stated, handing me the paper.

"What's this?"

"Open it and see," he instructed. Unfolding the small piece of paper, I almost passed out as I analyzed what it read.

"Oh my God! Seven, what the fuck?" I shouted, jumping up and down. I couldn't even contain my excitement as I examined the check for over one hundred and fifty thousand dollars. "Are you serious?"

"Harlow, I love you more than you ever could imagine. I told you from the beginning that I was going to make you my queen and this here is the foundation for you to live out your dream," he confirmed.

"Thank you! I love you so much," I beamed as I ran and jumped into his arms.

"Aren't you forgetting something?" he hinted.

"What, you want me to suck your dick?" I asked confused.

"Yeah, that too," he laughed. "No, but seriously, you're forgetting to check out your new car."

"I almost forgot," I squealed as I jumped down from his arms and took off running outside. "You got me a Benz!" I gasped as I marveled at my new set of wheels. I couldn't wait to take my car for a spin. "I'll be right back," I exclaimed while opening the door and climbing in the front seat. "I'm about to cruise the city and stunt on these hoes real quick."

"Just make sure you don't forget to bring me and the kids back something to eat. I had to throw away all the food you brought just so that I could have an excuse for you to go to the store," he confessed as he threw his head back in laughter.

"You are so stupid," I stated as I poked my head out of the window and joined in. "You really had me fooled. I'm going to have to pay extra attention to your sneaky ass from now on," I teased before I started my truck up and proceeded to back out of the driveway.

"Ugh! I hate breaking a new car in," I muttered as soon as I got around the corner. I guess I was used to driving my beat up Acura because everything in my new Benz felt funny, from the tires to the steering wheel. It definitely was going to take some getting used to being as though I never drove a big body truck before. I wasn't complaining though because my boo went out of his way to surprise me with this exclusive car and I was going to do my best to show him how much he meant to me.

Instead of driving to the local supermarket around the corner from our house, I decided to make a special trip across town to Wegmans to pick up something nice so that I could prepare a big, fancy breakfast for my king. Since it was still early in the morning, the roads were clear of drivers, making the typical thirty minute drive easy for me. Mashing my foot on the gas, I hopped on the highway and sped the majority of the way there.

"What the hell!" I yelled.

Maycen

10 hours earlier ...

"So you're saying that he's in there right now?" I questioned as Tiran peered across the street through a pair of binoculars. We've been parked a few feet from the dealership for the last twenty minutes, waiting for Seven to drive off in his new car.

"Yeah, I'm looking at him right now," Tiran replied while zooming in with his spy gear.

"So what's the plan? You haven't said anything about your bright idea since we've been here."

"I was thinking that since Seven pretty much fell into our lap that we should follow him home and decide what to do from there. My cousin loaned me his gun just in case you wanted to ambush him and hold him hostage," he offered as he hunched down in his seat.

"Text Khia and see how much longer he's going to be there

because I have to pee," I instructed as I shook my leg to alleviate the urge to use the bathroom. Tiran quickly pulled out his phone to send the message.

Tiran: Are you almost done?
Khia: Yes. He should be out within the next five minutes.
Tiran: Got it. Thanks again my ride or die. I love you!
Khia: I love you too!

"What she say?" I asked, wanting to know what the holdup was.

"She said that he should be coming out in the next five minutes." Ten minutes went by before a person appeared to be walking towards a shiny white truck. "That's him right there," Tiran stated as he dimmed his headlights and discreetly started up the car.

"Wait a few seconds until after he pulls off and make sure that you keep at least a five car distance between you and him at all times. My uncle trained him well, so I already know that he's going to be hip to our plan if he sees anything out the ordinary," I warned.

Following my instructions to a tee, Tiran kept his distance as we tailed Seven all the way to his house without being detected.

"Now what?" he asked as he parked the car farther down the street but still within view of Seven's house.

"We sit and wait for an opportunity to present itself," I schooled.

"Maycen, we don't have a lot of time. Who's to say that he's even going to be home that long?" he reasoned.

"Well do you have any suggestions then?"

"Actually I do. I know something that we can do that's quick and easy," Tiran revealed before pulling out a cigarette.

"When in the hell did you start smoking?" I asked, surprised that my friend developed a nasty habit.

"Long story," he paused. "But what was I saying? Oh yeah! How about we cut the brake line to his brand new car so when he goes to accelerate it he won't be able to stop," he theorized. "It'll take all of thirty seconds to do the job and is guaranteed to cause some serious damage to him and his precious vehicle. He'll either die or end up paralyzed in somebody's hospital."

"That idea may actually work. When did you think of that?"

"Just now. I remember seeing it on the television before. A woman caught her husband cheating and she tried to kill him so that she could collect the insurance policy. It worked too," he stated as he recollected the events that transpired on the show.

"So how are we going to do this? Both of us can't go down there. We'll stick out like a sore thumb," I challenged.

"I'll go. He'll probably spot you before he does me. Just make sure you watch my back," he stated before flicking the bud of the cigarette to the ground and lowering his fitted cap over his eyes.

The street lights sparsely illuminated the pitch black sky as Tiran slowly crept down the street towards Seven's secluded house. The neighborhood was calm and quiet with not a single person roaming the streets. The only noise that could be heard was the sound of crickets chirping in the distance. Tiran was only a few feet away from his target before he hid behind a massive tree, waiting for my signal that the coast was clear for him to execute his plan. I held my breath as I closely watched his every move. Waving my hand in the sky quickly, I signaled for him to continue on.

"Steady. Steady," I whispered as I observed him crouching down low so that he could crawl under the truck.

In one fast motion, he slid under the front bumper and placed his hands up to slash the brake line with a box cutter that he usually carried in his car. Seconds later, he reemerged from under the car and rolled a few inches before he finally was on his feet again. Tip-toeing, Tiran crept back down the street unnoticed to where we were parked.

"It's done," he panted as soon as he jumped in the car.

"Let's go!" I ordered as I slammed my hand against the steering wheel, indicating that we needed to get the hell out of there.

For the rest of the car ride I remained silent as I thought of the possible outcomes of the crime that we'd just committed. To be honest, my adrenaline never stopped pumping until I was safely across town, pulling up in front of my house.

"That was some real stand up shit that you did back there," I acknowledged as I turned in my seat towards Tiran. "We can't tell nobody about what we just did. Not even Aunt Crys or my mother," I added.

"I'm not saying a word," he promised as he stuck his fist out for pound.

"And neither am I," I agreed as I dabbed him up. "Aight, now get some rest," I stated as I unlocked the passenger's door to exit. "We have a long day tomorrow."

Seven

The Present Time…

"I don't understand what is taking her so long to get back from the store," I mouthed to no one in particular. There was no use in calling her phone to find out her whereabouts because she rushed out of here so fast that she forgot to take it with her. I was starving and Harlow had yet to return back home with some groceries for us to eat. All we had left was two boxes of cereal on top of the cabinet and I was seconds away from saying fuck that eggs and bacon and pouring me a bowl. I'm pretty sure she was somewhere running around town with Logan, flossing in her whip. I swear to God though as soon as she stepped foot inside of this house I was going to choke her ass and then fuck her into a coma for making me wait so long to eat.

Propping my feet up on the table in the living room, I sat back and flipped through the channels until I found something interesting to watch. I was tired of watching the same basketball highlights over and over again on Sports Center and as soon as I changed the channel to the news station, my eyes were automatically glued to the television. Turning the volume up to the max, I couldn't believe what I saw as I looked on in fear.

"Hi, I'm Peggy O'Neal with breaking news coverage. I'm live on the scene of a crash where a young pregnant woman was pronounced dead and two others seriously injured following a car crash on interstate 695. Police have confirmed that the crash has killed the driver of the white Mercedes-Benz GLE 350 SUV. It happened sometime around 9:45 this morning going westbound on the highway near Exit 23. First responders quickly hurried to the scene and rushed the victims to the hospital by ambulance. There has been no update of the drivers of the 2012 Chevy Impala, however, officials say that the child of the young woman driving the Mercedes-Benz may survive the crash. Police and firefighters are still on the scene investigating the cause, but it appears that it wasn't accidental. According to a witness, it was said that the young woman tried to slam on her breaks but couldn't stop due to a punctured brake line. Any information as to who the victims are please call 555-654-8901."

As soon as the news reporter stepped aside to display the damage of the crash, my vision blacked out as I felt my breath leave my body.

Chapter 1

Omari

"You've reached Seven. I'm busy at the moment but if you leave your name and number, I'll be sure to hit you as soon as I become available. *BEEP*"

Seven's voicemail recited this same message for the tenth time and I was tired of hearing his corny greeting. "Answer the damn phone, it's important!" I yelled into the receiver clearly frustrated that my brother had yet to return my call. Once my message was successfully delivered, I pressed my finger on the red button on my iPhone and ended the call.

I had just seen Seven the other day and it slipped my mind to ask him about the details for our upcoming job. He and I were both partners of a lucrative car theft ring that was passed down to us by the late neighborhood legend "Buck" and thanks to him my brother and I became millionaires overnight. No job was too big or too small for us to take on and we had a solid team of workers that put their life on the line everyday so that we all could eat.

"I bet you he's digging into Harlow's guts right now," I said to myself as I slid my phone across the coffee table. It wasn't unheard of for my brother to place his phone on Do Not Disturb and go missing just so he and Harlow can have some uninterrupted, alone time.

"I know one thing for sure though, if he doesn't call me back before I finish this game of Madden I'm going to run inside his house and punch him dead in the eye." Harlow was my sis and all, but ain't no pussy on this earth worth the amount of money that Seven and I were about to make after this deal. Not Harlow's, not Sister Mary's, or Beyoncé's. Then again Beyoncé's might be worth it because the way the world worships her has me believing that thing is lined in gold.

Grabbing the remote off the couch, I pressed the power button and turned on the 64 inch flat screen television that sat inside of my plush living room. Flipping through the channels, I paused when an episode of *Law & Order: SVU* caught my eye. I was so tuned into the show that I completely forgot about playing Madden, giving Detective Stabler and Benson my undivided attention. Call me a hypocrite if you want but Benson and Stabler were some real OG's. They were the only officers that I respected in law enforcement and if I ever ran into them it would be free donuts on me. Just as I was about to get comfortable on my couch and watch a marathon of the series, my phone went off alerting me that I had an incoming text message.

Stranger: Hey handsome, it's me Candy. I met you in the club the other day. I was wondering could we do lunch today, if you're not busy.

Leaving the message left on read, I tried to rack my brain on who this Candy character was supposed to be. She claimed I met her in a club, but her name didn't ring a bell to me and that alone told me that she wasn't worth my time. Ever since Piper's shiesty ass tried to pin that baby on me a couple of years ago, it caused me to have a new outlook on women. No, I didn't believe that every woman I came in contact with was capable of doing me dirty, however I did think that majority of them were sneaky and had their own agendas. Until God tapped me on the shoulder and whispered in my ear that "she's the one", I was going to continue to drag my nuts on these whores and be emotionally unavailable.

Glancing at the time displayed on my cable box, I became even more agitated than I was before. I was so caught up into the show that I didn't even realize that it was going on one o'clock in the afternoon and there was still no response from my brother. Sighing, I got up from off of the couch and walked over to an outlet so that I could charge my phone. I hated the fact that I now had to make a drive all the way to West BumbleFuck just for some information but it was what it was. I wasn't the type of nigga to pop up at someone's house unannounced unless it had something to do with my money, my family, or my respect. Other than those three things, I tended to stay in my lane and do my own thing. On everything, Seven was going to have to hear my mouth for a week and I damn sure was going to remind him how irresponsible it was to have me waiting for pertinent information pertaining to our business.

After taking a quick shower and completing my hygiene, I slid on an Under Armor track suit and was headed out the door and in route to my brother's house to kick him in his shin for ignoring me. Jumping into my 2018 gray Audi RS 5, I adjusted my seat, placed Young Jezzy's mixtape on repeat, and sped off towards the direction of Seven's house.

Although it was only two o'clock in the afternoon, the streets were still crowded for it to be a Thursday. School buses and dirt bike riders both cluttered the road as I weaved through the lanes on a mission. I was only ten minutes away from Seven's mini mansion when my stomach forced me to take a detour so that I could grab something to eat. A nigga was starving, even though I just smashed the other half of the cheesesteak I got from the carry-out place last night. I don't know if it was my metabolism or a tapeworm but nothing seemed to satisfy my appetite. I needed to put something on my stomach fast though because I was almost positive that I would transform into the Incredible Hulk and I knew for a fact that Seven wouldn't feel like dealing with my hangry attitude.

Swerving my coupe into the right lane, I damn near hit an older woman who clearly wasn't paying attention to the traffic light as she attempted to cross the street. I thought New York pedestrians were bad, but once you drove in the slums of Baltimore a few times, you would begin to appreciate the regulation of New York foot traffic. As soon as I stopped at the light before me, my stomach began to rumble uncontrollably. *Do I want a corned beef sandwich or a chicken box?* I thought to myself as I sat impatiently waiting for the light to turn green. "Let me get a chicken box because I know Seven's greedy ass is going to try to DeeBo me for a wing," I mumbled to myself. "Matter of fact, I'mma get both. Ain't no telling what time I'mma leave Seven's spot and I know Sis ain't going to want to cook."

BEEPPPPPPP!

I was interrupted from my thoughts by the sound of an impatient driver's horn. "I don't care! Y'all gonna wait!" I shouted through the tinted window, even though the driver couldn't hear me. Adding insult to injury, I decide to be an ass as I slowly crept my car forward at a turtle's pace in search of a parking spot. I hated coming to the infamous Lexington Market because there was never any parking, but my taste buds craved a chicken box with salt, pepper, and ketchup and an ice cold half and half. As I peered through my rear-view mirror, it made me chuckle as I witnessed the angry driver yelling obscenities as I took my time maneuvering my car into the first open parking space. Placing my car in park, I quickly hopped out and offered the irate driver a smirk and a middle finger before I proceeded to the parking meter.

"Ayeee, my man! I got aahhh, I got some tickets right here for that, there pretty car," slurred an obnoxious junkie as he approached my coupe.

"Nah, I'm good slick," I stated as I walked away; attempting to dodge the scent of his foul body odor.

"All I want is, let's say two dollars and you can park your pretty car all day without worrying about them people," he proposed as he flashed me a toothless smile.

"I'll give you a quarter."

"A quarter? What the hell am I supposed to do with that? How about seventy-five cents," he countered.

"You're going to take this quarter or get the fuck out of my face. I'm not about to support your habit."

"Sold!" he yelled as he produced a balled up meter ticket from his pocket and handed it over to me.

"This shit better not be expired," I warned as I examined the once white parking pass. Satisfied with the accurate data printed on the paper, I gave the junkie a head nod and tossed him his fee.

As I walked over to my car, my stomach rumbled again reminding me the purpose of my pit stop. Placing a little more pep in my step, I quickly smoothed out the wrinkled piece of paper before opening my door and placing it onto my dashboard.

I pray it's not crowded in here today and hopefully them Koreans at Parks have some fresh chicken prepared because I

don't have time to wait for a fresh batch. If they don't have any
ready, then corn beef it'll be because never again will I eat that
raw cat them Asians served me the last time at the stand across
from them.

Walking inside of the establishment, I kept my fingers crossed as I made my way to the back towards Park's chicken stand.

"Hi. How can I help you?" the cashier greeted as she wrapped up the order of the previous customer.

Surveying the food in the glass window, I was relieved that the food god's saved me a few wings. "Let me get an order of four wings and fries with salt, pepper, and ketchup on the fries." Pointing to the glass display, I instructed exactly which wings I wanted because I'll be damned if Su Young tried to sell me some old shit. "Give me those two right there, this one and that one."

"Do you want drink?"

"Yeah. Give a jumbo half and half with a little bit of ice."

"That'll be $6.50," she advised before she walked away from the register to package up my food.

Moments later Su Young returned to the register holding the white carry-out bag that held my food and a large Styrofoam cup filled with tea and lemonade. "Got damn! Do you listen? I said a *little* bit of ice," I scoffed while examining the contents of the of the large cup.

"You said little. This little!" She fussed while moving her hands to each syllable she spoke.

Reaching into my pocket, I pulled out a ten dollar bill and threw it on the counter. "Keep the change," I stated before I grabbed my food and proceeded towards the doors that I entered from.

"Damn Americans," she muttered before turning her attention to the next customer.

As soon as I stepped foot outside of the building, I spotted several junkies surrounding my car and instantly became furious.

"Deodorant…Detergent…Soap! Two for ten or one for seven," yelled a scroungy middle-aged man as he walked up and down the strip.

Jogging towards my Audi, I hissed at the thought of me possibly having to lay one of these niggas down. No matter how many times I tried to count to ten to ease my temper, I couldn't erase the fact that I was hot-headed and a loose cannon.

"The fuck is going on!" I barked, while tossing the bag of food on the roof of my car.

"Your tire," replied an older dope fiend by the name of Skip.

"You caught a flat and I was gonna change it for you; hoping that you could spare a few bucks," hinted the older gentleman that sold me the parking pass earlier.

"Move out the way!" I demanded as I bent down to expect the damage. After close examination it appeared as though a nail punctured my tire and I was going to need a spare. "Fuck!" I yelled as I walked to the trunk of my car. I was hungry as hell and I seriously wasn't in the mood for this shit today.

As soon as I retrieved my tools and the spare from my trunk, I overheard the same man who was once selling deodorant and detergent now selling lug nuts.

These niggas is up to something. I thought to myself as I walked back over to the damaged tire and squatted down in front of it. The sun was beaming down hard on the back of neck; making the position I was kneeling in even more uncomfortable. Reaching for the hubcap, I successfully removed it with a screwdriver and gently placed it on the ground next to me; careful not to crack the rim. "Ain't this bout a bitch," I muttered under my breath as I quickly rose to my feet. Just as I suspected, these niggas was playing games. Canvassing the crowd, my eyes immediately fell on the man that I believed was the mastermind of this scheme. Discreetly moving through the small group of people that was gathered in front of the building, I slowly made my way over to the main culprit. He was so busy with trying to find his next target that he didn't see me sneak up behind him, until it was too late.

"Ah —!" he attempted to scream, but the pressure of my hands silenced his voice box.

"Run me my shit!" I growled as I tightened my grip around his neck.

"I don't... I don't have them. Oscar does!" He blurted out as he clawed at my fingers.

Diverting my attention up the street, I released the hold I had on the junkie's neck and walked off in search of Oscar.

"Lug nuts! Lug nut's y'allllllll!"

This nigga Oscar had some nerve to try and sell the lug nuts he stole from me only a few feet up the street. He could've at least had the decency to wait until I was out the area, but I guess when that monkey was on your back anything goes.

"How much you charging for two?" I asked, trying a different approach.

With goggley eyes, Oscar pondered for a second before responding. "Give me twenty dollars and you can have them both."

Reaching into my pocket I pretended to retrieve some cash; pulling a switch blade out instead. "If you don't want your intestines on this pavement I advise you to hand over my shit," I uttered through my clenched teeth. With his eyes wide as saucers, Oscar dropped the lug nuts on the ground and hauled ass in the opposite direction from where my car was parked. "Dumb ass," I grunted before I reached down and grabbed the lug nuts up off the ground and headed back down towards my car.

Twenty minutes and shirt full of sweat later, I was finally finished changing my tire. I was so in a rush to get away from the area, that I completely forgot that my food was still sitting on top of my car. Soon after I pulled off, I heard the unfortunate sound of my container crashing to the ground. "Damn, I wanted that!" I cursed as I thought about the mouthwatering food that was now wasted in the middle of the street. Glancing down at the cup holder, I shook my head as I realized that that too was a memory of the past. With the way that my day was going already, I prayed that Harlow at least had some left overs for a nigga to eat because clearly it wasn't in the plans for me to have those four wings and fries.

After fighting with traffic to get over here in a timely manner, I was happy to finally be pulling up behind Seven's parked car in his driveway. Jumping out of my barely parked coupe, I swiftly made my way in front of Seven's front door and immediately started banging. Although I had a key to his crib, I refused to use it in fear of that I could possibly be walking in on my sister being bent over and twisted up like a pretzel. I could only recall one time that I've witnessed my brother having sex and that was years ago when he was smashing our neighbor who acted more of like a sugar momma. It took me months before I was finally able to get the image of her droopy ass dislodged from my memory so I knew seeing Harlow in the same position would be even more haunting.

BANG BANG BANG BANG

"Open the door it's Detective Stabler, I'm with the FBI!" I yelled from other side of the door; disguising my voice. Hopefully my brother knew a thing or two about *Law & Order: SVU* or else he was going to be one unhappy camper. Placing my ear against the door, I listened for any sudden movement that would indicate that Seven or Harlow was in a panic. Nothing. "They must be asleep," I assumed; while placing my key in the door and entering their home.

Due to the unbearable hunger pains that my stomach was causing, I trotted my ass straight to the kitchen and made myself at home; opening both cabinets and drawers in search of a quick snack I could consume while waiting for my food to warm up. After about a minute or two of searching I almost gave up looking and went straight to heating up some of Harlow's left overs, but lucky for me Khloe had one more pop-tart hidden in the back of the pantry. Snatching the wrapper completely off the snack, I quickly shoved damn near half of the pop-tart in my mouth and was instantly bought to my happy place. "Mhmmm. These motherfuckers are good!" I burst as I peeked at the name of the flavor written across the box beside me. "I'mma have to get some of these for the house," I stated while walking over to the trash to discard the wrapper and empty box. Although the pop-tart I was chewing briefly curved my appetite for the moment, I was still planning on raiding Harlow's oversized refrigerator for a nice home cooked meal.

Turning on my heels, I shuffled my feet over to the stainless steel appliance and gave the handle a light tug. My eyes lit up with anticipation when the light from the fridge slipped through the opening, but as soon as they landed on the cool vacant shelves I immediately caught an attitude. "Who would eat up all the food like that," I grumbled in disappointment. Irked to the max, I slammed the refrigerator door shut and left the kitchen in search for some answers. "Sis, where y'all petty asses at?" I hollered as I wandered through the house. "Y'all know a nigga come here at least four times out the week for a hot meal, so why in the hell didn't anybody go to the market?"

"Shhhhh! Daddy Seven sleeping," Charli informed me as I

stumbled across her playing with her toys in the living room and a sleeping Seven sprawled out across the floor.

"I don't —," I attempted to speak but was cut off by Charli dramatically placing her pointer finger to lip and shushing, emphasizing for me to be quiet.

"I don't care," I replied, mimicking her voice tone. Charli was my little baby and every chance I got, I picked with her. No, we weren't related by blood, but I still looked at her as if she was my first-born niece. "Your daddy needs to wake the H-E-L-L up," I insisted as I noticed a half-empty cup of water sitting off to the side on the end table. A smug smirk formed across my face as bright idea formed in my mind. Slowly creeping over to retrieve the cup of water, I tried my best not to wake Seven. Once the cup was secured tightly in my hands, I quietly tip-toed back over to him and positioned myself directly over his body. "One...two...three," I whispered to a clueless Charli; before throwing the room temperature water in her father's face. "Wake your ass up nigga!," I yelled as I watched Seven jump up in panic.

"Ahhhhhhhh Harlow! Harlowwwwwwww! Oh my God, not my Harlow!"

<u>Seven</u>

"Ha ha ha ha, ha ha!"

I listened closely as I heard the faint sound of children giggling nearby. Wiping my eyes with my fist, I slowly walked around in small circles; staring at the breathtaking view around me. Where am I? I thought to myself as I felt a wave of calmness wash over me. Inhaling and exhaling deeply, I allowed the smell of mother nature to invade my nostrils.

"Ha ha ha ha!"

There it was again, I thought as I pushed through the tall grass, searching for where the laughter was coming from. Acting as a guide above me, the sun illuminated the sky as it beamed it's rays down upon the open field.

"Come to me Seven."

"Harlow, baby where are you?" I questioned while I stopped and surveyed my surroundings.

"I'm right here," I heard her say as I followed the sound of her soothing voice. Shifting through the large amounts of grass on the open field, I began to pick up my pace as I moved closer to the sound. With each step I took, my heart began to thump faster; anxiously awaiting to see her face.

"Almost there," she directed while her voice echoed in the distance.

Inching closer down the field, I squinted my eyes as a barely visible silhouette appeared a few feet away from me.

"Seven, come here. I've missed you so much," she cooed, while extending her arms for a hug.

"Harlow," I hesitated, "Is that you?"

Without speaking, Harlow emerged from the shadows and gracefully floated into my embrace. Eager to be in her presence, I quickly pulled her body closer for an intimate hug, but as soon as

46

my fingers caressed her soft skin, it felt different. Almost as if I was touching an angel. Removing myself from our embrace, I took a step back so that I could admire the beauty of the woman standing before me. Covered in the finest threads, Harlow wore a thin, white flowy maxi dress that exposed her sun kissed skin. Gazing into her eyes, she looked angelic as the wind blew through the loose curls that were framed around her bare face.

"Stop staring at me," she blushed.

"I can't... you're just that beautiful."

"Ha ha ha ha ha ha," the same, familiar sound of the small children laughing interrupted our short staring match.

"Where are we? And who's that laughing?" I pondered as I attempted to wrap my arms around her waist.

"Eternal paradise," she answered; offering a soft smile.

"It's peaceful here...how long have we been here?"

"This is my new home Seven...but you're just visiting," she

informed while dropping her head.

"What you mean I'm just visiting? I'm not about to go anywhere and leave you here by yourself," I stated; holding her body tighter.

"I'm not by myself... he's here with me."

"Who the fuck is he?" I barked; jealous that someone else held her attention.

"Our heavenly father. I'm here with him now Seven."

"No you're coming back home with me!" I demanded.

Frightened, Harlow suddenly snatched away from my grasp and nimbly backed away. "Stop it Seven! It's not safe for me there! They hurt me and if I don't stay put, they'll hurt you and our family too! Promise you'll protect our son and daughter and never let them forget about me! Promise meeeeeeeee!" she implored, before vanishing into thin air.

Confused, I attempted to grab her hand but it was too late;

she was gone.

"Ahhhhhhhh Harlow! Harlowwwwwwwww! Oh my God, not my Harlow!" I shouted as I woke up from my dream drenched in water and sweat. Hastily jumping to my feet, I ran around the room like a chicken with its head cut off as I tried to comprehend what was going on.

"Calm down! It's just water nigga," Omari announced while throwing me into a bear hug. "You act like you're scared of water. It's the same thing that you wash your ass with."

"Get the fuck off of me," I howled as the veins began to rise on my forehead. "Where is she? Where is my wife?"

"Calm down Seven! What are you talking about?"

"I saw her! I saw her in my dreams!"

"Nigga, you tripping over a damn dream? The fuck you want your blanky?"

"Omari don't fucking play with me! That dream felt as real

as this conversation that we are having now. She was trying to tell me that someone hurt her, but then she disappeared," I described while trying to decipher what Harlow was trying to reveal to me.

"It was a dreammmmmmmmm," Omari stressed while releasing his hold on me. "She's probably somewhere running around town with Logan."

"Be quiet and let me think! Something isn't right and —," the familiar voice of the news reporter simultaneously caused all the hairs on the back of my neck to stand and my head to pound.

Directing his attention to the news bulletin, Omari's facial expression went from clueless to shock. "Isn't that the —," he attempted to say but was cut off.

"We gotta get to the hospital! I gotta get to my wife! Grab Khloe from her room and let's go," I spat before snatching Charli from off the floor and rushing to the front door.

__Maycen__

Somewhere Across Town…

Although I tossed and turned majority of the night, getting little to no sleep, I still woke up eager and full of energy; anticipating the news of Seven's downfall. With the local news station blasting on every channel throughout the house, I sat in my recliner front and center with a permanent smile plastered on my face. As my eyes trailed off to the large clock above the big screen, I knew that it would only be a matter of minutes before I received verification that my good deed to society was complete.

"We interrupt your regularly scheduled programming with breaking news…"

"It's showtime," I crowed as I got up and pulled my seat closer.

"Hi, I'm Peggy O'Neal giving you an update on our breaking news coverage. I'm still live on the scene of the crash that claimed the life of a young pregnant woman driving a Mercedes-

Benz GLE 350 SUV. All victims of the crash were rushed to Sinai Hospital and two of the three are reported to be in critical condition. The accident happened today sometime around nine o'clock this morning going westbound on interstate 695. Police have confirmed that the crash is being investigated as vehicular homicide, however they won't release any additional information to the public. We will give you an update as soon as the information becomes available. Any information as to who the victims are please call 555-654-8901."

"What the fuck?" I frowned, while I sat back in my chair perplexed. I was almost positive that the car that we sabotaged was the exact same car that was on my television now, however the news reporter clearly had the drivers mixed up. As soon as the thought of Harlow being the driver entered my mind, it quickly exited. As much as I stalked my child's mother there wasn't no way that she could ease a pregnancy by me without me detecting it. *Maybe it's a coincidence. Yeah. It had to be that for sure.* I thought, trying to convince myself that the news reporters made a mistake. *Let me call Tiran and see if he heard the same thing.*

Standing up from my seat, I walked to the other room in search of my phone.

Six minutes and two mini heart attacks later, I finally had Tiran on the line as we both sat in silence while I tried to gather my thoughts. On edge, I released my breath before I spoke, "I think we fucked up."

Paranoid, Tiran stopped and looked around his room before he continued to listen.

"Tell me you saw the newscast a few minutes ago?"

"Nah, I missed it. My ass just got up," he informed.

"Well hurry up and turn on channel thirteen! They're broadcasting live footage from the scene of an accident."

Reaching for the remote on his nightstand, Tiran powered on the TV and switched to channel thirteen. As he examined the totaled cars on the screen a small chuckle escaped his lips. "Why you tripping? This is what we wanted to happen, right? What you feel bad now?"

"You must not have been paying attention to what the reporter just said."

"I was paying attention. She said that there was an accident leaving one driver dead and the other two badly injured, so what's the problem?"

"The problem is the driver of the car that we assumed was Seven's is a pregnant female!" I screeched.

"Pregnant female?" He paused. "Well maybe this isn't the accident that we're looking for."

"How many people do you know that can afford a Mercedes- Benz GLE 350 *and* happened to be in an accident the very same day we're anticipating one?"

"So what are you saying? You think someone else was driving his car?"

"Unfortunately, I do," I confided in a somber tone.

"Well who?"

"I think it's Harlow," I mumbled as my voice trailed off.

"But you *just* said the driver was pregnant," Tiran reminded.

"I know, but what if she was?" I pondered as I tried to ignore the feeling that my heart was telling me was true.

"When was the last time that you saw her?"

"Like two weeks ago," I answered as I tried to recollect my last encounter with her.

"Well, did she look pregnant?"

"No."

"Then it wasn't her in the accident then," he convinced. "As much as this city gossips about everything, I'm sure that somebody would have hit your phone by now with the news that she was pregnant."

"I don't know…it just doesn't feel right to me," I expressed. "I'm praying that it's somebody else, like an aunt or cousin."

"I really think that you're thinking too much into this. Just relax and we will —," Tiran paused. "Aye Maycen, let me call you back in a few minutes; that's someone on my other line," he announced before ending the call.

Tiran

"Hello," I answered on the third ring.

"What did you do?" Khia screamed through the phone as she paced her bedroom floor. "I told you that I didn't want no parts of what you were doing to that man! None! Now look at this shit, you killed that girl didn't you!"

"First off, calm the fuck down and lower your voice," I growled through clenched teeth. "Second of all, NO I didn't kill anybody."

"So you're gonna lie to me?" she rhetorically asked. "That's the same car that I sold Omari's brother yesterday! You promised me that you weren't on no shady shit, now Seven's going to kill me! Oh my God! What did I do?" she hysterically cried.

"Shut that shit up and pull yourself together!" I ordered. "Now what happened to that girl was an accident."

"Do you think I'm stupid? The news reporter said —"

"What did I say!" I stressed while getting up off of the bed and turning off the television. "All you did was sell him a car. Nothing more, nothing less. If you keep your gums quiet and stick to that story, you'll be fine," I coaxed.

"That's easier said than done. What if the police get involved Tiran? I'm not going to jail for you... or anyone for that matter."

"So you snitching now?" I challenged, flabbergasted at her revelation.

"If I have to I will," she admitted.

"Mannnnn get the fuck off my line!" I scowled before I

abruptly ended the call.

Everybody tripping! I concluded as I attempted to rub away the headache that was slowly nearing. Until the news reporter disclosed the identification of the victims, I was going to stand firm and believe that this was a mere coincidence. I refused to work myself up over a stupid theory that Harlow was indeed the driver. Yeah we never factored in the possibility of Harlow or Charli being in the car, but still what were the odds that either one of them would actually be in the car? All I know is that Seven deserved everything that he had coming to him for abusing my goddaughter and because of that my conscience was clear.

<u>Seven</u>

As soon as Omari pulled the car into the roundabout in front of Sinai Hospital's emergency room's entrance, I quickly hopped out without even allowing him to bring the car to a screeching halt first. My mind was all over the place as I tried my best to stay in good spirits about the outcome of the accident.

Although I wasn't one hundred percent sure of Harlow's condition, I knew that without a shadow of a doubt that she was some way involved.

The whole ride over to the hospital I kicked myself repeatedly for being so stupid. Why would I gift her that truck without getting it inspected first? Why did I send her out for food when we could have just ordered breakfast from Uber Eats? This was all my fault and if Harlow didn't survive this accident I don't know if I could stomach the fact that I would have to continue on through life without her. I rarely ever called on God for a favor but right now I needed Him to reassure me that everything was okay. I know it may sound selfish but I needed Him to tell me that my queen was one of the survivors. That she was the one that put up a fight and won.

Running to the registration desk with my siblings hot on my heels, I bombarded the first nurse that I saw available with question after question.

"Hi yes excuse me, umm I saw on the news that this is

where the victims of the accident on I-695 were being treated. Could you tell me what room they're in please? I need to make sure that my wife wasn't in that accident. She's average build, a little lighter than yourself. Ummm what else… what else… oh yeah she has a scar on her face. Do you know where she is? Can you help me?" I rambled until I heard the small commotion going on behind me.

"Sir, this is my last time telling you to move your car. You're blocking the entrance and preventing others from dropping their loved ones off," the security guard pressed while grabbing his radio; ready to call for back up.

"I don't give a damn about you calling your flunkies. I'm not moving my car. So if you can excuse me, I'd like to go check on my sister," Omari stated before turning to walk away.

"Officer Benjamin to base. I have a 10-33 on post 7. Can you send back up and radio in a tow truck?" the security called over the radio.

"10-4, en route," replied an officer posted in the control center.

"Sir...Sir," the nurse called out attempting to get my attention.

"Uhh yes," I answered diverting my attention back to the task at hand.

"Did you say that you were here to identify one of the victims of the accident?" she inquired, while making a notation on her clip board.

"Yes, I think my wife was one of the drivers injured."

"Can you wait right here until one of the officers from the crash comes out here to speak with you?" the nurse morosely stated before rising from her seat and disappearing behind the double doors.

Fifteen minutes passed before two white officers, one of which I recognized to be Officer Jacob McNair, emerged from the double doors and approached my family and I in the waiting room.

"Are you the alleged family member to one of the victims in the accident?" the unknown officer questioned with a straight face.

"Yes, I'm Seven Freeman. My wife Harlow was driving the white Mercedes-Benz," I fretted while studying both officer's body language.

"I think maybe you should take a seat," Officer McNair dismally suggested before allowing his partner to finish speaking. McNair lacked the usually cocky and confident persona that he typically possessed which instantly caused me to be on high alert.

"No, I'm good. I rather stand," I demurred as I wiped my sweaty palms against my hooping shorts.

"Sir, I'm afraid that I have some bad news for you," the tall, buff officer hesitated while he tried to find the right words to deliver the heart wrenching information. "Our emergency responders tried their best to resuscitate your wife, but sadly she didn't make it."

As soon as the words left his lips I could feel all the air leave my body as my legs began to get weak. "What…what do you mean she didn't make it?" I stammered as the tears began to pour from my eyes. "No! That can't be true! No…no it's not true! I don't believe it! I prayed for her safety! God wouldn't do this to me!" I bawled while Omari pulled me into his embrace for a brotherly hug.

"Shhh.. I got you. I got you," my brother whispered while he too shed some tears of his own.

"Why Mari? Why?" I wailed as my brother rocked my body in his arms.

"I don't know, but we're going to get through this as a family. I promise you that. At the end of the day, we all we got." he consoled as he continued to rock.

"Wait! We forgot to mention that there's good news too," Officer McNair offered trying his best to uplift my family's spirits.

I was so out of it that I completely forgot that both officers were still standing there.

"There isn't shit you can tell me that would make me feel good about losing my wife!" I growled while stepping away from my brother's embrace and approaching McNair.

"Not even the life of your son?" McNair countered.

"My son? You must be mistaken. My wife and I only have one child, and she's seated over there with my sister," I advised while pointing to Charli and Khloe.

"So this means you delivered the bad news to the wrong family, right? That my sister is still alive, rightttt?" Omari pestered while trying to sound optimistic.

"Unfortunately no, it doesn't. The woman driving the Mercedes Benz SUV that you identified as Mrs. Harlow Freeman, is in fact deceased. Her son however is currently being monitored in the Neonatal Intensive Care Unit on the third floor. If you would like, I can escort you upstairs so that you can see him," McNair's partner informed.

"I already told you that I don't have a son! Why won't you listen?" I spat as I began to become frustrated with both officer's lack of hearing.

"Sir, I understand that you're upset, but I'm only telling you what the doctors reported to me," the tall officer stated. "Allow us to take you to the third floor so that the doctor can explain the situation to you himself."

"We'll follow you," Omari interjected before he turned his attention towards me. "Look, let's just go see for ourselves what's going on. We can't leave that baby up there by himself without being sure that he's not yours first."

Omari was right. If in fact it was true that Harlow was gone, I'll be damned if I left my only connection to her abandoned in a hospital full of strangers. "Take me to my son., I vacillated before walking off to grab Khloe and Charli.

The walk through the dungeon of the hospital seemed longer than it actually was but that was only because I felt uneasy.

"Right this way," Officer McNair instructed as soon as we stepped off the elevator and into a room full of chaos. "Doctor Tolbert," McNair called out as soon as he spotted the middle aged man about to walk into another room. "This here is the father of our Jane Doe's offspring. He's here to see his child."

"Oh why yes," Dr. Tolbert stated as he rushed over to greet my family. "I'm Doctor Tolbert, the head doctor in charge of all the patients in the Neonatal Intensive Care Unit," he stated while reaching for a handshake.

"Hello doctor, I'm Seven Freeman, the husband of Harlow Freeman and this here is my family," I stated as I shook his hand.

"Nice to meet you Mr. Freeman. Why don't we go talk in a private room away from all of this commotion?" he suggested as he lead us to a quiet area down the hall.

"First of all I would like to say, I'm sorry for your loss and offer my condolences. I was told that the emergency responders did everything that they could and by the time she was in our care she already lost too much blood," he said before taking a pause. "I am, however, happy to say that my team and I were able to perform an emergency C- section in an attempt to save your son's life."

"She never said anything to me about being pregnant," I croaked as I wiped away the tear that was threatening to fall. "How many months was she?"

"Twenty-three weeks. She was in her second trimester of her pregnancy."

"This explains why she was always so tired and cranky. I just chalked it up to her not getting enough sleep," I affirmed while shaking my head. "Where's my son? I need to see him."

"He's down the hall in his incubator. I have to forewarn you though, he only has a twenty-five percent chance of survival. Your son was born with several complications due to him being born premature, including respiratory distress syndrome which is a breathing syndrome caused by the immature development of his lungs and Intracranial Hemorrhage which causes bleeding inside of the brain." Dr. Tolbert confirmed.

"I swear I can't take another loss like this. I just can't!"

"Mr. Freeman, our doctors are closely monitoring your son around the clock. They are all equipped with everything they need to keep your son calm and comfortable. He's fragile and at this moment he needs your love and support to help him push through."

"I hear you Doc, I just need to see him so that I can make it better. I need him to know that he belongs to a family that loves him."

"Absolutely, I'll have one of my nurses take you and your family to him," Dr. Tolbert stated while paging an available nurse on his beeper.

"Mari," I acknowledged while turning to face him. "I appreciate you bringing me here and acting as my support system, however I need you to do me this favor and take the girls home for me. I'm not ready for them to see Harlem in such a fragile condition just yet because it'll scare them. Hell, it'll probably scare me too. I just know that I need this time alone to bond with my son."

"You don't have to explain yourself to me, bro. All I ask is that you tell junior that his uncle loves him and when he gets older I promise to buy him his first hooker," Omari joked, while trying to lighten the mood. "After I drop them off to Ms. April, do you want me to swing back pass to get you?"

"Thanks, but I'm good bro. I'll find my way home."

"Okay cool, but if anything changes make sure you hit my phone and let me know." He stated before reaching in for a brotherly hug. "Oh and another thing," he added while taking a step back and looking me in my eyes. "Before I leave to take them home, I just wanna say that that name you chose… it's dope. Harlow would be happy to hear that you named y'all son after her." He finished before rounding up the girls and making his exit.

Chapter 2

Logan

One Week Later…

Ducked off in the corner on a cold, brown leather chair, I

sat stone-faced as my mind checked out into LooneyVille. As each

minute passed, I could feel my body getting number to the pain

that I was currently feeling. What started out as a need for a

Percocet here and there to take my mind off of things eventually

turned into me popping damn near the whole prescription drug

bottle back like mints. In no way did I consider myself addicted to

the drug, but any day that I went without them had me ready to call

it quits on this thing called life. Sadly, a week ago while I watched

my son being bought back to life in one hospital room, my best

friend of over eight years was losing hers in another. Harlow was

more than a friend to me, she was my sister and now all that I had

left of her was our sweet memories. She was my strength through

the storm and now that she was gone I was terrified of going

through life without her. It pained me that God took her away from me so soon but I guess he needed his angel more than I did. The numbness from the drug only temporarily took my mind off the reality that she was gone forever, however I was grateful for the distraction.

"Bae, you good over there?" Jabril questioned as he peered over his shoulder in my direction.

Ignoring his question, I sat in silence as my mind state begin to drift into euphoria. Closing my eyes, my head slightly nodded forward as I enjoyed the feeling that the drugs were giving me.

"Logan, did you hear me?"

"Huh…what?" I stammered as I popped my eyes open and wiped the imaginary drool from around my mouth.

"I asked was you good," he reiterated.

"Oh yeah, I'm fine," I lied as shifted my position in the chair that I was sitting in and drifted back into another brief slumber.

"Is everything set for the funeral tomorrow? I mean I know that Seven took care of the financial part but is there anything else that y'all need help with?" he offered before returning his attention back onto our son.

"Mhhhhhmmm," I grunted. "We good, thanks," I added, my voice barely above a whisper. *I wish he would shut up and stop asking questions! He's fucking up my high!* I complained, while placing my head against the leather.

"Oh okay, cool. Well I'mma stay at the hospital with baby boy tomorrow so that you can go and pay your respects to your sister. You're probably going to want some time alone after the funeral to you know... grieve... and that's cool. Just know that I'll be here if you need a listening ear or a shoulder to cry on."

Slamming my hands against the arms of the chair, I was finally fed up with his small talk, "Alright already! I heard you! Damn! All I want right now is some peace and quiet! Can I get that?" I erupted.

Instantly turning on his feet, Jabril took a minute to stop and stare at me strangely. Careful not to piss me off any further, he cautiously choose his words before he spoke, "I get that you're hurting right now Logan... I do, but you can't push away the people that love you. I just wanted you to know that you have a support system, that's all."

There goes my high. "Don't tell me what to do. You don't know what it feels like to lose the only person in the world that knows you better than they know themselves. That acted as your human diary and never judged you for not even the raunchiest of raunchy information. The only person that would give you her last so that you wouldn't have to go without. No one can replace her! No a single motherfucking soul! That's my sister that I have to lay to rest tomorrow so don't tell me what to do or how to feel!" I was exasperated as I shot up from my seat and walked towards Jabril's face with spit flying from my mouth.

"Excuse me, can you keep it down in here? Some of our other patients are trying to sleep, thank you," the nurse stated as she poked her head in Logic's room to address the ruckus.

"I'm sorry ma'am, we will try our best to keep the noise down," Jabril vowed as he offered the pale nurse a phony smile.

"Great! Thanks," she restated before closing the door to the secluded room.

"Look Logan, I don't want to argue with you. If you want me to leave you alone until you get yourself together, I will."

"To be honest, I could care less what you do. I'm about to get up outta here. Text me if anything changes with the condition of our son," I announced while grabbing my purse out of the window ledge and walking towards the door to open it.

"I love you!"

SLAM

I need a drink! Don't nobody got time for his shit today! Making my way to the elevators on our floor, I repeatedly pushed the elevator button so that I could leave this depressing place.

"Come on...come on," I mumbled to myself as I watched the downward arrow light up indicating that an elevator was en route. Pulling out my Galaxy, I sent my brother Seven a text to see if he wanted to meet up to grab a drink and blow off some steam.

Me: Hey bro. How you holding up?

Three minutes later*

Seven: Barely. Between tryna get a lead in the investigation to being on pins and needles with my son's status, I'm ready to lay some shit down!

Me: Man who you telling? I'm going through the same thing! Trying to mourn the loss of my sister and make sure that my son is good. I feel like I need to be selfish and take some time out for myself! Shit! How's Harlem doing anyway?

Seven: He's a fighter! The doctors said it's a 25% chance he will survive being born at 23 weeks but he's holding on.

Me: Just keep the faith! Even though I don't like it, all of this is God's plan!

Seven: I'm trying to see the bigger picture. But it hurts like hell knowing that I have to go through life without my soulmate.

Me: Just know I'm here for you! Shit if you want we can have a crying session at any time.

Seven: I'm good Sis. I'mma just paint the city red until I get the answers I need.

Me: DO WHAT YOU FEEL IS BEST! I love you and I will see you at the funeral tomorrow.

Seven: You not going to the viewing tonight? I need you there to make sure everything is a go tomorrow while I take care of some business.

Me: I wasn't planning on it. I really don't think I can stand to look at my best friend laying in a casket twice, but if you need me to make sure she looks like the true her, then I will.

Seven: Thanks Sis! I appreciate it. See you tomorrow.

Damnit! I really need a drink now. In no way shape or form was I prepared to go see Harlow's lifeless body lying in a metal casket a few hours from now, but Seven needed me to put my big girl panties on and handle the final affairs before her funeral. Knowing that my promise wouldn't get done without a drink, I hopped in my car and headed straight in the direction of the Windsor Inn for their infamous long island iced-tea on the rocks.

Walking through the doors of the restaurant, I immediately made myself at home and took a seat in the back by the bar.

"Hey stranger! What can I get you?" the upbeat bartender inquired while I sat on the stool scrolling through Instagram.

Never lifting my head up from out my phone, I dryly responded, "You can get me the usual."

"Got you! Coming right up," she announced before strutting away to make my drink.

"These bitches don't even like her like that. Now all of sudden they throwing up R.I.P post about my sister. Fuck out of here!" I huffed as I dropped my phone on the counter.

"Someone making you upset?" a familiar voice whispered in my ear as he took a seat next to me at the bar.

"Maycen, what are you doing here?"

"The same reason you are. I had to get some air before I went crazy," he answered while staring off into space.

"You just got here?" I quizzed while my face matched his same exact facial expression.

"Nahhh, I been here for a while now."

"I didn't see you when I came in."

"You walked right pass me looking like a zombie, so I let you go ahead without speaking."

"Here you go," the waitress interjected as she returned to where I sitting and placed my drink on a napkin.

Grabbing my credit card from out of my purse, I slid it across the counter so that I could pay for my drink.

"Don't worry about it. This one is on the house. I made it a little stronger too because it looks like you need to unwind. Call me if you need anything else," she gloated before walking back to the other side of the bar.

"Thank you...now back to you," I continued. "Why aren't you home with Charli?"

"Why aren't you at the hospital with Logic?" Maycen countered.

"Touché´!"

"But all jokes aside though, it's hard looking at Charli without thinking about her mother," he admitted. "She cries for her all the time and I don't be knowing what to say."

"Maybe you should let someone else keep her for a few days."

"Like who?"

"I know this may sound crazy, but maybe you should let

her go visit her brother and Seven at the hospital."

"Hell no! The fuck do I look like letting my daughter play house with that fuck nigga! It's his fault that Harlow's not here to begin with! Had he would not have given her that car we wouldn't be in this predicament," he grimaced.

"I understand that you don't care for the man, but as much as you hate to admit it you know that Charli does. Everyone is hurting behind this loss Maycen, including him. If you don't feel comfortable going to the hospital to accompany her, then I will take her myself. Charli needs to be surrounded around love right now because she's going to need all the support that she can get being as though she has to go through life without her mother," I explained.

"Nah Lo, It ain't going down like that. Whatever Harlow and that nigga had going on is none of my business or Charli's so you might as well dead that mission. I'mma raise my daughter and he can raise his child and that's that. It won't be no daddy daycare around here, I can promise you that."

"You're so fucking selfish and stubborn! Get out my face! Move!" I shot before throwing my drink back and storming out the door away from him.

Seven

After Omari came to switch shifts with me at the hospital, I finally was able to get a moment to myself to organize my thoughts. For the last seven days I've been racking my brain trying to understand why my soulmate was stripped of her chance at a happily ever after. She was the underdog and out of all the people that I knew that dodged the grim reaper she too deserved to have a second chance at life. I was a firm believer in karma and maybe, just maybe losing Harlow was mine. I wasn't quite a saint in this world, but I did have a good heart and I thought that at the end of the day that would at least count for something in God's eyes but I guess not. He snatched the life of the only woman that I have ever loved and left a permanent void in my heart, but I was still thankful for the fact that he decided to spare my son. Harlem Nazir Freeman was the only piece of Harlow that I had left in this world and I promised through him and Charli her legacy would live on forever.

As I cruised through the city on a mission, I thought about all the police officers and detectives I had scattered throughout the districts working Harlow's case. Out of the twenty-three police officers I had on payroll, all but two were advised to make Harlow's accident their number one priority. While the majority of her friends and family believed her death was truly an accident, I happened to believe otherwise. Every night since her death, I've been having the same on-going nightmare where Harlow tries to explain to me what happened the moments leading up to her death. As crazy as it may sound, my gut instincts told me that Harlow was attempting to speak to me through my dreams and that alone forced me to probe a little deeper into what sources were speculating actually happened. Between the information I obtained from the streets and the information I gathered so far from the officers, somebody's mother was going to be wearing all black, I promise you that!

Reaching my destination in under thirty minutes, I parked

my car in the customer parking lot and swaggered my way into the entrance of the Mercedes-Benz Hunt Valley dealership. As soon as I stepped foot between the double doors, I made sure that everyone in that bitch knew that I was not to be fucked with on this good Thursday. Searching around the establishment for a particular face, I was surprised when a tall, frail car salesman had the courage to stop me in my tracks.

"Hi, I'm Tom. Can I help you find anything today?" he greeted as he reached in for a hand shake.

Trying my best to tame the beast that was desperately awaiting to be released, I put on my best fake smile and then shook his hand and spoke, "Hello yes, I'm Michael Smith and I'm looking for one of your employees who sold me a car last week. I think her name is Kita."

"Oh yes, you must mean Khia. I believe she's on her lunch break right now. Is there anything that I can help you with?"

"No sir. I prefer to speak with her if you don't mind."

"No indeed! She should be returning back from her lunch in a few minutes. If you like, you're more than welcome to wait in the customer's lounge over there until she comes back," Tom suggested, pointing to the lounge.

"Thank you for your help," I paused while I read his name tag, "Thomas."

"No problem! And if you need anything else just give me a shout and I'll be glad to assist you."

"Will do," I reassured him as I turned on my heels and walked towards the direction of the customer's lounge. Half way through my walk across the dealership, I spotted an empty chair near the door that was in the ideal position for a stake-out. As if a fire had been lit under my ass, I walked to the lounge with a little more urgency to ensure that no one would steal that particular seat.

Positioning my chair in the corner of the lounge, I made sure that I could monitor everyone entering and leaving the establishment while still being undetected. I needed the element of surprise to be on my side because I knew for a fact that if Khia spotted me before I spotted her, she would have more than enough time to concoct a well-thought out lie.

While peering at the foot traffic traveling in and out of the doors, I was pissed that there was still no sign of her. Antsy, I subconsciously bounced my leg against the freshly waxed marble floors attempting to take my mind off of the time, which seemed to be at a standstill. Just as I was about to get up and go search for Uncle Tom's chipper ass, Khia came waltzing through the double doors with a Starbucks iced latte in one hand and her cell phone in the other.

Clearly late from her lunch, she quickly scanned the room for her boss before scurrying over to her desk in a hurry. Like a lion stalking their prey, I followed Khia's every movement with my eyes. She must have felt me burning a hole through her soul because she warily peeked over her shoulder, and as soon as her eyes landed on my face I knew her memory registered exactly who I was. She was petrified and it showed when her face froze and turned a ghastly pale shade. As if that wasn't enough to suspect her guilt, Khia then clumsily dropped her cool drink, splattering its contents all across the marble floor.

Yeah, she's guilty. I thought as I calmly walked over to her desk and took a seat.

"Ummmm…Hi Se.. Seven. How…How can I help you," she stuttered while smoothing out the imaginary wrinkles in her skirt and taking a seat.

"You know why I'm here," I stated coolly before placing my feet up on top of her desk.

Khia refused to make eye contact with me as she shifted through the top drawer of her desk, looking for napkins to clean up the spill. With her eyes still glued to the drawer, she kept her head down and nervously spoke. "Is everything ok? You know with…with the car?"

I remained quiet, allowing my silence to make her uncomfortable.

"Is…Is there anything I can help you with?" she asked while fiddling through some papers.

"Khia I didn't know you had a stuttering problem. You nervous?" I asked, shamefully taunting her. With nothing to say, Khia ignored my comment and allowed me to speak. "Let me ask you a question, do you watch the news?" I inquired as I crossed one leg over another.

"Sometimes. I'm not a big fan of it, but I do like to get an update on what's going on in society here and there."

"Interesting. Well I *am* a fan of watching the news and the other day I happened to come across something that rubbed me the wrong way. Would you happen to know what that something was?"

"No."

"You remember the white Mercedes-Benz GLE 350 you sold me last week?"

"Yes," she uttered.

"Well it was involved in a pretty bad accident because of some vehicular malfunctions. Would you know anything about that?"

"No...the car I sold you was in per— perfect condition. It was brand new."

"Show me the Carfax then," I badgered, as I removed my feet from her desk and stood up to get in her face.

"Umm sir... this isn't CarMax. We...We don't offer that," she gulped while taking a step back.

"Khia, do me a favor and look me in my face. Does it look like I'm playing with you?" I retorted as I took a step forward; getting so close to her face that she could smell my minty breath. "I will shoot this entire dealership the fuck up if you don't start producing the answers that I need," I threatened while discreetly flashing her the gun that I had tucked away in my hip.

"Mr. Freeman, I don't know what to say. We don't have that," she fretted. "I wish there was something that I could give you, but I don't have it. Maybe you can che…check the vin for —"

"Excuse my interruption," Tom broke in, "Khia did you spill something on the floor over there and leave it?"

Thankful for the distraction, Khia admitted to the spill and promised to get it up immediately.

Chuckling at the sight before me, I simultaneously flashed her my gun and my smile; reminding her that this conversation was far from over. Khia was hiding something and although she denied it now, I knew if I continued to apply enough pressure sooner or later she would break. She was my only lead thus far, even if all she did was sell me the car. I needed proof that the car I brought was in tip-top condition prior to me owning it and she was going to be the one to provide it to me. After I made it clear that I would return, I back- pedaled out of the dealership and proceeded to my car so that I could finish taking care of business before Omari called me to relieve him of his duties at the hospital.

****

If the weather were to reflect the way that I was feeling at this exact moment, there would be nothing but lightning and thunderstorms cluttering the dark gray skies. Today was the day that my beloved soulmate Harlow was being laid to rest and not even the hurricane of tears I shed the night before alleviated the pain. If it wasn't for the fact that I knew Harlow would cuss me out for not attending her funeral, I would rather grieve the loss of my wife in private.

There were so many things that I didn't get a chance to tell her, that I wish that I could go back and say. So many things that we didn't get a chance to experience, that I wish I would've put aside the time to do. I wish that I could hug her one last time and tell her how much I loved her. I wish that I could make her drive me around like Ms. Daisy again; me riding shotgun with her driving off into the sunset of eternity. I wish that we could have cooking classes with our son, daughter, my sisters, and of course Omari's greedy ass. I wish I had the chance to take her to the Super Bowl to let her watch her favorite team lose. These were the simple things that life had to offer that we both enjoyed doing together. And yet, the one wish I hoped for the most was for my children to have a chance to have one last walk in the park with their mother, holding hands, laughing, and eating ice cream.

TAP TAP

As I slightly rolled my car window down, I gave the intruder just enough space to speak from the outside of the car.

"Come on bro, you've got to come say your final goodbyes," Omari urged as he squatted down in his suit and spoke through the small opening of the cracked window.

"I already told you that I wasn't coming inside."

"I know that, but this is the last time that you'll ever get to see her."

"I know what my queen looks like, and the woman lying in that metal box isn't her," I expressed as I slowly began to roll up the window.

"Mannnnn, if you don't get your rabbit ass out this car, I

swear on my momma I'mma tell Harlow to haunt you in your sleep," Omari threatened as he banged on the glass window.

"I said I wasn't coming Omari, don't make me repeat myself again," I warned as I reclined my seat all the way back.

"You know what? You right! I'mma leave you be but when Maycen chump ass gets the last kiss don't come running in there on your Jet Li *Romeo Must Die* shit! Because I'mma trip you and let him get the first hit," Omari blurted out before turning around and going back inside of the Empowerment Temple.

It was times like this where I wished I was an only child. Here I was sitting in the car minding my own business and BOOM Omari's ass comes out here wanting to play and shit. Yeah I get that he was only trying to cheer me up, but he still, I was five seconds away from a mental meltdown and he was agitating the shit out of me. As much as I tried to ignore it though, Omari's last comment replayed in my head over and over, causing my body to cringe. The mere thought of Maycen being in the same room as Harlow alone, made me push my stubbornness aside and get out of

92

the car to say goodbye to my queen on last time.

Logan

"Let us bow our heads and pray," Pastor Brown directed while lowering his head and closing his eyes.

Tightening my grip around Charli's hand, I bowed my head and welcomed the Pastor's warm words.

"Excuse me. Excuse me," Omari whispered to the guests as he slid down the pew into the open seat beside me.

Lifting my head, I looked around the church for any signs of Seven. "Where's your brother?" I sniffled as I continued to peek over my shoulder.

"Still sitting outside in the car," he revealed as he reached for Charli to come sit on his lap.

"He's coming right?" I probed with my eyes glued to the doorway of the church.

"I doubt it. He's not in the right state of mind to see Harlow laying in a casket and I don't blame him," Omari answered while rocking a peaceful Charli back and forth into his embrace. "I'm not going to force him to come inside either because I'll be damned if I poke the sleeping bear and he shoot up this church while I'm in it," he added.

"I know exactly how he feels. I promise you if it wasn't for the fact that Harlow and I made a pact to carry each other to our last resting place, I would be home right now with a bottle of wine and a blunt mourning my sister," I whispered while trying my best not to disturb the ceremony.

"I just want him to cheer up. I'm not used to seeing him moping around looking like a lost puppy. It's kind of depressing."

"Give him some time Omari, your brother is hurting. The fact that Seven had enough strength to even come to the funeral says a lot."

"That nigga ain't here, he in the car," Omari corrected.

"He might not have come inside but he's *still* here," I

stressed. "Cut that man some slack. Shoot, Tiran's ass didn't even have the decency to come at all. At least Seven put on his Sunday's best to pay his respect, even if it was from outside in his car," I defended.

"You're right, I'm being insensitive right now," he concurred while shaking his head. "But you know what's crazy though? Before you said something, I didn't even notice that Tiran wasn't here," Omari paused, while observing the sea of faces crowded around him. "I don't care what kind of problems they had, Harlow was supposed to be that man's sister. That little beef between them was petty and should have *been* squashed. He foul as fuck for that, but that's your man though."

"He WAS my man. He ain't nothing now but a memory of the past now —"

"Mari!" Charli blurted while fidgeting in his arms. "Mari, Logi said that my mommy is in heaven, Is that true?"

"Yes Charli, your mommy is in heaven cooking for all of

the angels," Omari confirmed while giving her tiny fingers a kiss.

"I want to go to heaven with my mommy," Charli proclaimed while staring Omari in his dark brown eyes.

Damn.

I don't care how heartless a person claimed to be, hearing a five year old tell you that they wanted to be in heaven with their mother had to tug at your heart strings.

"Sweetie, you don't have to go to heaven to be with your mommy because she's always right here with you in spirit," I reassured while pointing to her heart.

"What about Daddy Seven? Is he here too?" she quizzed as she placed both hands on her upper left chest, covering her heart.

"Yes baby. Daddy Seven is there too," I answered, while sending a silent prayer up to the big man praying that I'd make it through this.

Seated in the pew directly two rows behind me, Maycen

silently watched the fatherly exchange between Omari and his daughter. With a disapproving frown etched across his face, he quickly rose to his feet and in the blink of an eye ushered his way into the open seat on the other side of me. No sooner than his bottom touched the bench, Maycen was in my ear speaking in a firm, yet harsh tone that showed his discontent. "You must think that I like to hear myself talk for the hell of it. I thought I made myself clear that I didn't want that nigga or his family around my daughter."

"Now is not the time nor place for you to be in your feelings over whose dick is bigger than whose," I shot as I attempted to create some space between Maycen and myself.

"If you don't want me to make a scene is this motherfucker I advise you to get my daughter from that nigga's lap and hand her over to me, NOW!" he threatened as he scooted over; closer than he was before.

While turning to the left in my seat, I could feel Maycen breathing down my neck as I removed Omari's hold on Charli's small frame and promptly returned her back to her father. Despite the fact that Maycen's threats didn't hold any true weight, I still obliged to his demands simply because I refused have my best friend's funeral be made into a spectacle. I already knew that Omari and his brother were on edge and weren't wrapped too tight; combine that with the sudden loss of their loved one and BOOM you were destined to have a war zone.

"Mari!" Charli whined while extending her hands for Omari to grab her. "Daddy, I want to go with Mari," she fussed while falling out into a temper-tantrum. "Get up or I'mma whip ya butt," Maycen muttered loud enough for Charli to hear him.

Ignoring her father, Charli remained sprawled out across the church floor.

"Charli, listen to your daddy and get up from off that dirty floor," I chimed in, offering my assistance.

"I don't need your help with parenting my daughter," Maycen spat while trying to conceal his jealousy. "But since she's being a spoiled brat, we about to get up outta here."

"Up out of where? The funeral just started Maycen! You're not that damn mad that you can't wait at least until they close the casket?" I protested while openly displaying my disgust.

"Nah, we out! I'm good off this shit."

"Fine then, you can dip! But leave my goddaughter here with me. I'm not about to allow you to let her miss her own mother's funeral. She needs to be around love right now, not that negative energy that you have harboring in your heart."

"I don't have to explain myself to anybody. We're leaving. My daughter, my rules," Maycen obstinately stated before snatching his stubborn daughter off the ground and proceeding towards the back of the church towards the exit.

"Maycen!" I yelled after him. "Maycen, come back!" I yelled again, but it was no use; he continued walking. Snapping around in my seat, I turned towards Omari and released my frustrations on him. "Why didn't you say something to stop him?

What you a mute now?"

"Man I'm not about to disrespect my sister's funeral like that by going back and forth with his bitch ass. There's a time and place for everything, and now wasn't it. I know what I'm capable of and the last thing I need is for me to expose my dark side in front of these here white people and I get locked up, again. Let him go and do him, we'll cross paths eventually. And if it's not with me then I'm sure it'll be with the Grim Reaper parked outside."

<u>Maycen</u>

I can't believe Logan really just tested my gangster back there in that church, and in front of the enemy at that. She had me so hot that I was five seconds away from choking her ass right there in the front pew because she knew not to play with me when it came to mine. Whatever I say pertaining to Charli, that's law! So when I said keep Charli from around them people, I meant that shit. Her blatant disrespect rubbed me the wrong way and at this point had me second guessing her future role in Charli's life.

Reaching into my suit jacket, I retrieved my iPhone and proceeded to dial Tiran's number; desperate to blow off the steam that his untamed bitch caused.

"Yo what's good," Tiran answered on the second ring.

"Your bitch, that's what's good! Her ass can't even follow simple directions!" I barked into the phone as I searched the parking lot for my car.

"I already told that bitch not to fuck with me or that was her ass. What? She ran her mouth already?"

"Man she had that bitch ass nigga around my daughter just a kee-kecing, like they were one big happy family."

"What was Khia doing around Charli? Better yet why the fuck was she around Seven?" Tiran fumed.

"Nigga I'm not talking about no damn Khia! I'm talking about Logan. Focus up and pay attention."

"You calling me for some damn Logan? I don't care what

that bitch does! We not together!"

"Well up until now she was fine in my book! But now, I don't even know. Can you believe that bitch had the nerve to crack slick with me in front of Omari like we haven't been family over all these years? I swear if it wasn't for the fact that we were sitting in the Lord's house, I would have ran in her mouth for disrespecting me."

"Shit you should of, maybe then she would learn how to talk to people."

"It's your fault that she's so treacherous. Maybe if you would have tamed that hoe a couple of years ago she would've had some etiquette by now."

"Man, coulda, woulda, shoulda. She's not my problem now. But speaking of problems, I *do* have a major one."

"Speak on it. But don't think I'm finished talking about your unloyal hoe," I mouthed after finally spotting my car.

Grabbing a hold of Charli's hand, I dragged her small

frame in the direction of my Acura. "Owwww! Daddy that hurts," Charli whined as she attempted to loosen my grip on her hand.

"Shut up and come on," I hissed as I let her hand free for a brief second.

"Y'all still at the funeral?" Tiran questioned after hearing the sound of Charli's voice.

"No, we're in the parking lot about to leave," I informed while still walking towards my car.

"Where y'all about to go?"

"Fuck is this? Twenty-one questions? I thought you said you had something important to tell me," I said, exasperated.

"Ayo chill with all that aggressive shit," Tiran warned before he continued on with our original conversation. "Now back to what I was telling you. Don't you remember the other day when we were watching the live broadcast of the accident on the news?"

"Yeah. What about it?" I dryly replied.

"Remember I had to go because somebody clicked in on my other line?" Tiran recounted.

"Yeah," I answered as I remembered Tiran suddenly cutting me off mid conversation that day to answer his other line.

"Well that somebody just so happened to be Khia's psycho ass. That bitch had the nerve to call me accusing me of setting her up and threatened to expose the truth about the accident."

"What you mean expose the truth? I thought we agreed to take this shit to our grave. What, you told her?" I grilled as my blood pressure began to rise.

"Hell no! I didn't tell her shit! She concocted her own theory of what happened. And get this, she threatened to go to the police about it if Seven finds out that she was involved."

"Yo what's up with you picking these ain't shit ass bitches? And why the fuck are you just telling me this shit now!"

"Because I'm not worried about Khia. She knows not to play with me."

"You need to be worried! If she said it, I'm sure she meant it! You act like she wasn't raised in the county around all them white folks. They don't believe in the code of the streets my nigga, they tell!"

"I know they do, but Khia knows better than to cross me. She was just talking her shit so that she could get under my skin. All I gotta do is drop this dope dick in her and then shorty's back in compliance," Tiran boasted, ignoring his best friend's concerns.

"Check this out, I don't care about none of that slick shit you're spitting. You're not about to play with my freedom or livelihood. It's sad to say but baby girl's time is up! She gotta go! And fast, before our secret becomes the talk of the town. Handle that situation and holla at me when it's done so that I can put you with my uncle's cleanup crew. Make sure —," I paused as my eyes zoomed in on the figure standing next to a car that was parallel to mine, "make sure you're discreet with this shit too. We don't need another body attached to our name. I gotta go though, I just came across an unexpected visitor," I advised in a hushed tone, while acknowledging the stranger that was staring me dead in the eyes.

Out of all the places that I could've parked, I ended up next to this nigga. I thought to myself as I ended the call and continued inching towards the unwelcomed guest.

As soon as Seven fell in Charli's line of vision, she immediately snatched away from my grasp and ran into his open arms. "Daddy Seven! Daddy Seven! Guess what?"

"What princess?" he cooed while glancing back and forth between Charli and myself.

"I saw my Mommy!"

"You did?" he exaggerated with excitement.

"Yes!" she answered in between giggles. "Logi told me not to cry when I saw her cause she lives right here," Charli added while pointing her heart, "with you!"

"She sure does! Always and forever! Now it's my turn to tell you a secret. Guess what?"

"What?" she beamed.

"You're gonna be a big sister again," he revealed, more so to me than Charli. A small smirk appeared across his face as he studied my body language.

"No way! Daddy did you hear him? I'm a big sister!"

"That enough Charli! Get over here!" I demanded as I mean mugged the person responsible for my baby mother's demise.

"But Daddy —" she attempted to speak but was cut off.

"I said now!" I repeated as I raised my voice an octave louder.

"It's okay princess you can go back over there with your daddy. I promise to introduce you to your baby brother when he gets better, okay?"

"Okay," she pouted as she slowly walked back over to where I stood.

"Don't make promises that you can't keep," I taunted as I observed him bite the inside of his cheek.

"I'm not even gonna feed into your bullshit. You know what's up with me," he calmly stated while slightly opening his suit jacket to flash his gun. "Niggas out here putting on like El Chapo but the whole time they really Ezell. I swear you can't make this shit up," he mocked before giving me his back and walking towards the entrance of the church.

If he wasn't strapped I would have said something back but unfortunately for me he was. I was so tired of losing to this nigga that I could literally taste his blood on my tongue. "You escaped death the first time, you won't be so lucky the next," I mumbled to myself before jerking the car door open and securing Charli in her booster seat. Every dog has it's day and his was soon coming.

Chapter 3

Khia

"Girl, I'm glad you called me to come and join you because I couldn't walk around another day with these raggedy nails," Inez proclaimed as she followed me inside of the luxury nail spa.

"Hi. How can I help you?" the nail technician greeted from the back of the salon.

"Hi, umm… we have a three o'clock appointment with Mimi and Theresa for both a fill-in and pedicure," I informed her as I approached the front counter and signed Inez's and my name on the sign in sheet.

"Okay. Pick ya color and then I'll be with you very soon," Mimi assured as she applied the final coat to her client's fingernails.

"What color you getting?" I queried as I searched the rack to the side of me for a pastel colored polish.

"I don't know. I just want something different. I know I'm tired of pink and I just had bright red. I'm thinking I might a try royal blue this time," she voiced while picking through the multiple colors displayed on the nail rack.

"Every time I come here I have a specific nail color in mind but as soon as I get in front of this rack right here, my mind draws a blank and I end up picking the same color over and over again," I avowed as I chose three colors that appeared to be in same color family.

"Girl that happens to everybody. I remember there use to be a time when I would only wear French manicures. It was cool for a season or two but after a while I started getting bored with it and reverted back to wearing colored polish."

"I swear men don't know our struggle. This is real life harder than an algebra test," I complained. "I'm dead ass about to play eeny, meeny, miny, moe to pick a color."

"You a fool," Inez chuckled. "What you think about this

color? I think it would go good with my new tattoo."

"I didn't know you got a new tattoo. What you get this time?"

"If I tell you, you gotta promise not to laugh?"

"I promise that I'll *try* not to laugh. Keyword *try*," I emphasized.

"Okay. So you know how after the release of that *For Colored Girls* movie, women started to get in touch with their African roots?"

"Bitch don't tell me you got Janet Jackson's face tattooed on you somewhere?" I teased as I broke into a light laugh.

"No smart ass, I don't. If you must know, I got black power tattooed on my wrist in Chinese," she answered, matter-of-factly.

"How much sense does that make? Why would you get black power written in Chinese instead of English? How do you know that even says black power? For all you know it could say black pepper," I burst out, no longer able to control my laughter.

"Honey, go over there and sit in chair. Rachel run water for you." Mimi instructed to the short, mocha complexioned woman that was seated in her chair. "You two," she directed while pointing in our direction. "You come sit in my chair, I ready for you. And you sit here and wait for Theresa."

"Shit! She ready for us. Hurry up and help me choose a color." I rushed as I held up the three colors in front of Inez.

"I shouldn't help you do shit since you laughed at me," she considered. "But if I had to choose between those three colors, I would go with the one in the middle."

"Thank you," I beamed while blowing her air kisses. "Now come on so I can fill you in on the latest tea that's been happening in my life." I motioned while moseying over to Mimi's station.

"Ooooo! Now you know I love when you spill the tea!" Inez squealed as she squeezed her voluptuous hips down the narrow pathway to her chair.

"When I say I had crazy ass week. Babyyy, I mean exactly that. You wouldn't even believe half the shit that I've been through in the last seventy- two hours."

"Don't tell me it's Tiran again," Inez fished while rolling her eyes.

"How you know?" I shot before dramatically releasing my breath.

"Because you're always going through it with him. What his conniving ass do this time?"

"I don't even know where to begin," I huffed as last week's events replayed in my head.

"Well start somewhere," she urged.

"Aight, so get this. Do you remember who Omari is from back in the day?"

"Yeah. He used to mess with my cousin."

"Well his brother Seven —," I attempted to say but was cut

off by Mimi.

"Honey, I know you say you want fill in, but do you want to keep the acrylic or try gel?" Mimi asked before gathering her tools.

"I want the acrylic and can you cut them down some, please? They're getting too long to type with."

"You should get the gel instead, it lasts longer," Inez suggested while she watched Mimi reach for the acrylic powder.

"You sure? Because I thought I heard someone somewhere say that it chips too fast."

"I can only speak for myself and when I get it, it lasts weeks."

"I'mma take your word for it but if it doesn't last, our next nail date will be on you," I warned before quickly snatching my hands away from the acrylic powder that was piled on top of Mimi's brush. "Mimi, don't cuss me out but I want to try the gel instead."

Dropping the brush on the desk, Mimi pulled down her face mask and cussed me out anyway.

"Deal," Inez agreed, cutting into Mimi's short little rant. "Excuse me, but how much longer do I have to wait before Theresa is ready?"

"Theresa!" Mimi shouted to the back, followed by a short dialect in her native tongue.

A few seconds later, Theresa emerged from the back of the salon fussing. "I heard you the first time! I no get break all day!"

Mimi continued jabbering about who knows what until Theresa was finally in ear shot and seated at the station beside hers.

"Hello girly. I haven't seen you in a long time. You go somewhere else?" Theresa inquired while she inspected Inez's nails that was desperately due for a fill in.

"No. I've just been so busy with work and my kids that I haven't had much time for myself."

"Well I take good care of you today. Just relax and talk to your girlfriend."

"So what's been going on with you lately? How's the kids?" I asked while I observed Mimi in her element.

"Christian still bad as hell and Imani, Lord don't get me started on her. She keeps... hold up wait a minute. You think you slick don't you. Don't try and change the subject and forget the real reason why we're here," Inez pointed out.

"I came for a fill-in," I lied.

"Yeah, okay. Spill the tea missy," she demanded.

"Damn, you one impatient chick. I was only trying to see what was new with my god babies."

"Yeah, yeah, yeah. Now spill!" she scoffed.

"Fine but promise that this stays between us."

"Okay," she promised with her face full of glee.

"No, I'm serious. This some take to your grave type ish," I

116

stressed.

"I said okay! Dang."

"Okay. So last week, out of the blue, I get a phone call from Omari asking me if my job had any exclusive cars on the lot that I was able to sell him. He told me that his brother was looking for something nice to give his sister and that he was willing to pay cash for. You know me, I'mma paper chaser so I automatically saw dollar signs and agreed to help him out. Now fast forward to a few days ago when I was damn near held hostage at my job for supposedly selling Omari's brother Seven a faulty car," I divulged, while looking around the salon to see if anyone heard me.

"Wait what? Why would Omari's brother think you sold him a faulty car?" puzzled Inez.

"Because, Seven's girlfriend was involved in that fatal accident on Interstate 695 the other day," I explained.

"Oh my God! I heard about that! That poor girl died. I thought they said that somebody cut the break line or something."

"They did. But for some reason that little piece of information went over Seven's head and he thinks I'm involved. This nigga came to my job with a gun and demanded that I give him the Carfax of the Benz I sold him."

"Wait! Did you say he asked for a Carfax?" she asked while covering her mouth and trying her best not to chuckle.

"It's not funny Inez," I whined. "You should've seen the look in his eye. I really think he might try and hurt me."

"If you seriously think Seven's crazy enough to do something to harm you, you need to go to the police," she insisted before replacing her smile with a serious expression.

"I am, but in the meantime take this letter and only open it and give it to the police if something happens me," I instructed as I reached in my oversized handbag and pulled out a sealed envelope containing a confession letter.

"Be careful, your nail," Mimi yapped as she poured acetone on a paper towel and fixed my polish.

"Oh my God, you're really serious!" Inez spoke in sympathetic tone.

"Just promise me that you'll do what I said."

"I promise!" she said while offering me a hug.

<u>Piper</u>

Once a week I allotted myself a spa day to help me unwind from the madness and today was no different. Typically, I was Mimi's last client of the day but for some reason today of all days, my husband felt the need to throw a monkey wrench in my plans and schedule us a romantic dinner date. I really wasn't in the mood to be around his sensitive ass because he was always in his feelings, but I guess if I wanted to be Mrs. Kirkland I had to play the part.

"Mimi, the water is getting cold. Can you run me a new batch?" I yelped as I removed my feet from the water and placed them on the towel.

"Sure," Mimi answered as she called to the back for some assistance. "Kim, a customer needs fresh water. Can you help please?"

While I was waiting for the nail technician to replace my pedicure water inside the bowl, I made myself comfortable by adjusting the massage handles in my chair and reclining my seat all the way back. Closing my eyes, I could feel myself drifting off into a mild somber and I welcomed the few extra Z's that I was about to receive. I was almost sound asleep too until I heard a woman mention a name that caused my ears to perk up and my eyes to shoot open.

Because of my ties to my fiancé I've tried my best to steer clear of the unnecessary drama, however once the name Seven was mentioned, I just couldn't help myself. I had to listen. At this point, I took it as a sign that God really wanted me to be all up in the mix of things because every time I tried to mind my own business and stay in my lane, he put me smack dab in the middle of the drama and I always ended up knee deep in someone else's shit.

I mean like seriously, it wasn't like I planned on eavesdropping into the two ladies' conversation, it just kinda happened. The woman, who I'm assuming went by the name of Khia, was spilling all types of the juicy tea about Seven and his brother and I was loving it, up until the point where she mentioned the accident.

Pulling my phone from my bag, I immediately went to the internet and googled Harlow's name; praying that the information I heard wasn't true. After a few scrolls and clicks, I finally came across the news bulletin that named Harlow the victim of the fatal crash on Interstate 695. Instantly, my heart sank to the pit of my stomach as I thought about the loss of my former friend.

It's sad to say, but I was more pissed that I was left out the loop than I was about the actual accident itself. I mean yeah, I knew it wasn't a secret that I didn't like Harlow, everyone knew, but I still thought that someone would at least have the decency to tell me the news. Instead, I had to find out about her death from two bitches gossiping in a nail salon.

The good die young, and in Harlow's case that was true. It

angered me that Harlow had to leave this earth so soon because I was just in the process of getting my payback for the pain that she caused me all these years. I had only began to scratch the surface with all the things that I planned to do to her and now she was gone for good.

In the past, when I fantasized of her dying it was always gruesome. She was either being badly tortured or shot with her blood, guts, and brain matter being scattered everywhere. Either way, I was always the one responsible for bringing her life to an end, not God. That's the kind of death I would have preferred and had I known she was going to take the easy route, I would have been killed her when I had the chance. I wouldn't be surprised now though if she was all the way in heaven doing cartwheels all because she didn't have to put up with my shit anymore.

*****

It was such a beautiful night in Philadelphia. The stars, along with the moon aligned in the sky while the trees swayed lightly in the cool breeze. Everything about the night seemed

122

perfect except for the fact that I wasn't sharing it with the one man that I truly loved. Nights like this made me want to call up my old lover and beg to come home but the idea of him dismissing me for his bird brain bitch bruised my ego and deterred me from making that call every time. It was hard to let go though, and as much as I hated to admit it, I often wondered if I was making a mistake by moving on and starting a new life with Larry.

Larry was a nice man and all, but I learned from my mother a long time ago that everything that glittered wasn't gold. I wasn't a fool to believe that Larry's closet didn't have skeletons, however, until it was proven that the grass wasn't greener on the other side, I was gonna continue to ride this gravy train and enjoy the perks while it lasted.

"Babe, are you okay? You haven't touched your food all night," Larry wondered as he stared me lovingly from across the candlelit table.

"Yeah, I'm fine. I just haven't had much of an appetite today. Maybe I'm coming down with something," I lied as I pushed the untouched plate of food from in front of me. "How was your day though?"

"Long. Today I had to hand over every officer's file in my department to the Internal Affairs investigator. She's going to go through each and every file with a fine tooth comb and honestly, I'm afraid of what she might find. Because of the shooting it's obvious that my officers haven't exactly been keeping their noses clean off all illegal activities. I just hope that Internal Affairs doesn't hold me responsible for one bad apple out of the bunch. I've been in charge of this city for the last twelve years and I pray that it stays that way."

"Now why would she hold you accountable for that? What those officers do on their own leisure time has nothing to do with you."

"Because she's a bitch and I think that she has her own personal vendetta against me," he cursed before taking a sip from his Hennessy. "She's mad that her husband got overlooked for the job as Police Commissioner years ago, that's all. I told him that when I retired he could have my job, but I guess that wasn't what he wanted to hear because eventually he went back to school to study law instead. That was well over ten years ago though."

"Tell that bitch she better stay in her lane or else I'mma pop up and introduce her to the real Piper. I'm talking about the Piper that used to drag bitches up and down Montford Avenue. I've been real chill lately but if she wants to take it there, we can!"

"That's not even necessary. Once she finds what she's looking for, she'll be out of my hair and hopefully I won't have to deal with her again. I'm tired of talking about her though, tonight is supposed to be about you and you only," he expressed before asking, "How did your meeting go with the wedding planner? Did you find anything you liked?"

"I'm not about to let her play with you Larry. She's trying to take food out of me and my daughter's mouth and I'm not having it!"

"Babe, I said let it go. I don't need you to worry your pretty self about the bullshit that goes on at my job. I can handle it all on my own. All I need you to do is look good, deliver me my pussy whenever I ask, and take care of our daughter. Now you can either tell me about your meeting with the wedding planner or you're gonna tell me that you're sorry after I give you this spanking. Either way, you're going to tell me something."

"There isn't anything to tell. All the venues she showed me were trash. I want something that screams chic, not cheap. That churchy look is wack and seems cliché to me."

"I'm sure they weren't as bad as you're making them seem."

"Honey, they were horribleee," I claimed as I shook my head for emphasis. "I wouldn't dare have my wedding in any of those places. I rather go to Vegas and get married in a chapel there first."

"Vegas isn't a bad idea at all," he considered as he rubbed his chin hair.

"The hell if it isn't! Don't play with me Larry! You know I was only being smart when I said that."

"I'm just saying. You love all the flashy shit that Vegas is known for, so why not?"

"Larry we are NOT getting married in no damn Vegas and that's final! Next question please!"

"Damn, your little ass is feisty. I see now why you don't have any friends," he chuckled as he removed his napkin from his lap and placed it onto the table. "You trying to get out of here? Because I know I am. I'm tryna get my dick sucked real good before Penelope comes home. You with that?"

Now he was talking my language. It was nothing like a good ole fuck to help me release my frustrations about missing out on that hoe's death. "You ain't saying nothing but a word. Let's go before it turns into a crime scene right here in this fancy ass restaurant. Cause you know I'mma soul snatcher," I concurred as I tossed my bag over my shoulder and sashayed to the exit in my six inch heels.

__Tiran__

If you would have told me a week ago that I was going to be the one responsible for my sister losing her life, I probably would have cussed you out and told you to get the fuck out of my face. Despite what anyone thought, I still loved her and would never wish any type of harm her way. I had all intentions on rebuilding our relationship because truth be told I missed our closeness; I was just too stubborn to admit it. We literally went from one end of the spectrum to the next, from siblings to strangers. And because of my foolishness we would never get the opportunity to go back to how things used to be. Sadly, she was a causality of a foolish war and now that the damage was done, it rocked me to my core.

When I say that the guilt hit me hard, I mean it hit me hard! And the more that I thought about it the more it made me want to go and hide under a rock to escape my reality. I couldn't even bring myself to attend Harlow's funeral because I felt like the word 'murderer' was permanently etched across my face and I was ashamed for the world to see it. And as if that wasn't enough to make me want to check into a mental institute, the fact that my best friend wanted me to orchestrate yet another murder was getting to me. In no shape or form did I consider myself a killer, so the fact that Maycen even hinted that Khia had to go left a bad taste in my mouth. Don't get me wrong, I understood where he was coming from because at the end of the day Khia knowing our secret could possibly place both of our lives in jeopardy. I just didn't want to have to be the one to send her to meet her maker.

The fact that I haven't spoken with Khia in days didn't help the predicament I was currently in either. It's like she disappeared off the face of the earth without leaving so much as a single trace as to where she was. It's not like we haven't had plenty of arguments before, but never has she ignored all lines of communication and went into hiding like this. Even the nights when I randomly drove past her house, her car still was never there, which raised my suspicions even further because Khia was a homebody and didn't play the clubs or nightlife too heavy. I didn't know if her absence meant she needed more space or if it meant that she was up to something; either way enough was enough. It was time to clear the air and address what caused this strain in our relationship once and for all.

As I was on my way home from picking up my food from Moe's Seafood, something told me to try my luck and swing past Khia's apartment to see if she was home. It might've been the angel sitting on my shoulder that told me to make the detour or hell maybe even the devil, whoever it was though, was pretty convincing and obviously knew something that I didn't.

It was late afternoon on a Friday so everybody and there Momma was outside enjoying the warm weather and crowding the block. Some girls could be seen outside playing Double Dutch with their friends while others chased the neighborhood boys around being hot in their asses. The old heads were even out today, playing dominos off to side of the court and drinking their infamous Colt 45's.

As I drove my car through the highly populated area, I acknowledged a few old heads here and there and even went out of my way to pull over to talk to some. If it wasn't for the fact that I was on a mission, I would have probably stayed and talked to them a little longer because they were always kicking knowledge. Unfortunately for me though, time was of the essence and I didn't want Khia to sneak off and leave if in fact she was even there.

As I maneuvered my car into the first parking space inside of Khia's lot, I surveyed the cars that were randomly scattered around and was shocked when my eyes landed on Khia's royal blue Honda Accord. Grabbing the bag of food along with my Humble Brand Clothing backpack from out of the front seat, I quickly exited my car and made my way over to the entrance of Khia's building.

I knew that in order for this encounter to go the way that I needed it to, I was going to have to catch her off guard. Otherwise there was no way in hell that she would agree to talk to me, let alone open the door and invite me in. Thinking fast on my feet, I came up with the perfect ruse that would allow me to meet with her face to face. I just hoped she fell for it.

Placing my hand over the peephole, I knocked three times on her apartment door and anxiously awaited for an answer. After several minutes went by without an answer I knocked again, but this time a little louder. *I know she can hear me,* I thought to myself as I checked the time on my Movado watch and released a deep breath.

KNOCK! KNOCK! KNOCK!

I was almost about to give up until I heard Khia's voice from a distance. "Damn! Could you give me a minute? I was in the bathroom, geez!" I heard her fuss as the sound of her footsteps got louder the closer she got to the door. "Now who is it?"

"Hi, I have a package for Ms. Wade," I lied as I tried to disguise my voice as best as I could.

"You can leave it right there by the door," she said sounding uninterested.

"I'm sorry ma'am but this package requires a signature."

"Ughh!" she huffed as she snatched her front door open and received the shock of a lifetime. "You said you had a package for me you fucking liar!"

"I do," I smirked as I held up the bag of food.

"What do you want Tiran, I'm busy? Why are you even here?"

"Dang, it's like that? I can't stop by and see my girl?" I cajoled as I watched her cross her arms and stand in defense mode in the doorway.

"See me for what? Last time I checked you didn't want anything to do with me so I'mma need you to keep that same energy and leave me the fuck alone."

"What? You still mad at me?" I chortled as if I didn't just threaten her life last week.

"Nope! I'm not mad at all. I just don't fuck with you like

that anymore."

"Well damn! That's how you feel? That's real fucked up."

"No," she corrected. "What's fucked up is the fact that you put me in the middle of your bullshit after I asked not to be. You claimed you fucked with me but the lie detector test determined that was a lie. Because ain't no real nigga gonna do no cruddy shit like that to a bitch that he claimed to be his girl. You a fraud and because of you, I now have niggas gunning for my neck," she chastised as she got in my face.

"When you start talking like this, all hood and shit? Let me find out you done found you a little chicken head to teach you a few things," I gibed.

"It doesn't matter who the fuck I've been hanging around, you're missing the point!"

"No, you're missing the point! Can't you see that I'm sorry? That I'm waving my white flag? I admit that I was wrong for getting you involved and all I'm trying to do right now is make it up to you. I even bought your greedy ass some food because I know you're hungry," I coaxed as I raised the bag of food in my hand for emphasis.

"Fuck, you think I'm a dog? Food is not gonna fix this!"

"It might not fix it completely, but it's a start."

"You think it's just that easy, don't you? That all you gotta is throw a few I'm sorrys here and there and POOF! You're back in my good graces."

"I didn't say that."

"You might not have said it verbally but your actions show that you damn sure was thinking it. Tiran, I'm not some doormat that you can walk all over."

"I know you're not," I said as I agreed with her. "You're my queen and I wish you would give me another chance to show you how much you mean to me. It's not every day that you meet your soulmate and it took me almost losing you to learn that. Matter of fact, I'm not even about to talk you head off. Actions speak louder than words, so watch out," I instructed as I excused myself and squeezed pass Khia through her front door.

"Move Tiran!" she yelled as she tried to stop me from walking any further into her house.

Ignoring her protests, I continued to walk through her house with not a care in the world.

"Tiran, leave now or else I'm going to call the police," she threatened as she paused to watch my reaction.

There she goes with that police shit again. I grimaced as I kept my back turned so that she wouldn't see my face. I didn't care if she was only joking, shorty was starting to throw around that police word too freely and it bothered me. They say that there's some truth in every joke and at this point I had already made up my mind about what I had to do.

As I was power-walking over into Khia's kitchen, I thought about all of the possible ways that I could kill her without drawing any attention to myself. Shooting her with a gun wouldn't work because it would make too much noise and stabbing her with a knife wouldn't work either because I'm sure she would put up a fight. The last thing I needed was to leave my DNA all over her body, or worse a fingerprint smeared in blood. Just as I thought that I was going to have to postpone my plan, I saw a small mouse run out from under the refrigerator and instantly I thought of a bright idea. *Rat poison for a rat.* I thought to myself as a mischievous grin spread across my face. I knew that Khia always kept rat poison under her kitchen counter because she was always complaining that her leasing office never acknowledged their mouse infestation.

Quickly retrieving the poisonous powder from under the sink, I checked to see if there was just enough powder to deliver a lethal dose and lucky for me, there was. My adrenaline was pumping fast as I looked over my shoulder to ensure that Khia was nowhere in sight. When I realized the coast was clear, I immediately snatched open the container containing the Cajun shrimp and chicken Alfredo and poured the rat powder in until I felt that it was enough.

"Tiran! I know you heard me!" I heard Khia yell from the other room. I knew I had a minute max before she was going to be on my ass so I had to move fast. Rushing over to the drawer that contained her silverware, I quickly grabbed a spoon and then ran back over to stir up the poisonous meal. "What are you in here doing?" she quizzed as she looked at me suspiciously.

"I was fixing you a plate. You can fake if you want, but I know that ass is hungry."

She thought about it for a second before she walked over and grabbed the spoon from out of my hand. "You're lucky that I'm starving because if I wasn't, you'd probably be in the back of a Paddy-wagon right now," she swore before taking a huge bite of her food. "Mhmmm. This is soooo good, I'm literally in bliss right now," she advised while she continued to chew her food. "Why you looking at me like that? What, you want a bite?"

"Nah, enjoy your food baby," I insisted while I continued to watch her body closely.

"Good because I wasn't gonna share with you anyway," she admitted.

"Damn, is it that good that you wouldn't even let me get a small bite?"

"Yes! This food is to die for," she moaned as she took another bite of her food.

"I bet it is," I chortled.

For the next few minutes or so we sat in silence as I continued to watch her demolish her dinner. For a minute I almost thought that my idea wasn't working, until I heard Khia erupt into an uncontrollable cough.

"Cough. Cough. Cough. Cough. Cough. Whew! This Cajun Alfredo is a little spicy. *Cough. Cough.* I think I need a glass of water. *Cough."*

"You okay? You don't look so good," I questioned as I feigned innocent and went to go retrieve her a glass of water.

"I don't know. *Cough.* I was just. *Cough.* Fine a minute ago but now all of a sudden I feel weak. Maybe I need to go lay down."

"You probably ate your food too fast. You know how you get when you haven't eaten all day," I reasoned as I handed her the water.

As soon as the glass touched her hands, Khia threw back the water in an attempt to alleviate her terrible cough. "Oh my God, my nose!" she screamed as blood began pouring from her nostrils and onto her clothes. "What is happening to me?" she howled as she slowly began to panic.

"Here, let me help you go lie down," I offered as a sinister smile spread across my face.

Khia was barely able to take four complete steps before her body went into shock and she fell out onto the floor.

Officer Jacob McNair

Two and a Half Weeks Later ...

"Why is it that no matter how much sleep I get at night, I'm always tired?" I wondered as I took a sip of my Dunkin Donuts coffee.

It was Monday, and my first day back to work after being off for three days. Although I'd just began my shift, I could already tell that today was going to be a long day.

"You probably have too much going on Jake. I already told you that you needed to slow down before you wind up having a heart attack," my partner Bill said as we drove around patrolling the streets.

"How can I when Sarah has Girl Scouts and cheerleading and Timothy has soccer and karate?" I challenged. "It wasn't a problem at first because Kate used to be the one to accompany them to their extracurricular activities, but now that she's pregnant again with our third child she can only do so much since the doctor ordered her to be on bedrest."

"I definitely tip my hat off to you man because I don't know how you do it. Especially on a crappy salary like ours. I'm surprised that I was even able to send Amber off to camp this summer after that huge pay cut that we just received."

"Shoot, I'm barely holding on myself. If it wasn't for the few stocks I owned and my small side business, I probably would have been filed for bankruptcy by now," I declared.

"You're probably right. Something is gonna have to give though sooner or later because I'm hurting right now. I've been working so hard trying to pick up some extra hours to try and compensate for the money lost that I can't recall the last time I even had a date with my wife. I'm losing out on my family time and that's not going to work because I'm not getting any younger."

"Well maybe you need to get yourself a little business like I did because trust me, the few extra dollars help a lot."

"That might not be a bad idea. I probably should talk it

over with —"

"All available units. We have a 269 that was just reported on 713 Moravia Road. Any units available in two or less?" the Dispatcher transmitted through our radios.

"815 in four," I radioed back.

"674 in ten," another police unit answered.

"10-4! Unit 815, Unit 674 respond code 3. Paramedics are on stand-by," the dispatcher announced before advising the paramedics to stand back until the scene was cleared.

"10-4," I acknowledged before turning on the police sirens attached to my patrol car. "I guess I better finish my coffee now while it's hot because there ain't no telling when the next time we'll be able to get a break."

"Forget the break, I'm just hoping that this call is nothing major because I already have enough reports to finish," Bill stated before busting a U-turn in the middle of the street.

"Got damn! You trying to make me spill my coffee or what?" I scoffed as I held onto the door handle with one hand and my cup with the other.

"Stop being a baby Jake. You've seen me drive way faster than this."

"I'm just saying, slow down some. I'm not trying to be forced to ride in the back of an ambulance because my partner gave me third- degree burns," I complained.

"I swear sometimes you complain more than Rebecca. Either offer to drive next time or shut up," he bickered as he wildly turned the corner forcing other motorists to slam on their brakes.

"Next time I will. Maybe then you'll see what it feels like to have front row seats to the Fast and the Furious," I shot as I placed my drink in the cup holder. Not even two minutes passed before Bill was pulling up and parking inside of Parkside Gardens' parking lot. "See what I mean, we're here already," I pointed out as I matched the address with the one that was sent to my computer.

"Oh be quiet and get out of the car," Bill said in an exasperated tone as he climbed out of the police cruiser and double checked his equipment.

Following my partner's lead, I exited the car and did the same before I proceeded towards the direction of the 911 caller's home.

"Do you want me to talk or you?" I asked as we both approached the caller's door.

"You can ask the questions while I read their body language," he answered before I raised my hand to knock on their door.

KNOCK! KNOCK! KNOCK! KNOCK!

"Good morning, it's the police!" I yelled from the other side of the door. "We'd like to talk to you. Would you mind opening the door?"

A few seconds later, we heard loud shuffling coming from inside of the house followed by the sound of a security latch unlatching. Placing one hand on the Glock 22 that was in my holster, I waited for the owner of the house to come into view.

"Good morning officers," the older woman greeted before stepping out of her apartment and closing the door behind her.

"Hello Ma'am. We were called here on the report of a possible dead body. Would you happen to know anything about that?" I inquired while my partner stood beside me silently.

"Why yes, I do! I'm the one that made that call. I'm not one-hundred percent sure, but I believe something happened with my neighbor above me. We usually cross paths every morning when she's on her way to work but for the past week or so I haven't seen her."

"Well ma'am you do know that it is possible that she could be on vacation?" I offered as I jotted down a few notes on my notepad.

"I know. I thought that too at first until I started smelling this horrible odor seeping into my apartment. I've never smelled a dead body before but if I had to guess what it smelled like, my guess would be that."

"Where is it again that you say your neighbor lived?" I questioned as I stuck my small notepad back into my pocket.

"She lives above me in apartment 2C," she answered before opening her door and preparing to step back into her apartment. "If find her and she's alright can you just let her know that I was concerned? I know she hates it when other people stick their nose in her business and I don't want to catch any backlash if that's the case."

"Will do ma'am," my partner finally said as we both walked off and headed up the flight of stairs to see what was going on.

As soon as we reached the top step to the second floor, we instantly knew that was something was wrong. The rotten smell that filled our nostrils was enough to cause us both to spill the continents of our breakfast all over on hallway floor.

"I think we both know what's on the other side of this door," Bill mouthed before covering his nose with his hand.

"This shit smells horrible! I don't know how in the hell that lady able to stand this smell for so long."

"Me either!" he agreed. "Do you want me to make the call for the paramedics or you?"

"You can do it because right now I'm trying to get my stomach together before we have to go in there and examine what went on."

Taking a few steps back, I allowed some space in between the victim's front door and myself while my partner dispatched the paramedics to the scene. I could literally taste the bacon, egg, and cheese sandwich my wife made me earlier in the back of my throat and I knew that if I didn't step away fast I was going to be wearing it all over my shirt.

"Alright. They said that they are on their way," he informed me as he walked over to where I was standing. "This heat that we are experiencing today probably isn't helping the smell either," Bill added as he tried to make some small conversation while we waited.

Just as I was about to comment, my cellphone rung alerting me that I had an incoming call.

"Hey what's up," I answered as I stepped away for some privacy.

"Where are you?" Commissioner Larry Kirkland questioned before he continued talking any further.

"I just entered a crime scene as a first responder."

"Is Bill there with you? Just say yes or no."

"Yes," I answered as I looked over my shoulder to ensure that Bill wasn't close enough to hear what was being said.

"Okay, but just a heads up I'm letting you know that we

need to have a talk. Things with you know who have been getting out of hand lately and we both need to take a step back before Donna has both of our asses fired or even worse, in jail," he cautioned in a voice that was barely above a whisper.

"But I've been keeping my hands clean," I mumbled as I stepped further away from Bill.

"Look, we'll talk more in person whenever he's not around. But just make sure you stay on a straight path until at least the investigation is over."

"I understand."

"Good! Now I gotta go, I've already been on the phone with you for too long," he stated before hanging up the phone.

After placing my cellphone back inside of my pocket, I adjusted my holster belt and walked back over to where my partner was standing.

"Who was that?" he quizzed as he stared at me strangely.

"Oh nobody, just Kate complaining that she's hungry again. You know how pregnant wives are," I joked as I attempted to change the subject.

"You couldn't pay me to get Samantha pregnant again."

"Well hopefully after this time around Kate gets her tubes tied," I stated as I heard the sirens to the ambulance echo in the distance. *Saved by the bell, literally.*

"It sounds like the paramedics are about to pull up. Do you want to go ahead and secure the area inside the apartment now before they have to enter?" Bill suggested as if he could read my mind.

"Yeah! Let's go," I commanded as I held my breath and banged on the door. "POLICE! OPEN THE DOOR!" I announced before placing my hand on my weapon and then kicking the front door in.

As me and my partner both entered the apartment, we wasted no time securing the area to ensure that it was safe for others to come and do their job.

"Clear!" Bill yelled as he checked the living room for any possible suspects.

Advancing further into the apartment, I finally found where the smell was coming from. "I have a dead body over here," I yelled as I swatted away the flies that were around the female's body and covered my nose with my shirt.

"Look what I found," Bill spoke as he held up a piece of paper with a gloved hand.

"You weren't supposed to touch that."

"I know but look," he pressed.

"What is it?" I queried as I reached into my belt pocket and pulled out a glove.

"Looks like a suicide note to me. What do you think?" he speculated as he handed it over for me to examine.

It read:

To whom it may concern,

First of all I want to start off by saying that I'm sorry for all of the confusion that I've caused in everybody's life. If you're reading this letter that means that more than likely you have found my body lying somewhere dead. You probably are feeling bad for me right now but I encourage you not to because I deserved this. I killed an innocent woman by the name of Harlow Stevenson and let others believe that it was an accident. It was foolish of me, but now I had to take that up with the man above at my judgement day. I didn't personally know Harlow but I did know her boyfriend Seven Freeman and his brother Omari from a mutual friend. Seven was my secret crush and after all those years of trying to get him to notice me, I became enraged when I found out that he was in love with another woman instead. My plan stemmed from pure anger and I created it that very same day that Seven Freeman stepped into my dealership and told me that he wanted to purchase an all-white Mercedes-Benz GLE 350 for his girlfriend. (You can cross check it with the footage from the Hunt Valley Mercedes-Benz dealership to see that I'm telling the truth). After the night that

153

Seven left my job, I copied his address down on a piece of paper and paid a drug addict twenty bucks to cut the brake line to his car. At the time it felt good because I knew that since I couldn't have him, no one could but now that Harlow is dead behind my actions I feel so stupid. I couldn't go on with life knowing that I killed an innocent woman so I made the conscious decision to take my own as a peace offering to God. I know that suicide is a sin, but Jesus died on the cross so that I wouldn't have to suffer for all of the nasty things that I've done. Time heals all wounds and I pray that one day Seven and his family forgive me for taking the life of their loved one. Justice is now served. An eye for an eye!

P.S Once you match my finger prints to the ones that are on this letter you will find out that everything that I just mentioned is true.

I'm sorry again,

Khia

After rereading the letter for what felt like the hundredth

time, I knew in my heart that I had an important decision to make regarding the information that I just found. I was advised by my boss not even ten minutes ago to steer clear of any communication with Seven Freeman due to the nature of our illegal business dealings, however at the end of the day I had to remember who was responsible for putting food on my table. My partner Bill was right when he said that we officers were being paid next to nothing to put our lives on the line. For that very reason I decided to make a deal with the devil so that my family could eat for a lifetime.

I was glad that we now had the person responsible for killing Harlow in our custody and that we now could finally put that case to rest.

Chapter 4

Maycen

Thanksgiving Day Three Years Later...

"Daddy, how come Charli doesn't have to wear a dress and I do?" Penelope pouted as she pulled at the itchy fabric that covered her knee.

"Penelope, what did I tell you about questioning what I say? When you have children of your own you'll be able to make your own rules. Until then stay in a child's place." I chided as I handed her a sweater so that we could leave out of the door.

Saddened, Penelope tucked her tail in between her legs and placed the navy blue cardigan over top of her dress. "Yes sir," she acquiesced.

"Charli!" I yelled to the top of the steps. "Come on before you make us late for dinner!"

"Coming Daddy," she beamed as she ran down the steps in

her favorite jeans and sweater. As soon as Charli's feet she touched the bottom stair her eyes fell on her sister's attire, immediately causing her to laugh.

"Nice dress," Charli teased as she grabbed her coat from off of the railing and placed it on her little body.

"Shut up," Penelope shot back as she stuck her tongue out at her sister.

"Enough already girls! Now, let's go before your grandmother calls me again inquiring about where we're at," I ordered as the three of us exited the house and made our way over to my mother's for a thanksgiving feast.

For the entire car ride over to my mother's house, I was forced to listen to my two daughters bicker back and forth. No matter how many times I threatened to pull the car over to hand out some ass whippings, they both ignored me and continued to press each other's buttons.

"Daddy! Charli called me a bad word," Penelope shouted

from the back seat.

"I did not! Daddy she's lying," Charli defended as she mustered up her most innocent face.

"You two just got lucky," I taunted as I pulled into my mother's driveway. "Now wait until I tell your grandmother how you have been acting. I promise you when she finds out, you two can kiss all those cookies and cakes goodbye."

"Nooooo! Daddy we're sorry," they said in unison as they unhooked their seatbelts and prepared to get out of the car.

"Nope! Don't apologize now," I gibed as I exited the car and unlocked their door for them to get out.

"Apologize about what?" my mother chimed in as she emerged from the shadows and onto the porch.

Charli and Penelope both stood quiet as they studied my next move. "Apologize about being late," I paused as I looked at the two of them sigh in relief.

"Awww, don't you two worry your pretty little selves about your Daddy's slow driving. I'm just happy that you're finally here so that we all can eat." She smiled while opening the door wide for us to enter. Happy to be in the clear, both Penelope and Charli skipped up the stairs and into my mother's house without a care in the world, but as soon as I reached my mother's front door she stopped me dead in my tracks and closed the screen door. "Don't you ever threaten my babies like that again," she whispered in my ear before she opened the door back up and allowed me to enter her house.

"Nephew!" my uncle Rick slurred as he drunkenly walked towards me holding a bottle of E&J.

"What's up Uncle Rick?" I greeted as I reached my hand out for some dap.

"How you been boy? I haven't seen you in a while."

"I've been good. Just trying to stay out the way and provide for my children."

"How many of them babies do you have now?"

"Two. One is eight and the other is seven," I advised as I removed my coat and placed it in the closet.

"Oh them not babies, they almost grown," he said, surprised.

"Yeah, I know right. Before you know it, I'll be paying for college."

CRASH!

"Ooooooooooooo you gonna get in trouble!" Penelope told Charlie as she stepped away from the shattered flower vase on the floor.

We weren't even at my mother's house for ten minutes yet and they were already breaking something.

"Charli go in the living room and have a seat!" I instructed as I grabbed the broom from out the closet and proceeded to clean up the mess.

Petrified, Charli followed my instructions and got out of my sight quick, fast, and in a hurry.

"Daddy do you want me to help you?" Penelope offered as she attempted to reach down and help pick up the glass.

"Move Penny before you cut yourself!" I barked as I pushed Penelope out of the way.

Penelope carefully rubbed her arm, while her eyes welled up with tears. "I...I was only trying to help," she whimpered.

"Go find your sister and have a seat next to her!" I hissed as I swept the glass up.

While Penelope was running off to find her sister she accidentally ran into my mother full speed, almost knocking her down. "Ohh, baby you almost made me fall," my mother yelped as she held onto the wall for support.

"I'm sorry Grandma," Penelope apologized as she wiped the tears from her eyes.

"Penelope what did I just tell you?" I badgered from the other room.

"To go sit down," she answered with her head down.

"Baby, what's wrong?" my mother consoled as she rubbed Penelope on her back

"Daddy is mad at me," Penny sniffled.

"It's okay sweetie. Your Daddy is probably being a big meanie right now. He'll get over it and if he doesn't, I'll give him a spanking. How does that sound?" she offered while reaching for a handshake.

"Good," Penelope giggled as she secured the deal.

"Now go over there and grab a little piece of cake for you and your sister off the table. Don't show nobody though, you hear?" my mother instructed before she winked and walked away to find me. "Just the person I'm looking for," my other scolded as she walked up on me still cleaning the mess.

"What I do?" I asked clueless as to what I did.

"How many times do I have to tell you to stop yelling at that poor girl?"

"What do you mean? I only told her to go in the other room and sit down," I corrected as I swept the last bit of glass into the dustpan.

"Oh I heard you! You told her to do that *after* you practically let Charli get away with murder," she articulated.

"I did not! I told her to go sit her ass down somewhere too," I defended.

"Boy you better watch your damn mouth in my house!" she warned before continuing. "I don't know how many times I have to tell you it's not what you say, it's how you say it."

"How did I say it Ma?" I puzzled.

"You know how you said it. You yelled at her."

"Only after she tried to touch the glass with her bare

163

hands!" I explained. "What was I supposed to do? Let her cut her hand?"

"Don't be a smart ass! Penny was only trying to help you clean up HER SISTER's mess. I'm sure if the roles were reversed the conversation would have went a different way."

"No, because I would have corrected Charli too."

"Maycen you can't lie to me, I'm your mother. I know you better than you know your own self. You're more lenient with Charli because of what happened to her mother and I get it, but you can't be that way because eventually you're going to create a monster. Charlie is either going feel like she can get away with murder or Penelope is going to feel like the black sheep of the family and hold resentment towards you. Either way, you'll have a problem on your hands," my mother, Pamela advised.

My mother sure did have a way of calling people out on their bullshit, and I hated it. When I thought that I was doing a good job at hiding my distaste for Penelope and her mother,

Pamela Drew was always there to check me and tell me that I wasn't. It wasn't that I hated Penelope or anything, I just loved my other daughter Charli more. What people didn't understand is Charli was created out of the love between me and her mother. She was planned and accepted from day one. She was a true daddy's girl and my little bundle of joy. Penelope, however, was different. She wasn't created out of love, but out of deception instead. She was a mistake and was never was supposed to happen. She was the true reason why my family was broken up and thus far, I didn't think that anyone noticed that I harbored these ill feelings towards her. But leave it up to my mother to make it known that she knew.

"Ma, it's not like that. I love both of my daughters equally. I just... I don't know. I'mma try and do better. I'mma fix it."

"You better because I would hate to say I told you so," she responded before strutting away to round up the children for Thanksgiving dinner.

Omari

Out of all of the days to be late to a family dinner, I picked today. It was Thanksgiving, the national fat boy's holiday and I was excited to finally be able to chow down on some good food after being forced to eat a bunch of bull crap these last twelve months. After a lot of begging and pleading, Seven was able to convince Ms. April to offer her cooking services to our family this year because truthfully my family hasn't had a big Thanksgiving feast since the passing of Harlow three years ago. Although Harlow was only in our family for a short period of time, she managed to claim the title as top chef and no one has even come close to mirroring her talent since.

Driving all the way from East Baltimore to West, I put the pedal to the metal and burnt rubber as I rushed to get to my brother's house just in time for him to cut the turkey.

DING

My iPhone sounded, alerting me that I had a message.

Seven: Where you at?

Me: On my way to your house.

Seven: Can you go to the store and get a bag of ice?

Me: What you need ice for? It's cold outside nigga!

Seven: For the drinks idiot.

Me: I knew that!

BEEEEEEEEEEEPPPPPP!

I was so busy engulfed into my phone that I didn't even notice the silver Volvo pull out in front of me until it was almost too late.

"Watch where the fuck you're going," the motorist cursed as she rolled down her window to deliver me a tongue lashing.

"Fuck you and yo Momma!" I fired back as I drove off trying to catch the light. It was just my luck that the light turned red as soon as I was approached it. The daredevil in me thought about running it but I the fact that I just barely escaped an accident

167

seconds ago caused me to change my mind.

BEEEEEEEEEP! BEEEEEEEEEP! BEEEEEEEEP!

Glancing in my rear-view mirror I tried to see where the beeping was coming from and low and behold it was the same feisty driver that I just cussed out.

Pulling her Volvo up to the side of mines, the angry driver unexpectedly parked and jumped out to finish delivering the tongue lashing that she started prior to us reaching the light. "Now what was it that you had to say about my Momma?" she spat as she approached my window with a bat in her hand.

"That's real cute baby girl," I taunted while rolling down my window to get a better view of her phat ass. "But I advise you to back the fuck up before I pretend that this is Grand Theft Auto and run your ass over with my car."

"You right about this being Grand Theft Auto!" she fumed before raising her bat to knock out my headlights. "I'm about to knock out all of this shit."

BEEEPPPPPPPPPPP! BEEEEEEPPPPPPPP!

"Fuck you!" we both said in unison before looking at each other and busting out into laughter.

BEEEEEEEPPPPPPPP!

"Move the fuck around us then! Impatient ass!" I barked as I hopped out of my car and slammed the door.

"Yeah moved the fuck the around!" she repeated as she walked to the other car with her bat in her hand.

BEEEEEEEEEEEEEEEEEP!

At this point I was getting agitated with the driver and I was almost positive that my little sidekick felt the same. "Aye my man, stop beeping ya horn before I get mad and trust me, you don't wanna see me upset."

BEEEEEEEEEEEEEEEEEEEEEEP!

"Get out the street asshole!" The motorist shot before sounding his horn again.

BEEEEEEEEEEEEEEEEEEEEP!

"Honk that motherfucking horn again! Go ahead I dare ya," she challenged as she tightened the grip around her bat. "Do it and I'mma show you why they call me baby Sosa." She warned before taking another step towards the car.

I guess the driver thought shorty was playing because he beeped the horn again.

BEEEEEEEEEEEEEEEEEEEEEEEEEEEP!

"Hold up! Hold up shorty!" I intervened as grabbed hold of her body to prevent her from attacking the other driver.

"Get off of me!" she hollered. "Y'all motherfuckers are going to learn not to play with me."

"Chilllllll, angry bird! It's not that serious," I tried to reason.

"Who you calling an angry bird," she chuckled.

"You!" I chortled before letting her go. "Your ass is worse

than them damn birds that purposely shit on your car after knowing that you just got a fresh car wash."

"Let me find out you're the next Kevin Hart. I'mma put your ass up in some shows so that you can make me some money."

"I'm sorry to bust ya bubble baby but you nor those comedy shows pay enough money to have me on stage telling jokes. I'd much rather sell dreams to these bitches out here."

"Okay Dr. King," she countered with a quick comeback.

"Now who's the comedian?" I laughed. "What's your name sweetheart?"

"Why?"

"Because I asked, that's why."

"My Momma told me that I'm not allowed to talk to strangers," she joked as she tried her best to look uninterested.

"Why is it that I always end up liking the short crazy girls?" I mumbled under my breath.

"Ohhhhhhhh, so you like me huh?" she badgered.

"Why are we still in the middle street?" I deflected as I ignored her question.

"Because you want to be. Now answer my question."

"My Momma told me that I'm not allowed to talk to strangers," I shot back, giving her the same answer that she just gave me.

"I like you," she smiled as she leaned against her car.

"If you like me tell me your name," I coaxed as I admired her beauty.

"I'll do you one better. Hand me your phone."

Reaching into my pants pocket, I unlocked my home screen and handed her my phone. "We really should get from out of the middle of the street," I suggested. "I would hate to have to hurt somebody already for trying to hit you."

"Stop whining. We about to get in our cars now," she

teased as she tossed me my phone and backpedaled to the driver's side of her car.

Glancing down at the name that she stored in my phone, I smirked as I read the letters that were on my screen. *Angry Bird.*

I might have just met my match.

Larry

"Nikki, please tell me that you have a turkey hiding in that bag of yours," I begged as I welcomed my older sister into my house for dinner.

"Nope!" she replied as she snatched her plastic shopping bag open. "All I have here is some sweet potato pie and some pound cake."

Exhaling, I closed the door behind her and took the bag of treats from her hand. "Do you think Boston Market is open on the holidays?"

"Wait a minute what's wrong? Why do you need to go to

Boston Market?"

"Because," I hesitated as I looked off to the side. I couldn't look my sister in the eye knowing that my wife dropped the ball, again. "We don't have a turkey or ham to cut at the table.

"I asked you did you need me to come over and help cook and you told me no! That your wife had it handled and that all I had to do was bring the desserts!" My sister shouted, not giving a fuck if Piper heard her in the other room. "Where's Tina? Does she know about this bullshit?"

"Tina's not coming," I revealed delivering yet another dose of unfortunate news.

"And why the hell not?"

"Because she doesn't want to be around Piper."

"And I don't blame her! That winch is bad news! You hear me? BAD NEWS!"

"Come on Nikki. She's not that bad," I defended as I tried

to keep my voice to a minimum. The last thing I needed was Piper to overhear us talking and start a whole World War Four in the middle of my living room.

"Not that bad? Sir, we're about to be forced to eat Captain Crunch cereal for dinner on Thanksgiving! Donna would have never did this mess to us!"

"Shhhh! Keep your voice down!" I shot while looking over my shoulder for any signs of my wife. "Piper doesn't know about me and Donna," I grunted.

"Well she needs to! Maybe then that'll light a fire under her ass and motivate her to learn to become domestic."

"No she doesn't! And we're gonna keep it that —," I ordered but was cut off by my wife when she entered the foyer.

"Honey, why didn't you tell me that Wendy Williams was here," Piper snickered as she came and stood beside me.

"Wendy Williams? How cute!" my sister sarcastically laughed. "At least we can say that she has a job. I'm wondering could we say the same about you?" she shot.

"If you must know I do have a job. It's to spend your brother's money," Piper quipped as I stood there silently, praying that is situation didn't escalate.

"You ain't nothing but a gold diggin' bitch!" Nikki scowled as she took a step towards Piper. "If my brother knew what's best for him, he would leave your ass and go find him a real woman."

"You're saying that to say what? Baby, there ain't no need to be greedy. I got mad friends that's pretty! It's nothing for me to let a bitch *think* that she can steal my spot," Piper boasted. "Ask your brother! He knows at the end of the day whose pussy he's coming home to."

"You sound stupid as fuck!" Nikki spat as she screwed her face up even more.

"And you look stupid! Next!" Piper countered.

"Bitch I oughta smack the shit out of you!"

"Do it and I'll have your brother lock your ass up right here!" Piper instigated.

Nikki turned her attention towards me and looked for me to defend her. When I didn't say anything she nodded her head and backpedaled towards the front door. "Oh I get it, she's your wife," she emphasized with finger quotes. "But when she shows you her true colors just remember you chose your side."

"Nikki! It's not like that!" I tried to reason.

"No it most definitely is! Have a nice life Larry," Nikki snorted before exiting out of my front door.

Just as I thought that my sister was out of my life for good, she surprised me when she reappeared in my doorway two seconds later. "I thought you were gone for good," I confessed as I reached in to give her a hug.

"Oh bitch I am. I just came back for this," she said as she snatched the bag of treats from my hand. "Now you and your bitch can eat oodles and noodles!" she stated as she walked back out of the house and slammed the door.

Logan

One Month Later...

It was Christmas Eve, the day before my favorite holiday and I was filled with cheer as I sat in the corner of my bedroom, with a cup of hot chocolate, wrapping presents for my family. This Christmas meant more to me than any other because it was the first time that Logic would be able to open his presents home with his family, instead of cooped up inside of a hospital, miserable. To celebrate the occasion, I went overboard with buying every Spiderman toy known to man just to bring a smile to my son's face. It warmed my heart to know that he would finally be able to experience the excitement of waking up to half eaten cookies and gifts left from Santa.

Creek! Boom!

From upstairs in my room I could hear the sound of my

front door open and close followed by a pair of footsteps. Jabril must have been back from his business trip, and I was ecstatic that it was just in time to enjoy the holidays with me and his son. Elated, I listened closely as Jabril climbed the flight of steps leading to our bedroom two at a time and I immediately rushed over to our door to greet him with open arms.

Jabril was so distracted with whatever that was going on in his phone, that he walked right pass me standing there and went straight for our dresser drawers.

"Well damn, hello to you too," I sassed as I rolled my eyes and sucked my teeth.

"Oh, hey bae. I didn't see you," Jabril stated as he paused from what he was doing to address me.

"Mmmhmm. I'm sure you didn't because whoever you're texting has your eyes glued to your phone instead of on me."

"Don't do that because it's not even that serious. I was only texting my boss letting him know that I was on my way back to the airport and that I would be meeting with him shortly."

"What you mean on your way back? You meant to say that you're on your way *home* from the airport, right?" I corrected as I placed one hand on my hip.

"Look, I was gonna tell you but I knew that you were going to get upset."

"Tell me what Jabril?" I challenged as I ice grilled him from across the room.

"That at the last minute my boss instructed for me and my colleagues to fly out today to Virginia for a mandatory meeting with a CEO of a large accounting firm."

"On Christmas Eve? Nigga you must think I'm stupid! Who is she?"

"Who is who?" he puzzled.

"The bitch that you're fucking!" I barked loudly, almost waking my son up in the next room.

"Logan I'm not sleeping with anybody but you and you know it," Jabril denied.

"You're lying!" I exploded. "It's funny to me that now all of a sudden you have all of these secret meetings that you gotta attend out of town. And for days on end at that. You haven't been home for a hot five seconds yet and you're already ready to run back out that door without even spending a millisecond with your son. So again I ask, who is she?"

"Logan...Baby...I promise you that I'm not sleeping with anyone. This meeting is strictly business. That's all," he reassured as he walked over to me and pulled me in for a hug.

"I don't believe you," I announced as I pulled away from his embrace and walked over and sat on the bed. "You do realize that this is the first Christmas that Logic gets to spend at home, right? The first time that he's not hooked up to all those loud ass machines and forced to stay in bed while other kids get rejoice over the fact that Santa came bearing presents. The first time that he can run around making airplane noises without having to worry about disconnecting a monitor somewhere. The first time that your son actually gets to be a kid! And you mean to tell me that you're going to miss all of this for some bitch or so- called job." I criticized. "At what point does your family come first Jabril?"

"You guys will always come first. You know that!"

"No, actually I don't! This right here proves where you want to be! And by the looks of it, it's not with us!"

"Why are you doing this Logan? This job puts food on the table for all of us to eat. Yeah I may not like it that I have to work long hours and yeah sometimes I have to be away for a few days but I chose to make that sacrifice for my family. When you quit your job so that you could be with our son more I'm the one that picked up the slack and not once did I bitch or complain about it, not once! Not one time did I give you a hard time or ask you to get another job so why are you giving me one?"

"Bravo," I sarcastically chuckled while giving Jabril a round of applause. "Thanks for doing all of the things that a man is supposed to do. What you want, a pat on the back for providing for your family?"

"Logan that's not what I meant."

"No speak your mind. What, you think I'm irresponsible for making the decision to quit my job?"

"I didn't say that."

"Then what exactly are you saying? Because the last time I checked, I was the one that was picking up your slack!" I retorted.

"How?" he opposed.

"Was I not the one who was forced to lie to *our* son when he asked where *his* daddy was at all of the time? Was I was not the one that had to wipe his tears away when he asked did his daddy love him?"

"You're seriously reaching right now. Logic knows that I love him, I tell him all the time," he disputed.

"Yeah, he knows because I'm the one that tells him," I shot

as I stood up from the bed and walked over to the walk-in closet that Jabril and I shared. "But since you don't see the error in your ways, I'mma just let you dig yourself into a deeper hole than you already are," I stated as I grabbed the carry-on bag from the back of our closet and tossed it to him. "Here! Pack your shit up and go before my son wakes up and sees you. I don't feel like explaining to him why once again his daddy has to leave."

"Yo, you bugging," he grunted as he turned his back towards me and proceeded to fill his carry on with fresh clothes from out the dresser drawers.

"I bet I am. But at least I can say that my old nigga would've stayed and spent the holiday with his son, no matter what," I mumbled under my breath as I exited our bedroom and went to go check on Logic.

As soon as I stepped foot inside of his room, I knew he was awake by the way that his body was positioned on the bed. Logic could only sleep on his back due to his breathing complications, so once I spotted him facing the wall on his stomach I knew that he

184

had heard what was said between his father and I.

"Hey prince charming," I cooed as I sat down on his race car bed and delivered a kiss to his cheek.

"Hi Mommy," Logic spoke, his voice filled with grief.

"What's wrong baby? Are you okay?" I questioned as I pulled his frail body onto my lap.

"I heard you and Daddy yelling and saying bad words again," he answered as he lowered his head to stare at the floor.

"Aw baby, don't be sad. Everything is going to be okay," I reassured as I rubbed his back with my right hand. "Me and your Daddy were just having a misunderstanding. That's all."

"Okay," he answered flatly with his eyes still glued to the floor.

"Now come give your Momma a hug."

Logic did as he was told and wrapped his arms around my waist. "Mommy."

"Yes baby?"

"Is Daddy leaving again?"

See this is exactly what I was talking about. Logic didn't need any extra stress to add to what he was already experiencing. And especially not from his father, the man that was supposed to be his hero.

"No baby, your daddy isn't leaving," I lied. "He's right there in the other room about to take a nap but when he gets up he promises to help us bake more cookies for Santa. Okay?"

"Okay Mommy," Logic smiled as he jumped off of my lap and crawled back into the bed. "I'm taking a nap too, like my Daddy," he announced as he twirled around in his blanket and closed his eyes to go back to sleep.

Seven

KNOCK! KNOCK! KNOCK! KNOCK!

"Coming!" the young woman called out as she rushed

towards her front door to answer it. Without even giving it a second thought, she quickly snatched the locks off the door and opened it for her unexpected guest.

"Hello Ma'am. Are you Misses Butler?" I asked as I looked down at the paper in my hand that held a woman's name and address.

"Look sir, whatever it is that I owe you, I promise to pay it with my next check. Please just bear with me. I'm a single mother trying to do the best that I can with the little that I have," she rambled off as a look of defeat appeared plastered on her face.

"No Ma'am. In no way am I here to make your day any harder. In fact, I actually have some good news for you, but first let me introduce myself. My name is Seven Freeman and this is my son Harlem. We're with the Harlow's Angels Children Foundation."

"Children's Foundation?" she repeated before prohibiting me to continue on. "I'm sorry, but there's been a mix up. My son

Saivon isn't sick. I think you have the wrong address," she stated before she took a step back preparing to shut the door.

"Please Miss Butler, if you give me a second I can explain," I pleaded as I placed my right foot in her doorway, preventing her from shutting the door in my face.

For a second she hesitated, probably assuming that I wanted something from her but against her better judgement she nodded her head and signaled for me to go on.

"Every year in honor of my deceased wife, my foundation gives back to the community by adopting a single mother and her small family for Christmas. This year after going over hundreds of applications, my organization came to a unanimous decision that the family chosen would be you and your son."

"Huh? What? Are you serious?" she gasped as her body began to shake.

"Yes Ma'am," I confirmed as a wide smile formed across my face.

"Oh my God! How did you? Why did you? Why are you doing this?" she sputtered as she jumped up and down, crying tears of joy.

"How did I know that you really needed this?" I chimed in as I finished her sentence for her.

"Yes," she nodded her head, barely able to speak due to the tears that were caught in her throat.

"Thank your co-workers over at Broadway cleaning services for nominating you for our single mother of the year contest. This is the first time in the three years that we've held the contest that we received over twenty nominations for the same woman. The fact that so many people felt that you were deserving of that title had us convinced and eager to meet you to present you with your gifts."

"I don't know what to say! Thank you! Thank you so much!" she cried as she ran out of her house to hug me.

"You are a phenomenal woman Ms. Butler. Your son

should be proud," I acknowledged as I returned the gesture.

"Oh my God! My son! You have to meet him!" she burst out before pulling away and turning towards the front door. "Saivon! Come quick! I have someone for you to meet!"

Moments later, a pair of little feet appeared in the doorway of Ms. Butler's home. "Mommy why are you yelling? Are you ok?" the young man questioned as he studied his mother's facial expression for any possible signs of worry.

"Yes baby! Mommy is fine!" she reassured as she bent down and pulled his tiny body in for a hug.

"Little man is protective over his mother. I like that. That's how I imagined my son was going to be," I mused as I stared down at my son holding his teddy bear beside me.

"Oh, I'm so sorry for your loss!" she apologized as a solemn look washed over her face. "If you don't mind me asking, what happened? How did she die?"

Although it was over three years ago, the pain from losing

my wife was still fresh. "She was killed in a car accident."

"Oh my God, that is so sad."

"Yeah I know. But at least I can sleep at night knowing that justice was served in the end."

"What do you mean?" she asked confusingly, urging me to explain further.

"The woman responsible for my wife's untimely death couldn't deal with what she'd done, so she killed herself."

"Wow! That's crazy."

"No! She was crazy!" I corrected.

"Mommy who's this?" the little young boy who I assumed to be her son interjected.

"Saivon baby, this is Mr. Freeman and this is his son Harlem," she advised as she pointed to both me and my son.

"Please, call me Seven," I interrupted as she gave her introductions.

"I'm sorry. This is Mr. *Seven*," she emphasized. "And he has something special to tell you!" she gushed.

"Hi Mr. Seven," he stated as he shyly waved his hand.

"Hey Saivon! How are you?" I greeted as I kneeled down so that I was eye level with him.

"I'm fine," he nervously responded.

"Saivon do you mind if I ask you a question?"

Saivon looked to his mother for her approval before answering. "Yes," he nodded his head and I chuckled.

"Who's your favorite superhero?"

"Batman!" he beamed as he exposed his toothless smile.

"Oh really? Well what if I told you that I had a truck full of Batman toys, what would you do?"

"No way! Mommy is he serious?" he cheered as he simultaneously clapped his hands.

"Yes sweetheart, he's telling the truth," she assured as she stared at her son, adoringly.

"I'll show you. Just wait right here for one second," I instructed as I grabbed a hold of my son's hand and walked down the porch to my truck.

Shortly after that, I reappeared on Ms. Butler's porch with seven oversized bags filled with dozens of toys and a small envelope in my hands.

After handing Saivon the bags of toys, I knowingly passed the envelope I had in my hand to Saivon's mother and stood off to the side as I waited for her reaction.

"What's this?" she quizzed as she eyed me curiously.

"Open it and see," I urged as I stared at her closely.

Doing as she was told, Ms. Butler slowly slid her finger through the crease of the envelope and pulled out the folded up piece of paper.

"I'm afraid to look at it," she admitted as held on tightly to the paper that was in her hand.

"Believe it or not, my wife was afraid to do the same thing when I presented her with the very same gift a few years ago."

"See now you're making me even more nervous! Why won't you just tell me what it is?" she chirped as she rocked back and forth on her feet, waiting for me to give her an explanation on what the writing on the folded piece of paper entailed.

"I'm not telling you. You gotta open it and see for yourself," I insisted.

Ms. Butler held her breath as she unfolded the small piece of paper, but instantly released it when her eyes fell on a check for Twenty-five thousand dollars. "Whose is this? Because ain't no way in hell it's mine!" she screamed as she tried to hand the check back over to me.

"It's yours! That's your name that's printed in bold lettering, right?" I hinted as I pushed the check back over into her hand.

Before I knew it, Ms. Butler dropped down her knees and sang out in praise. "Thank you Lord! Thank youuuuu! Hallelujah! My God is awesome! Yes he is! Hallelujah!"

"Mommy look at my toys!" Saivon smiled as he shoved the Batman action figure in his mother's face.

"Toy!" Harlem burst as he dropped his stuffed bear and reached for the action figure that was in Saivon's hands.

"You wanna come play with him in my room with me?" Saivon offered as he passed the toy over to Harlem.

"Toy!" Harlem sang again.

"Mommy can me and Harlem go upstairs in my room and play with my toys? I promise we won't make a mess!" he begged as put on his best puppy dog face.

"Sure I don't mind but it's up to Mr. Seven," she said as she got up off her knees and diverted the question over to me.

"Mr. Seven?"

"That's cool little man but he can only stay for a minute. We have to drop the rest of these gifts off to my family before it gets too late and they go to bed," I agreed. Not even a second after the words left my mouth, Harlem and Saivon both took off inside of the house.

After dusting the dirt off of her legs, Ms. Butler looked to me and offered a smile that expressed her genuine appreciation. "I don't know if I'll ever be able to repay you for what you have done for me."

"You don't have to. This gesture was from the heart. I'm not looking for anything in return."

"I know that but still, I don't think you even realize how this act of kindness has touched me and my family. Prior to you coming here this afternoon, I didn't have a single thing to give my son for Christmas this year because I was barely making ends meet. I was two months behind in my rent and trying my best to stay afloat. But thanks to you, I now have money to catch up on all of my bills. My son has a closet full of toys to keep him occupied and I now don't have to stress and worry about where we're gonna get our next meal from."

"Well I'm glad that I could help take the burden off of you so that you and your son could have a merry Christmas."

"How about you come on in here and let me fix you a cup of hot chocolate? It's cold out here and I don't wanna get you sick before the new year begins."

"I thought you'd never ask," I joked as I opened the screen door and followed her inside of the house. "What's your name by the way because I'm tired of calling you Misses Butler already? That name makes you sound old as shit."

"Sierra," she answered with a chuckle. "The Sierra Butler."

Later that Night...

Thanks to Sierra's goofy ass I lost track of time and was

out later than I originally intended on being. I had only planned on staying at her crib for an hour, but once we got to talking and she got to sharing her life story, I was hooked and I just had to hear more. Don't get me wrong, I've came across a lot of shorties in my day that fell victim to the struggle, but it was just something about her vibe that screamed she was different. Something that reminded me of my precious Harlow that made me yearn for more. Maybe I was tripping, or maybe I just missed my wife but when I talked to Sierra I felt the same familiar urge to protect her that I once had with Harlow and the same tug at my heart.

Sierra was a cool little caramel complexioned baddie with a nice pair of lips and a nice tall slender frame. She didn't seem like the type to drown her face in makeup which was a plus and she wasn't trying to keep up with the Jones' which was even better. She was quiet, she kept to herself for the most part, and she actually was quite funny; something that I didn't expect from such a lost soul. From her impersonations to her corny knock-knock jokes, she kept me entertained for the three hours that I was at her crib and I could tell shorty was someone that I wouldn't mind being around. I wasn't looking for a girlfriend and I damn sure was trying to replace my wife, but if we happened to cross paths again sometime in the future I could possibly see myself getting to know her a little more.

Reaching my second destination of the night, I prayed that I was just able to hop out, drop of what I came to deliver, and hop back in my car to leave. My California King was calling my name and I couldn't wait to make love to the one thousand thread count Egyptian sheets that covered it.

Me: I'm outside.

Jake: Great! I'm three minutes away!

Me: Cool! I'm parked over by the Checkers in the black Ford-150 pickup truck.

In under two minutes flat, Jake pulled his car in the parking space beside of me and placed it in park before getting out.

"Hey man! Long time no see," he greeted as he reached in

for a handshake.

"I know right. It's been a minute," I agreed as I discreetly slid him the envelope while we were shaking hands.

"The usual?" He asked while tucking the white envelope in his back pocket and pulling his navy blue North Face coat over to cover it.

"It's all there. Plus some," I answered as I opened my car door back up and proceeded to get into it. "Merry Christmas Jake. Make sure you buy your wife and kids something nice."

"Thanks man! I will!" he replied and like a thief in the night, we both disappeared.

<u>Omari</u>

Me and my little angry bird Shaniya aka ShyShy have been kicking it kinda heavy since the little incident we had in the middle of the parkway a month ago and honestly I couldn't get enough of her positive vibes. After dealing with Piper's scandalous ways and trying to dodge all them other gold diggin bitches, it felt refreshing to finally come across a shorty who was on her own paper chase and wasn't worried about the knot of money that I had in my pocket. That kind of shit made a nigga like me smile in the inside and go out of my way to do more for her, even though she declined the gesture every time. ShyShy liked that sentimental shit instead, you know the spontaneous flowers, the late night walks down by the water, and all the other corny shit a young nigga like myself wasn't used to. *But* since I planned to keep her around for the long haul, I was going to try my best to learn, which brings me to why I'm here now standing in the middle of the kitchen trying to be Chef Boyardee.

At the last minute, I thought it would be a good idea to plan us a cool lil date with just me and her cooped up on the couch, with some food, and movie, but now I was kicking myself for even coming up with this bullshit. I called myself getting brownie points by cooking the food instead of ordering it but the shit was more stressful then stealing a car.

Staring at the back of the Hamburger Helper box that I held in my hand, I reread the instructions for what seemed like the tenth time and still couldn't seem to grasp what I was supposed to do. *Brown hamburger meat? Reduce heat and let simmer? What the fuck is that supposed to mean?* I thought to myself as I placed the box of uncooked pasta on the kitchen counter and went to go retrieve a glass from the cabinets. When I brought this box of food, I assumed that shit was already done and all I had to do was heat it up in the oven for a minute and voilà, it was done.

"Why is this shit called Hamburger Helper if I still gotta cook all this? Like dead ass, where the fuck is my helper!" I huffed as I knocked the box of food over on the counter and walked over to my mini bar to pour myself a drink. "Now I'm about to have a bunch of soggy ass noodles with no meat."

DING! DONG!

"Ain't this bout a bitch! I shoulda known her lead foot ass was going to get here before 9 o'clock."

DING! DONG!

"Damn! Give a nigga a second to answer the door first, impatient ass!" I shot as I looked out of the peephole before unlatching the lock and opening the door.

"Move Mari! I gotta pee!" she ordered as she bounced her leg and unhooked her pants.

"Say please," I exasperated as I stood in the doorway blocking her from entering.

"Mari MOVEEEEEE! BEFORE I PEE ON MYSELF!"

"Say please," I reiterated as I smiled at the spectacle before me.

"PLEASEEEEE DAMN IT!" she barked as I stepped to the side and allowed her to scurry off to the restroom.

"ASSHOLE!" she yelled from the other room as she finally was able to release her bladder into the toilet.

Moments later, I heard the toilet flush and the water

running from the sink.

"YOU BETTER WASH YOUR HANDS TOO DIRTY!" I taunted as I closed the door behind me and walked back into the kitchen.

"Now what were you saying?" she sassed as she walked in the kitchen from the other entrance.

"I saiddddddddddddd that I missed your little dirty ass," I lied as I copped a deuce and pulled her in for a bear hug.

"Nahhhh, don't lie now," she said in between giggles while I nestled my nose in between her neck.

"You smell good. What you got on?"

"It's called soap and water," she joked as she stepped away from me and walked over to the pot that sat on the stove. "I thought you said you were cooking?" she probed while lifting the lid and examining the empty pot.

"I was but I forgot to get the ground beef for the

Hamburger Helper."

"Hamburger Helper? Nigga you said you were cooking me something special for the holiday."

"That *is* special. My ass don't know how to cook so that's the best that I could do," I admitted before taking a sip of the D'usse that was in my glass.

"I swear I hate you!" Shy chuckled as she walked back over to where I was standing. "But I appreciate the effort behind what you were trying to do," she stated as she stood on her tippy-toes to give me a kiss on the cheek.

"Damn, can I get a real one?" I pestered as I placed my glass back on the counter and pulled her body close.

"Hell no! I don't know where your mouth has been," she teased as she squeezed away from my grasp and took a step back.

"I'm trying to put them on you!" I cajoled as I eyed the skin-tight 7 for All Mankind jeans she had on with a HUEY brand shirt to match.

"Uhh Uhhhh. I already told you that it's not that type of party. Now hurry up and come on before we miss the Charlie Brown Christmas movie."

"Charlie Brown? I don't wanna watch that! I thought we were gonna watch something like This Christmas or The Best Man Holiday."

"We are! We're watching Charlie Brown THIS CHRISTMAS," she articulated before placing a bag of popcorn in the microwave and strutting off into the living room.

"I can't stand her smart ass," I mumbled to myself before grabbing my drink off the counter and joining her in the living room.

"Soooooo since you failed miserably at Chef Ramsay's cooking challenge, have you thought of a backup option as to what we're going to eat?"

"I already told you what I wanted to eat, but you shot me down so it's your turn to find something."

"Pizza it is!" she chimed in as she pulled out her phone and dialed a nearby pizza spot. "What kind do you want?"

"Get me a meat lovers with extra cheese."

"I should've known greedy ass!" she commented before placing the order through the phone and then hanging up.

"Watch your mouth when you're talking to me!" I shot while taking a seat next to her on the couch.

"Boy ain't nobody scared of you! I thought I showed you that the day I was about to bust your windows out in the middle of the street," she reminded as she gave me the *'yeah ok'* face.

"Keyword *about to*," I emphasized. "You don't get credit for no shit you were about to do. If that was the case I was about to choke your ass that same day and give you this dick."

"See there you go with that nasty shit again. What do I need to do in order for you to get the picture? Leave?" she suggested as she stood up from the couch and fixed her clothing.

The last thing I wanted her to do was leave. The night was just getting started and I was enjoying the laughter she bought on this lonely Christmas Eve.

"Man sit your cry baby ass down, Angry Bird! Wasn't nobody being serious. It was a joke!" I bellowed while grabbing her arm and pulling her back down to her seat.

"I told you to stop playing with me!" she chided as she mushed my head with her finger.

"No, I told you to stop playing with me," I retaliated as I gently pushed her off of the couch and onto the floor.

"Did you really just push me?" she queried before she threw a pillow at me and erupted into laughter.

"I see you didn't learn your lesson," I voiced as I reached across the couch for the other pillow. "Keep playing and I'mma knock your wig off next," I threatened as I tightened my grip around the pillow in my hand.

"I quit! I quit! I quit!" she surrendered as she dodged my

attack and shot up off the floor. "You don't play fair!" she cackled while she checked her weave.

"Now go sit in timeout and think about what you've done!" I ordered while pointing to the corner of the living room.

"Nigga you got me FUCKED UP!" she spat as she sprinted over to the couch and smacked in the back of my head with the pillow that she had hidden off to the side.

I had no choice but to laugh as I grabbed the back of head and rubbed the spot that Shy had hit me in. I could already tell that it was going to be a long night filled with nothing but laughter and positive vibes and I was looking forward to it.

__Logan__

Two Weeks Later ...

"Get up baby! You gotta get ready!" I instructed as I peeked my head inside of Logic's bedroom. I was so excited for the playdate that I had planned for us today that I couldn't keep the surprise to myself for not another minute. "Come on Logic! Mommy planned a day of fun for us at the Bounce place," I called out as I walked closer to his bed and noticed that he still wasn't moving. "Come on Logic. You can sleep when we get back," I stated as reached down and shook his body. "Logic…" I paused as I gently touched his skin again, this time noticing that it was cold. "Logic, baby did you hear Mommy? Wake up!" I yelped as shook his body forcibly, sadly he still didn't budge an inch. "Please Lord not again! Not my son!" I cried out as I frantically ran into the other room searching for my phone. "Hold on Logic! Help is coming! You hear me, help is coming!" I quavered as I punched 9-1-1 into the cellphone and waited for an operator.

"911, what's your emergency?" the operator sang into the receiver.

"My son! He's unresponsive! Please come help him! Pleaseeeeeeee!" I screamed.

"Ma'am calm down. Did you try CPR?"

"No! Oh my God! No I didn't think of that!" I bawled unable to control my tears.

"Ma'am emergency services are on their way to your house as we speak, but I need you to attempt to give your son CPR until they get there, okay?"

I didn't attempt to answer the operator, as I dropped my phone and raced back into the other room to perform CPR on my son. "One and two and three and four…." I continued to count out loud as I pressed down powerfully on his chest. "Eight and nine…" *Whewwwwww! Whewwwww!* I paused as I held Logic's nose and released all the air that I had in my lungs into his mouth. Holding on to hope, I continued to repeat this process over and over until I finally heard the ambulance off in the distance. "Logic they're here. Do you hear the sirens baby? They're coming to save you!" I cried as I pushed down on his rib cage harder. "One and two and three and four…."

KNOCK! KNOCK! KNOCK!

"Ma'am it's the paramedics! Can you open the door?"

"Yessss! I'm coming! Please help me save my son!" I shouted as I sprinted down the flight of stairs and damn near yanked the front door of the hinges.

"Where is he Ma'am?" the paramedic asked as he gathered his emergency equipment.

"He's upstairs in the bedroom to the right!" I blurted out as I ran after the paramedics who were now up the stairs.

As I stared at the scene unfold in front of my eyes, I could feel my heart shatter in a thousand pieces. Logic has yet to even attempt to take a breath and the more I thought about it, the more I realized that it was possible that this day has finally come. The day that every mother on earth dreaded. No mother wanted to see their child go before them and as many times as I tried to mentally prepare myself for this moment, nothing in the world seemed to soothe my aching heart. All I could do was stand there helplessly as I watched the love of my life slip away. There wasn't a single word that could describe the way that I was feeling as I cried from the depths of my soul out into the universe.

Seven Months Later...

It was eighty-nine degrees outside on a hot summer day and here I was once again in the house, buried under the covers, and high as a kite with my music on blast. The heat was the furthest thing from my mind as I sat in my cluttered room with my head in the clouds thinking back on the good times that I shared with my son. No matter what was going on around me, I thought about my him. I missed everything about Logic, from his laugh to the way that he used to suck his two fingers and roll his shirt. Or even the way he used to call my name a million and one times because he was scared of the dark. All of those things I took for granted and would give anything in the world to get back because life without Logic was miserable and just didn't make sense.

The dark circles under my eyes were proof that I haven't slept in days and the smell of onions coming from under my arms was enough to make even a homeless person cover their nose. I desperately needed a nap but the feeling that the pills bought me had me fighting my sleep just so that I could enjoy it while it lasted.

Closing my eyes, I allowed the music to take me to a place of peace and serenity. As my toes swayed to the soothing melody, I envisioned a tropical island surrounded by crystal clear water and lots of sand. The instrumental, along with the two Percocet pills I had just popped, had me feeling like I riding the wave off into Paradise with my son while my best friend sat of to the side of the beach in her shades laughing and joking. This feeling was a feeling that I wanted to last forever.

"Logan, get up! You can't just lay in the same spot all day," Jabril commanded as he walked in the room and pulled the covers back from over my head.

My body cringed immediately at the sound of his voice and for a minute I thought that I was experiencing Deja vu. "Logan, get up," sounded way too familiar for my liking and just that fast the flashback of the day I lost my son crossed my mind.

"Did you hear what I said? Get up!" he repeated as he pulled the pillow from under me and tossed it on the floor.

"Jabril leave me alone!" I grunted with an attitude. And as I attempted to reach for the covers to pull back over my eyes, I lost my balance and fell on the floor, making a loud thumping noise when I landed.

"See look at you! You look like a damn junkie! Can't even sit up straight without falling," he scolded as he grabbed me by the arm and pulled me from up off the floor.

"Leave me alone! I'm fine!" I slurred as I shooed his hands away. "You wasn't worried about me before so don't start now."

"Here you go with that shit again," Jabril huffed as he walked around the piled up clothes on the floor and took a seat on the bed. "When are you going to clean this mess up?" he probed as he examined the pigsty that he once called his room.

"I'm not cleaning shit! Tell that bitch to go do it!" I spat as spit flew from my mouth.

"HOW MANY TIMES DO I HAVE TO TELL YOU THAT THERE ISN'T ANOTHER WOMAN!" he growled as he stood back up and got in my face. "I'M TIRED OF YOU MAKING SHIT UP IN YOUR HEAD!"

"Making up shit? How fucking cute! For your info I don't have the time nor energy to make shit up about a deadbeat, scum of the earth, shoulda been swallowed person like yourself!"

"Logan you need help! You're taking your anger out on the wrong person!"

"Oh trust me, I got the right person! You're the reason why I feel this way now!" I cried. "You're the reason why my son isn't here!"

"How dare you blame my son's death on me! That's wrong on all levels and you know it!"

"No what's wrong was me choosing you to be his father! That's what's wrong! I would have been better of going to the sperm bank if I wanted a dead beat for a father!" I shrieked out in anger.

"Dead beat?" he wickedly chuckled.

"You heard me! D-E-A-D BEATTTTT! You standing in my face acting like you were father of the year but answer this question for me. Where were you when I was calling for help the day that our son needed you? Where was Superman at then, huh? Oh I'll tell you! He was ducked off somewhere across town with a bitch when *our* son was lying in my arms dying!"

"Logan for the HUNDREDTH TIME... I WAS AT WORKKKKK!"

"Work my ass! You can't keep using that as your excuse! It's played the fuck out! Just admit it! Your ass ain't shit and never will be! I hate you! Do you hear me? I FUCKING HATE YOUUUUUUUUUUUUUUU!"

"You hate me, but I'm the reason why you have a place to lay your head at now. I make sure you have food in your stomach and clean clothes to put on your body. How the fuck else did you think we were gonna survive Logan? I don't see your mother stepping up to plate and offering you anything. I rescued you! Or did you forget that!"

"I HAD MY OWN BEFORE I MET YOU! *You* came in *my* face, sweating *me*! You wanted a family and as soon as I give you one, you disappear. Holidays! Birthdays! Shit you couldn't even take your son to the park! But you expect me to think all of this was because of work? Yeah okay! Stick a red nose on me and call me Boo-Boo the fool. All you is, is an opportunist who preys on weak woman."

"You know what? I'm not arguing with you today. I've had enough. I'm tired of doing the same old song and dance with you. You keep pointing the finger at me but not one time did you own up to your own shit. Since I'm such a horrible person and you hate me so much, how about you get your things and get the fuck out of the house that I pay for! Matter of fact to prove my point even further, make sure you only take the things that you *came* with. Don't touch shit that this dead beat ass nigga brought!"

"Fuck you! I'm not going anywhere!" I protested as I laid back down and gave Jabril my ass to kiss.

"Oh you're gonna get the hell up outta here one way or another," he warned as he walked over to the dresser and retrieved his phone. "You've got five seconds to get hell out of my house before I call the police and have them charge you with trespassing."

"You can't do that! I live here too!" I reasoned as I jumped out of bed and attempted to snatch his phone from his hands.

"Get your hands off of me before I add assault and battery to the list of charges!" he sneered as he pushed my hands away.

"You know what? FUCK YOUUUUUU!" I roared as I knocked all of his belongings off the dresser and onto the floor. "I don't need you or the headache you came with! I'm outta here!" I announced as I snatched a pair of basketball shorts off the floor and stormed out of the room. I quickly slid the stained shorts on and held my head high as I walked out of that house with nothing but the clothing on my back.

With no particular destination in mind, I strolled the block from sun up to sundown until I came across someone I recognized.

"Logan? Is that you?" my neighbor from down the street asked as she stopped walking her dog to look over my disheveled appearance.

"Yeah Cree, it's me. What are you doing out here this late at night?"

"I should be asking you the same thing."

"I just needed a breath of fresh air to help clear my mind."

"I don't want to pry into your business, but are you okay? Do you need anything? I've been meaning to reach out to you and ask you if you wanted to go out for some drinks or something because I've noticed that you've been a little distant since... well you know," she hinted.

"Yeah I know," I said as I looked to the side and twiddled

my fingers. "I haven't really quite been myself lately. But since you asked, I actually do need a small favor from you. Do you mind if I borrow your phone for a second? I'm locked out of my house and I need to get in contact with Jabril so that he come and let me in," I lied as I mustered up a phony smile.

"Sure! No problem!" she agreed as she reached inside of her fanny pack and handed me her phone. "Here you go!"

Thinking of who I could call on to help get me out of this bind, I scrolled down my memory rolodex and dialed the first person that came to mind. "Come on... Come on... Answer the phone," I mumbled as I waited for the ringing to stop and the person to pick up the phone.

"Hello. Who's this?" Seven questioned as his voice boomed through the receiver.

"Seven! Thank God you answered! It's me, Logan! I need you to do me a hugeeee favor."

"What wrong Lo?"

"Can you meet me at the Wegmans off of Reisterstown Road? I rather talk to you about it person."

"Lo, I'm not on that side of town. It's gonna be a minute," he informed while I looked at the time that was on the cellphone.

"That's fine. I can wait," I considered as I calculated the distance that I had to walk. "Just make sure that you look for me because I don't have a phone."

"What happened to your phone?"

"It's a long story. I'll explain it to you when you get here."

"But how am I supposed to let you know that I'm there though?"

"You'll get creative. I gotta go now, I have to give this lady back her phone. I'll see you in a few. Oh and thanks again bro!" I rambled off before ending the call and passing Cree back her phone. "Thanks again Cree. My ride will be here shortly."

"Well do you want me to wait with you?" she asked,

concerned.

"Nah I'm good, you've done enough. I'm just gonna wait right here until he pulls up. He shouldn't be too long."

"I don't feel safe leaving you out here all by yourself with no phone," she voiced before handing me her phone, once again. "Here, hold mine until he gets here and when he does you can just drop it off by the house. If I'm not back in time from walking Monroe, just drop it off with Doug. He should be home by now."

"Cree, I don't wanna —"

"Take it!" she insisted.

"Thank you Cree," I said as I expressed my gratitude. "I promise that I won't take long."

"You're welcome Logan," she replied as she reached in for a hug. "And if you ever need to talk, just remember that I'm a phone call away."

"I will."

And just like that Cree continued on with walking her dog and left me alone to wait for my brother to come get me.

I was glad that Cree was nice enough to leave me with her phone because honestly, I was dreading that four mile walk in this heat.

BARK! BARK! BARK! BARK!

Then again on second thought, I better get to walking.

It took me about an hour to walk from my neighborhood to the shopping center where Wegmans was located. I was drenched from sweat from head to toe and surprisingly for the first time in a while, I actually craved a shower. Maybe it was all in my mind, but my body felt like a trillion bugs decided to have a parade all around it. I hated this feeling and immediately started digging my nails in my skin to alleviate the massive itching sensation.

I've never felt so out of place before as I caught the looks of other's unwelcoming stares while I stood out front and waited for my brother. I knew this area was too bougie for a person dressed like myself and now I was regretting not taking the high road anyway.

Why the hell are these people staring at me like they've never seen someone scratch their arm before. I cursed to myself as I mean mugged all the citizens passing by. My grimace seemed to scare all of them off, but one. In fact, to her it seemed that my scowl was even inviting.

"God bless you," the older woman sympathized as she passed me two dollars, a peppermint, and a number to a homeless shelter.

"What in the?" I asked puzzled as I surveyed the items in my hand.

"Don't worry Honey. Take this as a blessing from the man above. There is always light at the end of every tunnel. Just keep the faith and this too shall pass," she preached before pushing her cart into the holder and walking away with her groceries.

Damn. Did I look that bad where people could mistake me

for being homeless?

I needed to get out of here to get myself together because at this point I was even beginning to feel sorry for myself.

Checking the time that was displayed across the phone, I made a mental note that I only had about an hour until the store closed for the evening.

BEEP! BEEP!

Like a deer caught in headlights, I squinted my eyes so that I was able to get a better view of the person that was trying to get my attention. I said a silent prayer and hoped it wasn't another church member trying to do their good deed for the day because I'd had enough of the peppermints and scriptures.

Finally! I thought to myself as I recognized the silver Audi coupe pull up in front of me.

"About damn time you came and got me!" I jested as I pulled the passenger door open and jumped in the front seat.

"Oh hell nah! Logan you got some bags?" Seven screeched as he tried to prevent me for scooting any closer to him in my seat.

"What in the hell do you need bags for?" I quizzed as I looked at him clueless.

"For yo ass! You not about to sit on my seats smelling like that," he exaggerated by holding his nose.

"Shut up!" I warned as I playfully hit him in his chest.

"Damn King Kong! That hurt!" he teased as he rubbed the area that I had just hit him in.

"Why you keep picking with me knowing that I'm not in the mood?"

"Because I'm your brother and I can't remember that last time that I saw a smile on your face."

"But I'm not smiling though," I countered as I tried to fight the urge to show all thirty-two pearly teeth.

"You are now!" Seven corrected while he reached across

the cup holder and tickled my stomach.

"Aight! Stop! You win! I'm smiling now! You happy?"

"I am! Now what's up? What's been going on with you? And what is it that you need?

Although Seven was only a few years older than me, he made me feel like I was talking to my father and coming from being a daddy's girl that was sometimes kinda hard.

"Before I go in detail about what's been going on, I need you to promise me that you won't jump off the deep end and do anything stupid."

"Not making that promise. But go ahead and tell me what's wrong," he said as he urged me to continue.

"Seven!" I called out so that I could have his undivided attention.

"What?"

"This is serious! I need you to make a promise that you

won't go and do anything stupid," I pleaded.

"I'll try."

"Seven!"

"What! That's the best that I'm willing to do! You already know how I feel about my family and you know how I get down, so in my opinion asking me to give you anything other than that is crazy."

He was right. If I wanted to get the big dogs involved in my petty lovers quarrel, I better be able to handle the consequences. All I could do was cross my fingers and pray that I wasn't digging a deeper hole for him or myself.

After taking a deep breath and exhaling, I finally worked up enough courage to fill him in on today's events.

"I don't even know where to begin," I stated as I tried explaining the situation to him the best way I knew how.

"Start somewhere. Anywhere!" he pressed while growing

impatient.

"Okay! So look, I'm not sure if you're aware of not, but ever since I lost my son Logic, I've kinda felt like I lost my will to move on. I know it sounds crazy but the only thing that has been preventing me from calling it quits is the fact that I know that if I kill myself I will never be able to be reunited with my son in the pearly gates of Heaven."

"Logan why —" Seven tried to cut in, but I refused to let him cause me to lose my train of thought.

"Wait a minute. Let me finish," I stated as I continued to update him with what's been going on in my life. "Now like I saying, I was too afraid to end my own life, so the only other way I knew left to take away the pain I was feeling was... drugs."

"Logan please don't tell me that you're shooting that shit up into your veins."

Admitting to Seven that I was shooting up dope would ultimately solidify my title as a junkie and the last thing that I needed was for him to turn his back on me. So, instead of exposing him to *all* of my demons, I opted to just inform him on the less serious ones and hoped that it was enough to get him to help.

"I'm not a junkie Seven! I wouldn't dare put those type of drugs in my system," I defended as I pulled at the t-shirt that covered my arms.

"Then exactly what drugs do you mean?" he asked, wanting me to clarify which specific drugs I was hinting at.

"Oxys and Percs," I revealed as I tried to ignore the look of disappointment that was displayed across his face.

"How long have you been using?" he continued to probe.

"Honestly," I paused. "Since Harlow died."

Seven nodded his head as if to say he knew how I was feeling. "Logan, you should have been reached out to me. You know that I would have helped you. Shit, we're fighting the same battle."

"I couldn't bring myself to say anything Seven. I was too embarrassed."

"Well we're going to get you help. Now come on, let me get you out of this heat and take you home," he stated before putting his key in the ignition and starting the car.

"Wait! There's more," I blurted out, failing to remember the initial reason for this reunion.

"I'm listening," Seven acknowledged as he turned on his defrost and slowly pulled off.

"I kinda need a place to crash until I get back on my feet," I gulped as I sat back in my seat and anticipated his answer.

"You know that that's not a problem. I have more than enough space for you and Jabril."

"Jabril isn't coming with me. It's just me," I corrected as I reached for the dial and turned the air on max in his car.

"Is everything good between y'all? he pried.

"No. We got into a huge argument today. I finally got some things off of my chest that I've been holding in for a while and I guess he didn't like what I had to say because he got mad and put me out of his house."

"What you mean put you out his house? He put his hands on you Logan?" Seven fumed as he tightened his grip around the steering wheel.

"No. He just changed the locks and threatened to call the cops if I ever came back," I replied while shrugging my shoulders. "Oh well. It is, what it is."

"Well as long as his coon ass didn't put his hands on you I'm good. I can tolerate them police threats all day, but him putting his hands on you? Now that's different."

"Maybe this was what I needed. I mean I haven't seen you or Harlem in God knows how long. I'm sure he —".

BUZZ! BUZZ! BUZZ!

"What's that noise?"

"Oh shit! I forgot to give Cree back her phone! Can you drop me off around the corner to her house so that I can return it? Pleaseeeeeeeeeeee, I promise that I'll only be a second, I swear," I begged as I placed both of my hands together and pleaded for him to take me.

"Girl knock it off. You know that I'm willing to take you wherever it is that you need to go. All that begging shit is unnecessary."

"Thank you!" I beamed. "Whatever it is that I can do to pay you back, don't hesitate to let me know."

"You can start off by taking a bath," he implied as he looked at me with the serious face. "And then after that we can work on getting you to kick that nasty addiction of yours."

"Deal! But make this the last time you talk about the way I smell."

"Only if you make it your business to not smell this way again," he countered.

"Deal!"

And at my request, he left it alone for the rest of the night.

Three Weeks Later...

"Lo, I'mma be in the car. Just lock the door behind you whenever you're finished getting ready!" Seven yelled to the top of the stairs as he was leaving out of the front door.

"I'm putting my shoes on now!" I yelled back as I slid both feet into a fresh pair of white and black Adidas shell heads and then walked in front of the mirror to check my appearance. "Yeah, I'm getting my weight back in all the right places," I boasted while I twirled around to admire my juicy ass and my thick long legs. "I'm about to give em' hell all summer." I swore as I gave my bottom one last look. All it took was a few pep talks and a trip to Tyson's Corner for me to slip back into my old ways and thanks to Seven my ego was now on a trillion.

After giving myself the final look over in the mirror, I grabbed my wallet from off of the dresser and quickly exited the house; while I still had a ride to the T-Mobile store.

"So did you decide on which phone you were going to get?" Seven inquired as soon as my cheeks touched the smooth leather seats in his whip.

"I was thinking that since I'm starting to get my mojo back, I should probably try something new. You know, something that's outta of my norm," I expressed as I rolled the window down, allowing the air to hit my face.

"Like a Galaxy?"

"That's cool... and different. Well, for me anyway."

"I hope your prepared for all those broken text messages," He joked. "You gonna get message two after you get message four, which is before you get message one," he chortled as he held his stomach to help cease his laughter.

"Never mind! I'mma stick to what I know," I exclaimed as I too joined in on the laugh.

"Ahhh man! I can see you now, cussing and fussing every time you get a text message," he announced as he wiped the tears from his eyes.

"Yeah...yeah...yeah," I commented as I spotted the T-Mobile sign off in a distance. "Dang, we're here already?" I rhetorically asked as I unfastened my seat belt and prepared to get out.

"I told you that it was only around the corner. What? You thought that I was joking?"

"Heck yeah! Usually when most people refer to something being around the corner, it's really ten to fifteen minutes away. But with you. You actually meant *around the corner*."

"You should know by now that I'm not most people," he bragged as he shifted lanes and then turned into the parking lot.

"Shoot, for all of that, I could have walked here," I stated while I waited for him to put the car in park before I hopped out.

"Well next time I'mma let your ass walk then."

"Lies you tell!" I chirped as I walked up the ramp and opened the door to the cellular store.

"You running inside like you're the one that's paying," Seven commented as he entered the store several seconds behind me.

"Hi. Welcome to T-Mobile. I'll be with you in just a few minutes. But while you wait, you can check out all our electronics that are spread out around the store," the store manager greeted as she continued to help her customer.

"Oooooo, I like this!" I marveled as I picked up the Galaxy S9 model that was stationed directly in front of me.

"Aight. But when that thing blows up in your ear, don't say that I didn't warn you."

"Dear iPhone user, I can make decisions on my own without your input."

"Dear future Samsung user, please be sure to pick out your casket color and style before you purchase your phone. Signed, an iPhone user," he mocked while doing his best impersonation of me lying in a casket.

"First of all, I'm not even gonna look like when it's time for me to say my final goodbye.

"Well how you gonna look then?"

"Like this," I corrected as I put up my middle finger and pretended to be dead. "Middle finger to my haters even in the afterlife. Baby Babyyyyy."

"And on that note, I'mma go right on ahead and step on over here to look at these phones," Seven announced as he chucked up his deuces.

"Whatever," I replied as I resumed the task at hand and continued to look around the store.

About fifteen minutes passed before the cellular agent was finally ready to assist me.

"Good afternoon Misses…"

"Logan," I finished as I greeted her with a handshake.

"Oh I love that name! I was going to name my son that," the agent gushed as she flashed a warm and inviting smile.

"Why thank you. Believe it or not, I actually used to hate my name when I was growing up."

"Why?"

"Because all the teachers thought that I was a boy," I chuckled as I reminisced on my good ole' school days.

"I was going to say that," she admitted as we both laughed in amusement. "So anyway, what brings you in today?"

"I need to get a new cell phone because my last one was stolen."

"Yikes! That's not good. Do you have an idea of which particular brand you want? Samsung? iPhone? Nokia?" she rattled on until she sorted through all of phone options that they had available on hand.

"My brother thinks that I should get an iPhone, but I kinda want something new. What do you think?" I vacillated as I mused over the phones in front of me.

"I personally prefer the iPhone over the Galaxy, but that's just my opinion. But ultimately, you have to purchase whatever you feel is best for you because you're the one who has to use it."

"You know what? I'mma just go ahead and go with the iPhone because knowing me, it'll be just my luck that my phone happens to be the one that explodes," I said as I gave in. "And before you know it, you'll be calling this company L-Mobile because I'mma damn sure get my coins for it too. Okayyy!" I snickered as I gave the girl a high-five.

"I don't care what you do. As long as you let me keep my job, I'm good," she disclosed, as she lowered her voice so no one could hear her.

"Let me stop acting ghetto before I get you in trouble," I whispered as I saw Seven walking over to approach us. "Yeah, so umm… you can go in the back and get that there um… iPhone for me now," I deflected, while mustering up my best professional tone.

"Sure! Be right back!" she stated, as she took the hint and scurried off into the back.

"What was y'all over here talking about?" Seven quizzed as he looked back and forth between me and the back of the store.

"Nothing. She was just convincing me to get an iPhone," I responded while my rolling my eyes.

"Smart woman."

"Yeah well, I wish she would hurry up. I still gotta back up all of my data that was stored in my iCloud," I stated as glanced at the store clock for the time.

"Well you're about to get your wish. Here she comes," Seven advised as he nodded his head towards the direction the woman was coming from.

As soon as the cellular agent was within earshot, she immediately began rambling off, "so here's the dilemma. When I was in the back sorting through our inventory, I was only able to find a black iPhone 5 and a white and a rose gold iPhone. Are either one of these fine or do you want us to see if another store has what you're looking for?"

"The rose gold iPhone X is perfect!" I declared as I glanced at the clock again.

"Cool. Now hand it here, so that I can go pay for it," Seven instructed as he grabbed the phone from my hand and proceeded to pay for it at the counter.

"Hey, I have a quick question," I asked, before the cellular agent was able to walk off. "Do you mind if I connect to your store's Wi-Fi to back up my phone? I kinda been out of a phone for a while and I'm dying to check my messages."

"Sure, that's not a problem. I can give you the Wi-Fi code now while you wait for him to finish up."

"Thank you so much."

"Your oh so welcome," she mentioned as she jotted down the exogenous code for the Wi-Fi on a piece of paper. "Just make sure you fill out the survey on the back to tell them how awesome I was," she winked.

"Oh absolutely!" I agreed as I picked up the pen she once held and wrote her name on the piece of paper.

While I waited for my brother to take care of the financial part of things, I made myself a home at the small circular table that sat off to the side and reflected on all that he has done for me in these last few weeks. Just the other day I was homeless with not a pot to piss in or a window to throw it out of, but now look at me. I was laced from head to toe in the finest threads, I had a couple of dollars in my pocket, and I was happy; well for the most part. Every now and then I could feel the guilt creeping back into my thoughts, reminding me of that tragic day. But, just as soon as it appeared it was gone, thanks to a hefty dose of my special medicine.

"This damn phone better be able to read your mind," Seven complained as he returned back over to where I was seated with a T-Mobile bag in hand.

"Stop crying! It wasn't that much."

"Shiddddd. This phone cost more than both of my car notes, combined."

"You got it to blow Big Timer, so relax."

"Not on no damn phone," he mouthed as he handed me the bag.

"Correct me if I'm wrong, but I coulda swore that you was just over there ranting and raving over this piece of doggone metal. Acting like it was the best thing since sliced bread."

"And when do you ever listen to me?"

"Always. You know that."

"Well then let's go."

"I can't leave just yet because I gotta sign into my iCloud

to retrieve all of my backed up information."

"Can't that wait until after we go and pick up Harlem?" he hinted.

"No! Because who said that's gonna be the last stop before we get back in the house? You know like I do, anything Harlem wants from his precious Daddy, he gets. And I don't have time to wait because I need to know who's been hitting my shit since it's been off."

What I really was in a rush for was to see if my dealer reached out to me to inform me of his new shipment, but of course I couldn't tell Seven that.

"Ard impatient ass! How long is it gonna take to back up your phone?"

"No more than five to ten minutes," I grinned while reaching in the white bag to retrieve my brand new phone.

"Cool. While you handling that, I'mma go and stop next door to check and see if they got this new game Omari's been looking for at GameStop. Come and get me when you're done."

"Okay. I shouldn't be long," I informed him as I snatched the plastic covering from off the box.

Seven exited the T-Mobile store once I agreed not to too take long and went next door in search of whatever it was that Omari couldn't find.

As soon as Seven was out of my line of sight, I immediately snatched my phone from its box and quickly powered it on to start the set up process. It's been a long three weeks without any communication from the outside world and I desperately wanted to see what was waiting for me in my messages. I prayed that it was some good news though, because I was in need of a fix, and bad. The little bit of "medicine" that I had stashed away in my bedroom wasn't enough to hold me over until the weekend so if my supplier didn't act soon, I was sure to slip back into my former state of depression.

After drifting off to LaLa land for a few brief minutes, I

quickly came to and got back to the task at hand which was backing up my phone. Glancing down at the loading bar, I was elated to see that my transfer was almost complete and that I was one step closer to getting my hands on some product.

"Three more minutes," I read out loud as the anticipation killed me on the inside.

Deep down, those three minutes felt like an eternity but as soon as I read the words backup complete, I instantly forgot all about the torture of waiting. I opted to skip the introductions and went straight to message icon, ready to real all of my texts. Sliding my thumb across the glass screen, I scrolled through all the 'are you okay' messages and paused when my eyes landed on a number that I've never seen. I couldn't contain my excitement as I quickly clicked on the message with my thumb and read what it said.

Call me.

I smiled inwardly because I knew that it was no other person than him. My dealer. He was the only person I knew that would change his number every two weeks and he was the only person I knew that kept his text under a six word maximum.

Should I call him now or later? I thought to myself and after weighing my options I realized that now was the smarter choice. There was no guarantee that I would have the same privacy later and there was no way in hell that I would risk calling my dealer in front of Seven. After pressing my finger on the blue phone in the contact information, I put my ear to the phone and waited for him to answer.

"I see you finally stopped being stubborn and reached out!"

Tiran

I didn't expect for Logan to return my call, especially not after the way I left her high and dry to dwell in her feelings. Our last conversation didn't end off on a good note and I almost couldn't blame her for feeling the way that she felt towards me. At the time I didn't care that I was burning bridges with the only woman that I truly ever loved, however now after having to deal with Khia's disloyalty, I realized that I needed Logan just as much as I needed air in my lungs to breathe. Logan was my voice of reason and without her, I was slowly starting to lose my mind. I couldn't even remember the last time that I had a good night's rest and some of that was partially from the demons that I kept tucked away in my closet.

With everything that had been going on with Harlow and Khia, I was forced to go into hiding for a while and move somewhere off the radar where nobody recognized me. Even then, I never stayed in one place for too long because I was paranoid and knew eventually that my past was going to catch up with me.

"Tiran?" she asked, caught off guard by the voice that she recognized on the other end of the phone.

"Hey beautiful," I cooed, confirming that the voice that she heard was in fact mine.

"What do you? Wha…what is it that you want?" Logan stammered.

"I was calling to reach out," I informed but then paused before I finished my sentence. I knew that when it came to Logan, Logic was a soft spot and I was afraid to reopen an old wound. "And offer my condolences on your loss."

"That was months ago Tiran. Don't you think it's kinda too late for you to be beating down my door for that?"

"It's never too late to console a friend in their time of need," I corrected while shifting through the hand rest in my car for some spare change.

"Well when I needed a friend, no one was there," she recounted before continuing. "Which is fine though because it taught me who was in my corner and who wasn't."

"You can't fault me for me something that I didn't know about."

"I can do whatever my heart pleases. Now, is that all that you wanted to talk about? No better yet, am I free to place you on block now?"

"Logan, listen. Hear me out for a moment."

"My...my...my. Look how the tables have turned. It feels funny sitting at the other end of the table, listening to you plead your case."

"Are you gonna give me a chance to explain or not?"

"I'll take the latter. I hate to be the bearer of bad news, but I'mma pass on your little pity party."

"Logan!" I called out.

"What Tiran? I already know what you're going to say, so there's no need. I don't need you to feel sorry for me...or my son. Life happens and sometimes you gotta move on."

"Life happens and sometimes you gotta move on," I mimicked. "That part is for me isn't it? You being smart aren't you?"

"I said what I said."

"No answer the question. You taking shots now?"

"Nobody is worried about you Tiran. And you are delusional if you think that they are," Logan clarified as her voice began to rise a little from her apparent frustration. "You know what's funny to me? How now everybody and their Momma wanna come outta the woodworks all of a sudden and show their support and…ask me am I good. But where were all of y'all at when I needed ya'll? Where was all of this comfort and forgiveness? I'll tell you! Nowhere! I got to where I am because of ME. Because I decided to be strong. And now that I know I am capable of picking myself up and putting myself back together, I don't need y'all for shit. Y'all taught me how to live my life without y'all, I didn't ask for that."

"You keep saying y'all! What, that nigga got you mad at the world to the point that you're taking your anger out on me?"

"Don't no nigga have anything to do with how I feel about you!"

"He has to! Because all you keep saying is y'all and not you! Y'all did this and y'all did that! All *I'm* guilty of… is reaching out to a friend who I thought was in need of some kind words to help uplift her day. That's it, that's all! Whatever it is that he got going on over there that has you lashing out on everybody, has nothing to do with me."

"Are you kidding me right now? Like seriously! You disappeared off the face of the earth for years, do you hear me…YEARSSSS! And now that you mysteriously reappeared, you expect me to just sit here and welcome you back in with open arms? Like you never left? Like you didn't just shit on me *and* my sister. Matter of fact, speaking of my sister… you didn't even have the decency to come to her funeral and pay your respects! But you want me to believe that you care? Mannnn get the fuck outta here!" she fumed before I heard a voice say.

"Damn Lo! You *still* backing up your phone? I thought that you said that it was only gonna take a few minutes," the voice interrupted and caused me to forget what I was saying.

"I'm coming now Seven! Stop whining!" Logan acknowledged while pulling the phone away from her ear for a split second.

"I see you still deal with that nigga, huh?" I grunted while reminding Logan that she was still on the phone.

"That's none of your business," she hissed.

"What is it about that nigga that y'all hoes can't seem to shake?" I insulted as I finally got out of the car to walk over to the gas attendant to pay for some gas.

"I don't know. But whatever it is, it's probably the reason why you and ya mans can't stop hating on him."

"Hate on him for what? I get the same twenty-four hours in a day that he does so if I wanted to put the time and energy in outshining his organization, I could."

"Logan, who you over there talking to?" Seven quizzed from a distance.

"Nobody!" she replied. "I was just hanging up the phone now."

And before you knew it, the line went dead.

Chapter 5

Seven

Two and a Half Months Later…

For some reason today, no matter how hard I tried to sneak a few Z's in before my meeting, I couldn't. And part of that reason was because my phone wouldn't stop going off. Between Omari calling me to bitch and complain about our workers and Logan calling me for money, I could see now that a nap wasn't in my future.

RING! RING! RING!

"What is it now?" I rasped into the phone without looking to see who it was.

"Oooh, I'm sorry to disturb you. I'll just call you back at another time," she apologized.

"No! No! You're good. I thought this was my brother again calling about some nonsense," I explained as I sat up from my bed and wiped my eyes.

"Are you sure?" she asked, hesitant to state the reason for her call.

"Yeah, I'm sure. What's up?"

"You know that I wouldn't call if I really didn't need you, right?" she coaxed as she tried to put her pride to the side and ask me what she needed to ask.

"Yeah, I know. It must be something serious if Wonder Woman is calling on little ole' me for help," I joked.

"It is," she said with a light chuckle. "I have to work this evening and I can't find a baby sitter for Saivon."

"Where's Ms. April?"

"In New York again for one of her infamous bus trips," Sierra informed. "I thought about calling out, but my boss threatened to let me go the last time if I had one more occurrence."

"Don't worry Cee. We'll figure something out."

"I can't lose my job Seven, it's the only way that I'm able to put food on the table for me and my son."

"And I know that. I'm not going to let that happen."

"I'm not knocking Ms. April or anything, but this is the second time in three weeks that I had to struggle to find someone else to watch my son."

"Why didn't you call me the first time this happened?"

"Because you've already done enough."

"And I wanna do more. I already told you that I'm here for you if you need me."

"Seven no!" she blurted. "It's bad enough that you pressured me in to letting you pay for his daycare. I'm not about to feel helpless and become somebody's charity case."

"Stop thinking like that because we both know that you're not, you just fell on bad times. Just take it as me helping a friend get back on their feet."

"Thank you but no thank you. All I need you to do is point me in the right direction of your nearest daycare center that can watch my son on such short notice."

"I have an idea. How about I come and get Saivon from you so that you can take a nap before you go into work. I know that you're tired and that you haven't slept since you got off from your first job."

"Seven, I can't let you do that."

"And why not?" I challenged.

"Because I don't want to impede on what you already have going on."

"Trust me, you're not. I just thought of the perfect person to watch you son and you don't have to worry about her charging you a penny because she owes me."

"I am not about to leave my son around one of your little hoes," she sassed.

"Do I look like I'm ready to go meet my maker?" I chuckled. "Sike but nah, she's not one of my hoes, she's my sister."

"Did your Momma push her out of her womb?" she countered.

"No."

"Then she's not your sister. I don't want my son around no one who seems questionable," she spoke.

"Me and Logan don't have to share the same mother and father to make us siblings. Her loyalty to me is enough to make her family."

"Yeah, y'all fucking," she said more to herself than to me.

"Actually we're not. Since you must know, Logan is the best friend of my deceased wife and she's the god mother to my son and daughter."

As soon as I mentioned my deceased wife, Sierra changed

her tune quick. "Ohhhh that's the girl that you were telling me about that night that you dropped of those gifts off."

"Yeah," I affirmed while shaking my head.

"My bad. I assumed that you were talking about somebody else," she apologized while beginning to gather her son's things. "I don't have a problem with Logan watching my son. I feel comfortable now, knowing that you trust her with your life."

"Good! Now go pack Saivon a bag then go take a nap," I instructed as I got up off the bed to slide on a pair of basketball shorts. "Oh and before I forget, make sure you leave the key under the mat so that I can get in. I'm not trying to wake you up from your nap."

"Okay, I'm doing it now. How long do you think it's gonna be before you get here?"

"Depending on the traffic, I'll say thirty minutes. It shouldn't take no longer than that."

"Okay, I'm about to go and get him ready."

"Cool," I said, ready to end the call but just as I was about to press the end button Sierra called out.

"Hey Seven."

"Yeah?"

"Thanks again," she uttered, her voice laced with sincere appreciation.

"No problem shorty!" I replied before actually hanging up the phone this time and going to look for Logan.

After tossing my phone on my dresser, I slid my foot in the pair of Guardian Angel slides that sat at the end of my bed and left out of my room. Jogging down the steps, I went straight to the kitchen to retrieve a bottle of water out of the refrigerator and smiled when I spotted the duplicate set of keys I gave Logan hanging on the key hook. Taking a gulp of my water, I allowed the refreshing liquid to seep down my rusty throat and replenish my insides. Satisfied with the instant recharge, I placed my water on the counter and proceeded to locate Logan.

"Hey Lo!" I called out as my voiced echoed all throughout the house. "Lo, where you at?" I repeated as I walked back and forth in between the rooms.

"I'm down here," she yelled out from the basement bathroom.

"Why you all the way down there when it's a bathroom right by the kitchen?" I puzzled as I descended the steps into the basement.

"Because I ate a burrito today and I didn't want you or Harlem smelling my shit. Is that so bad," she stated as she washed her hands and closed the bathroom door behind her.

"It doesn't smell like shit down here to me," I voiced as if she was hiding something.

"That's because I sprayed. What's up with the questions though? You need something?"

"Yeah, I need you to do me a favor for tonight."

"I hope it's not anything crazy."

"It's not," I reassured her.

"Good. Because the last time that you enlisted my services, I found myself in the middle of a brawl that was World Star Hip Hop worthy."

"Uh uh! Don't blame that on me. I asked you to take Harlem to the park for me that day, not get into it with some boy's mother," I argued.

"Well she shoulda taught her son some manners then! That's what's wrong with these cap mouthed seeds of Chucky. They don't have no home training."

"I agree! And since the two children that I need you to watch *do* have home training, I don't expect to hear any complaints about their behavior," I said as I eased that small favor up in there.

"Two?" she questioned as she balled up her face.

"Yeah two," I confirmed.

"I already know that Harlem is one of them but who's the other child?"

"His name is Saivon. He's my friend's son. And before you start to go in, no I'm not sleeping with his mother and no he isn't a BeBe kid."

"Hell no! I'm not watching none of them chicken heads' you entertain offspring. That's against the girl code on all levels," she said as she expressed her disdain.

"I wouldn't ask you to do me this favor, if I didn't need it LoLo."

"But Seven that's wrong! Why can't she watch her own child? And don't tell me it's because you're trying to take her out on a date. Because that would be a double hell no!" she advised.

"I see this is going to take a little more convincing," I stated as I took a seat on the couch and made myself comfortable. "Look, the last thing that I want to do is put her personal business out there, but the reason why she can't watch her child is because she's a single mother juggling three jobs trying to make ends meet. Her baby sitter canceled on her at the last minute and now she's forced to either go to work and leave her son unattended or risk losing her job because she doesn't have anyone else to watch him."

"She can stay home from a night of stripping. I'm sure she can make it up another day," she shot.

"You over there screaming that girl code shit, but right now you being foul as fuck. You don't know shit about shorty and you already talking greasy on her name. Why she gotta be a stripper huh? Why she can't have a regular job like any other hard working woman? You wouldn't like it if people assumed the same about you after you quit your job to take care of your son!"

"But my son was sick!"

"And? There's no difference. You made a sacrifice for your son, and lucky for you, you had someone else pick up the weight that you weren't able to carry. I can't say that my friend has the same," I reasoned.

"Yes she does! She has you."

"And I have you! Which is why I'm asking you to look past your individual feelings and help me out."

After taking a minute to consider everything that I just said, Logan finally agreed to help a brother out.

"I'm only helping you because I know how it feels to be by yourself and have to carry the burden of your child all by your lonesome."

"I know and I promise that I'mma look out for you when I get back in the house from my meeting," I said as I got up from my seat and headed out the house to go and get Saivon.

Later That Night...

In the kitchen, while listening to my music, I stood at the counter preparing dinner for the boys while they sat in the living room watching a movie. I was in the process of putting a few chicken tenders on a metal sheet pan when Saivon quietly walked up behind me and startled me.

"Ms. Logan can I have some more juice please?" Saivon politely asked and then waited for my response.

"Whew! You scared me!" I shrieked as I damn near jumped out of my skin.

The chicken tenders that were once on the tray now decorated the kitchen floor.

Whelp, there goes dinner. I thought to myself as I kneeled down on the floor to pick up the frozen nuggets.

"Do you need some help Ms. Logan?" Saivon offered as he rushed over to the mess and started scooping up the pieces.

"Awww, you're so sweet," I smiled as I got up from the floor and tossed the remainder of the wasted tenders in the trash. That was the last of chicken tenders in the upstairs freezer and I prayed that Seven had a stash of kid-friendly foods somewhere else. All that was left upstairs was a few bags of frozen fries and that wasn't enough to feed these babies. "Saivon do me a favor and go over there and keep an eye out on Harlem for me while I go downstairs and find us something to eat."

"Okay," he replied so sweetly.

"And when I come back I'mma pour you and Harlem two big cups of juice."

"Okay!" he sang as scampered back into the living room to check on Harlem.

For a brief moment, I thought I needed a little pick me-up. But just as soon as the thought entered my mind, it left.

Nah. I can't do that while they're here. It's too dangerous. I'll just wait until Seven comes back so that I can leave. But wait, what if he doesn't come back until tomorrow? Shit! That's too long to go without anything in my system. You know what? I'mma just take a little pinch, to hold me over until tonight. Yeah! That's what I'mma do.

Using the small window of opportunity, I hurried down the stairs and secured myself inside of the basement bathroom so that no one could interrupt me. I only had a little bit of time before Saivon would start wondering where I was at, so I had to move fast while he was preoccupied.

Discreetly, as if someone could see me, I pulled the small plastic bag of white powder out of my bra and inspected through the bag before opening it.

"This shit better be worth the money I spent," I grumbled as I placed a tiny amount of the powdery substance on my pinky and rubbed it across my gums.

After a few odd seconds, I could feel my gums starting to numb and a smug smile crept across my face.

Jackpot!

Searching around the bathroom with my eyes, I tried to find something that I could use to help me distribute the cocaine evenly on the bathroom sink. I wanted more bang for my buck, so snorting the drug seemed liked the better decision instead of digesting it. I was moments away from saying 'fuck it' and improvising with what I had, until I suddenly remembered the expired I.D card that I had tucked away in the cleaning supplies box under the counter. Antsy, I immediately dropped down on my knees and opened the cabinet to begin searching for the plastic card. "Come on. Come on. I know it's here," I huffed while placing my body up against the bathroom counter and reaching all the way to the back. I continued to feel around for the hard piece of plastic and as each minute passed I grew more and more frustrated. Just before I was about to give up and save my high for later, my fingers brushed up against the item in question and I instantly used all of my might to try and grip it. "Ah ha!" I breathed, happy that the small card was finally in my hands.

Time was of the essence and once I realized that I had already wasted enough of it on searching for my I.D, I quickly poured the white substance in a thin line on the marble countertop and positioned my body so that I was eye level to it. My heart raced with anticipation, as I leaned down directly above the powder and released a deep breath before snorting the line of drugs like a vacuum cleaner. Tilting my head back, I welcomed the warm sensation that burned my nose before dripping down to the back of my throat. I was in heaven as this feeling of euphoria was unmatched and enough to put my mind at ease for the moment.

"Ms. Logan," I heard the innocent voice say as I stood there frozen with my mouth agape. It was almost like I could feel his eyes on me as I slowly turned around to address him.

Wow, I'm tripping! I thought as I looked and saw nobody there. "I gotta get myself together," I slurred as I pinched my nose to stop the snot from falling and stumbled out of the bathroom. I was so out of it that I wasn't even aware of what I was doing or for that matter, what was in my hand. It just felt like I was dreaming and the more my high escalated the louder the voices around me became.

"Ms. Logan, my mommy is here," the same innocent voice was calling my name and it sounded so surreal. "Ms. Logan! Ms. Logan!"

"Who is that?"

"Ms. Logan," I could feel a set of little hands gently tugging at my shirt, signaling to that it was time to come back to reality.

"Saivon did you find her?" I could hear a grown woman say as she called out to the little boy from the top of the stairs.

"Yes Mommy!" he responded back, causing me to snap my head in the direction in which is voice was coming from.

This high heightened all of my senses, but my sense of hearing was the most sensitive.

"Saivon what are you doing down here?" I questioned as I wiped the corners of my mouth with my hand.

"My mommy was looking for you. She told me to come down here and get you."

"Your mommy?" I asked as I stood there perplexed.

"Yeah, she's upstairs," Saivon informed causing my eyes to widen.

"Shit!" I hissed as my body began sweating profusely while my eyes started to twitch. "Think fast. Think fast," I rambled off in fear. My adrenaline was in overtime as the wheels in my head began to spin.

As I was scanning the room for a possible ploy, a drunken smile appeared across my face as I almost forgot the initial reason why I was in the basement to begin with. *The food!* I thought to myself as I dashed over to the deep freezer and grabbed and a handful of food. I was such in a hurry to get upstairs that I didn't even notice that I dropped the bag of cocaine on the steps behind me.

"Hi, I'm Saivon's mother. You must be —"

<u>Sierra</u>

Three Hours Earlier…

Usually working the evening shift was a breeze for me, but today it was different. I was surprised that I was even able to get my work done as fast as I did, especially not with the way that my son was weighing heavily on my mind. I wasn't too keen on leaving him with a stranger, but at this point what other options did I have? I was a single mother with no other support system outside of Seven, so I pretty much had to take what I could get. I swear though if it wasn't for my faith in God, I would have been left because Lord knows I was very overprotective when it came to mine. Still, I was grateful that my day was finally over, now all I had left to do was check in with my supervisor and I was out of here.

"Mr. Wilson, I'm done cleaning the bathrooms and all of the offices. Is there anything else that you need me to do before I leave?" I asked after peeping my head through his office door.

"Did you wipe down all the walls and the base boards? Did you clean the windows? Did you dust? You know we have a huge executive meeting tomorrow with a lot of big wigs running through here, so I need this place to be spotless."

"I know Sir. I've already wiped everything down and double checked the offices to see if they were neat and presentable.

276

Everything looks good for tomorrow. You don't have anything to worry about."

"You did all of that in," he paused for a moment to look at his watch, "four hours?"

"No Sir. It took me a little longer than that. I was just able to finish a little earlier than usual because I opted to work through my lunch today. I kinda have a family emergency that I need to take care of so I utilized all the time that I had."

"I understand, but you do know that you are only getting paid for the time that you are here, correct?"

"Yes, I'm aware."

"Very well then, you're free to leave."

"Thank you."

"You're welcome," Mr. Wilson responded while I pulled my head from out of his office and grabbed the door to shut it. "Oh, and Ms. Wilson," he called out, summonsing back into his office.

"Yes, Mr. Wilson?"

"Let's not make this an everyday thing. This is a place of business and I need people here who are reliable and dedicated to doing their job, not to say that you aren't. I'm making an exception for you this time because I understand things happen, but next time...never mind. Just know that there's not going to be a next time," he cautioned while locking his eyes with mine.

"I know Sir and it won't happen again," I assured as I took heed to his warning and got the hell out of dodge before he changed his mind.

As I sat in traffic waiting for the light to change, I couldn't help but to imagine the look on my son's face when he found out that I was coming to get him early. My son was a straight up momma's boy and due to the long hours I had to work, it was rare that he ever got a chance to lay up under me. Some days I could feel his heartache, but he never voiced his feelings because he

278

knew the effect his words had on me.

"About time!" I huffed as I looked up and noticed that the light had changed. I was beyond impatient and in a rush because I knew that every second that I was able to spend with Saivon counted for something. Pressing my foot on the accelerator, I zoomed through traffic like a bat out of hell; pulling up to Seven's mansion in a matter of minutes. "Ooooo, this is nice," I acclaimed as I got out of the car and surveyed the neighborhood. All around me I was surrounded by nothing but big beautiful houses and exotic luxury cars. "I didn't know Seven was touching this much money," I marveled as I pulled out my phone and cross checked the address that he sent me with the one that I was standing in front of. "I guess this is it," I confirmed as I placed my phone back in my pocket and jogged up the front steps to go knock on the door.

KNOCK! KNOCK!

Taking a step back, I gave the person a little bit of time to answer the front door before I knocked again.

KNOCK! KNOCK! KNOCK!

"What's taking her so long?" I mumbled to myself as I jiggled the door knob and pushed the door.

CREEKKKK

I presumed Seven to be a safe and cautious man, so imagine my surprise when the door to Seven's six-bedroom home slowly slid agape without anyone standing on the other side to open it.

"Hello!" I announced as I let myself in and roamed the house for the person in charge. "Hello!" I called out again as I wandered through the house, in awe of the rooms.

"Mommy!" Saivon screamed as soon as I turned the corner and was in his eyesight.

"Hey baby," I greeted as I bent down to shower his face with kisses.

"What are you doing here? I thought you was at work," he

questioned.

"I was sweetie, but I got off early so that I could surprise you."

"Does that mean we can leave?" Saivon beamed with admiration in his eyes.

"Yes baby, we can leave. But first, I gotta find Ms. Logan to tell her that I'm here to get you."

"I know where she's at! She's downstairs!" he squealed.

"Why is she downstairs if y'all are up here?" I frowned as I glanced over at Harlem, who was glued to the television.

"Cause when she was cooking, she made a mistake and dropped our food on the floor. She told me wait right here with Harlem while she went to go find us some more nuggets in the basement."

"How long has she been gone?"

"I don't know," he answered while shrugging his shoulders.

"Okay, well do me a favor. I need you to go downstairs for me and tell her that I'm here while I go and gather your things," I said while escorting Saivon into the kitchen.

It took me a while to locate his things because they were scattered all across the living room. I'm talking clothes, toys, and trash from his snacks were everywhere. But once I finished, I was ready to go.

As I was walking back into the kitchen, I noticed that Saivon nor his baby sitter had emerged from the basement and I was beginning to wonder if he even delivered the message. Marching over to the top of the steps, I opened the basement door up and called down to the bottom. "Saivon, did you find her?"

"Yes Mommy!" he shouted back.

Moments later, a tall voluptuous woman appeared at the top of the steps with her hands full of food.

"Hi, I'm Saivon's mother. You must be —"

"Ms. Logan! You dropped your sugar!" Saivon burst as he

jumped to the top of the step and dangled the plastic bag full of cocaine in his face.

"Where did you get that?" Logan roared while throwing the frozen food on the counter and then snatching the bag of nose candy from his hands.

"Bitch! Don't snatch nothing from my son!" I exploded as I advanced towards her and reached for the bag.

"Well tell your son to keep his hands off my shit!"

"YOU FUCKING DROPPED IT!" I scowled as I spoke every syllable. "All he did was pick it up for your ungrateful ass!"

"I didn't ask him to touch my shit! I knew where the fuck I left it at!" she spat in disgust. "See this is why I didn't want to watch the little rascal to begin with. Y'all motherfuckers need to learn y'all boundaries!"

"Little rascal? Bitch, who the fuck do you think you're playing with? I will smack the shit out of you! You better watch your mouth when it comes to my son or shit will get real gully in here…AND FAST!"

"Ain't no owls in here! You heard exactly what I said!" she provoked as she tried to stuff the half opened bag of drugs in her bra.

Logan didn't even get a chance to secure the baggie in her bra all the way because before you knew it, I was all over her ass like white on rice.

"I'm tired of y'all big amazon bitches playing with me," I growled as cocked my fist all the way back and punched her square in the nose.

"You bitchhhh!" Logan barked as she snapped out of the mini daze that she was in and grabbed her bloody nose. "You fucking broke my shit!" she bleated as she charged towards me.

I may have been small but one thing I wasn't, was scared. Balling my fist up into a knot, I waited until Logan was within arm's reach before I started raining blows all over her upper body. "Back the fuck up!" I snarled.

"That shit don't hurt! Come on! Hit me harder! Hit me harder!" she taunted while she was bent over, still grabbing her nose.

This bitch is looney! I thought to myself while I mustered up all of my strength from my pent up frustration and gave her what she asked for. As I tried to use one of my hands to grab a fist full of her faux locs, Logan jerked her body back just in time and it caused me to swipe her bag of nose treats onto the floor; spilling it.

"YOU DUMB BITCH! LOOK WHAT YOU DID! IT TOOK ME FOREVER TO GET THAT!" Logan wailed as she dropped down to her knees and began scooping the powder into a pile. Blood, mixed with sweat, oozed down from her face and fell on top of the cocaine creating a slimy substance. "I should spit on you!" Logan seethed as she analyzed the damaged product.

"Do it and watch me kick all thirty-two teeth down your throat," I challenged as I kept my eyes trained on her.

For a minute, I thought that she would take the hint that I

was not to be fucked with, but as soon as I let my guard down for a split second to turn and check on my son. BOOM! She was on her feet and her hands were wrapped my neck.

"Talk that shit now bitch!" she growled into my ear as she transformed into the Incredible Hulk.

"Help...me," I strained, while fighting for my breath.

"Get off my mommy!" Saivon yelled as he ran full speed towards Logan and shoved her hard in her back.

"You little..." Logan cursed as she eased her grip from around my neck just enough for me to steal a breath.

It was now or never because if I didn't make a move fast, I was surely about to become the next victim on Baltimore's Murder Ink Instagram page. Using the little strength I had left, I lifted my elbow as far as it could go and bought it down hard into Logan's side.

"Saivon run!" I panted as I took advantage of the distraction I created and darted towards the front door. I was almost out of the house, with Saivon hot on my heels, but I stopped running when I realized that I was leaving behind one valuable thing. *Harlem.* "Shit!" I hissed as the realization that I was going to have to go back to the area that I just was running from hit me. "Here, take these and go wait in the car. If I don't come back out here within the next five minutes, press this button and call Seven," I instructed as I passed my keys and phone over to my son.

"Okay!" Saivon agreed as he looked at me worried.

"And whatever you do. Do NOT come back into this house."

"I won't."

"I'm serious Saivon. It's not safe!"

And with that I left my son at the front door while I went back to rescue Harlem and bring him to safety.

<u>Seven</u>

RING! RING! RING! RING!

I was in the middle of a meeting with some pretty important people when my phone went off alerting me that I had an incoming call. Glancing down at the name displayed across the screen, I pressed ignore and continued on with my conversation.

"As I was saying. We have a shipment of exclusive parts ranging from Bentley's to Lamborghini's coming in two weeks. My team will arrange for you to get the parts at a secret location, which will be given to you the day of the drop off," I briefed the buyers, not wanting to disclose too much information.

RING! RING! RING! RING! RING! RING!

Ugh! What does she want? She knows that I'm busy right now. I thought to myself as I pressed the ignore button for the second time and flipped my phone over on the table. I was going to have to return her call later because right now I discussing business. My team was about to make a real good come up off of this sale so I had to ensure that everything was up to par for the Gomez brothers' liking.

BUZZ! BUZZ!

"You probably should answer that," Diego sarcastically shot. He was the asshole of the Gomez trio and definitely my least favorite.

"Whatever it is, I'll get to it later," I deflected as I tried to get back to the topic at hand. The drop off arrangements.

"You sure?" Diego chuckled before removing his toothpick and sitting it on the table. "I would hate for that to be your precious Harlem."

"Aye slick! Leave my nephew name out your mouth! He ain't none of your concern!" Omari barked from the other side of the table.

"He will be if this deal goes wrong," Remel, the muscle of the trio, answered. "We have a lot of money on the line so we need this exchange to be flawlessly executed or else people are going to start disappearing."

"On both sides," Omari advised as his trigger finger started to itch.

"I second that," I agreed as I chimed into the exchange between my brother and Remel.

RING! RING!

There she goes again! That was the tenth time Sierra called my phone in a matter of minutes and I was starting to get the feeling that something was wrong.

BUZZ! BUZZ!

"Are we holding you up?" Antonio finally spoke, causing all his workers to become silent. He wasn't a man of many words so when he spoke, everybody listened.

"Not at all," I reassured while picking up my phone to read the message.

Sierra: Answer the phone!

Sierra: Seven!!!

Pressing my fingers on the keys, I sent Sierra a quick message letting her know that I was busy and that I would call her right back.

Me: I'm finishing up now. I'll call you as soon as I get out into the parking lot.

When I saw that little gray bubble instantly appear in the left hand corner of my phone, I waited a few seconds to see what she had to say.

Sierra: I'll be in jail by then!

Jail? What the fuck? I thought she was at work!

Me: Give me two minutes to wrap up this meeting and I'll call you!

I didn't even give her a chance to respond as I stood up from the table and addressed all of those who were in attendance. "I appreciate everyone for coming out but unfortunately this meeting has to be cut short."

"Told you," Diego snickered to his brothers.

Without disclosing my personal business, I continued.

"This meeting will resume sometime next week when you're available. The shipment doesn't come in until the following week so that gives us enough time to discuss the details."

"I don't know if I trust that you or your organization is competent enough to handle what we need you to handle," Remel considered as he remained seated at the long table. "This is the second time that your "personal life" has intervened with our business dealings and I'm starting to think that maybe me and my brothers need to take our business elsewhere."

"Second time? When was the first?" I faked confused. I knew exactly which day he was referring to, I just wanted him to say it.

"Ohhhh! You don't recall, I see. Well here, let me remind you. Do the letters FBI ring a bell to you?" he hinted.

"Nah they don't. I don't fuck with the alphabet boys," I denied.

"I don't know how much of that, that I believe is true.

Aren't you affiliated with Mr. Larry Kirkland?" he questioned, while the others waited for me to answer.

"Yeah, he's on my payroll. What about him?"

"Nothing. I find it quite strange how the FBI got wind of our last major drop off and when it was all said and done my people were the only ones who were there."

"Larry isn't with FBI, the ATF, nor the DEA. He's the commissioner and I pay him good money to turn a blind eye while I do what I gotta do in these streets."

"A pig is a pig," Diego sneered, while siding with his brother.

"Man stop playing dumb! You know his wife died that day! Have some fucking compassion," Omari argued.

"That's not my problem. Business is business. And I don't like how your team is handling it," Remel replied coldly.

"You right, business is business. But don't sit there and act like you're not wearing the money that I blessed you with from that *same* situation. I know the rules of the game and I compensated you and your family for the fault that was on my end," I demurred as I stood firm.

"Those were mere pennies from a peasant," he quipped. "Me and my people have touched more money than you poor boys could ever imagine. Which is why we need to end this now because we're wasting our time waiting on these scraps."

"You're not the one that gets to make that decision though, now are you?" Omari retorted as he stood to his feet as well.

"No, but I am the one that gets to decided who lives and who dies," Remel calmly replied while daring Omari to challenge him.

"What you think after they made your gun, they stopped making them? You bleed the same way as me homeboy," Omari shot back.

"In my country we don't use guns. We prefer to be up close

and personal to our prey so that we can gut them like a pig and watch them take their last breath."

"Well we ain't in Mexico no more my nigga! Us, Americans, use guns!"

"How dare you insult me!" Remel raged as he shot up from his seat. "My people are from Guatemala you punta!"

"Did he just call me a bitch?" Omari quizzed as he rushed towards Remel, who was standing a few feet away from him.

"Enough already!" Antonio bellowed as his voice shot across the room. "You two are making a fool of yourselves in front of your organizations! Seven," he paused while turning his attention on me. "Take care of your family first. My people will reach out for another date and then we can resume from there."

I chose not to speak. I just nodded my head and allowed him to continue.

"And you," Antonio scolded while directing his attention back to his brother. "Don't you ever embarrass me like that again.

Understood?"

The look on Remel's face said it all. He was tight and judging by the way he stormed out of the meeting and slammed the door, you could tell that it was about to be World War Four in these streets.

"Alright then, since there aren't any more issues or concerns, the meeting is adjourned."

Once the Gomez organization began to disperse, I made sure my team was squared away for the next meeting before disappearing behind the door that we all came in from.

Snatching my phone from my pocket, I immediately dialed Sierra's number while I ran to my car and got in.

"Tell your brother this ain't over," I heard Remel snort before I whipped my head in the direction that he was standing, which was by my passenger side window.

Before I had a chance to respond, Sierra burst through the other side of the receiver reminding me that I was on the phone.

"About time you called me back!"

"Cee, let me call you right back," I promised before abruptly hanging the phone up in her ear. I had to handle what was in front of me first before I could scurry off to rescue her because if I didn't address it now, ain't no telling what might happen. "Aye son, all that subliminal shit is unnecessary. You either gonna shit or get off the pot. Do what you gotta do, it's no need to talk about it."

He didn't even get a chance to talk his shit before you know it, my car was in drive and speeding out of the parking lot. I was even halfway down the block when I sent Omari a text letting him know what just happened.

Me: Yo boy is salty about how his brother handled him in that meeting! He just approached me in the parking lot talking big shit so watch your back!

Omari: I'm already on it Chief!

Me: Aight, Bet!

My brother was smart enough to know not to take the threats that Remel threw at him lightly. I was a firm believer that there was some truth in every joke, and this situation was no different.

After I made sure my brother was on point with what was going on, I dialed Sierra's number and waited for her to answer.

"Seven I swear to God if you hang this phone up on me again, I'mma kill you *and* your sister!" she warned and I could tell that she meant every word.

"Oh Lord, what she do now?"

"WHAT SHE DO? I JUST HAD TO DRAG THAT BITCH BECAUSE SHE LEFT HER DRUGS UNATTENDED AROUND MY SON!" she barked through the phone and I was almost positive that if I was in front of her right now, she would have hit me.

Logan's not using drugs again. She can't be!

"Nah, that can't be true because I know Logan. She

wouldn't dare have that type of shit around my son," I defended.

"YOU A DAMN LIE! I SAW THAT BITCH WITH MY OWN TWO EYES SNIFFING THE FLOOR WHEN I WENT BACK TO GET HARLEM."

"Why the fuck was she sniffing the floor?" I asked, confused.

"BECAUSE SHE'S A JUNKIE! Me and her got to fighting and after she snatched the bag of drugs out of Saivon's hand they fell on the floor."

"Wait a minute, y'all were fighting?"

"YESSSSS! Were you not listening to anything that I was saying? Me and her just went toe to toe in front of my son. Shit, your son too!" she added.

"Yeah, I'm listening. But it's not making sense to me. I mean listen to yourself. You're saying that Saivon "found" a bag of drugs and showed you in front of Logan. That doesn't necessarily mean she was the person he got it from. He could have

299

found those drugs anywhere for real. In an alley, on the street. Anywhere!"

"I know my son! And I also know that he's not gonna bring home no shit like that! So you can even believe what I'm telling you and do something about it or I can find somebody who will."

"Look, chill with all that. It's unnecessary. I'm about to hang up with you and call Logan to see what's going on and when I'm done, I'mma call you back."

"You know what? Don't even worry about it! Because I can already tell that you're gonna take her side. I'mma handle that bitch the way that I see fit and if you have a problem with it then you can jump in line behind her."

"Sierra!"

"No fuck you! You think that I'm lying about that dope fiend so I'mma let you see for you self. Don't call my phone trying to apologize either because when it's all said and done, you're gonna learn the truth about your sister."

"How you gonna tell me not to call your phone? You have my son."

"That's right, I do. And right about now you should be thanking me because I coulda left him there with her."

"Man chill the fuck out until I get to the bottom of this! You throwing dirt on my sister's name without allowing me to hear her side of the story first. Just let me hear her out to see what she has to say so that I can fix this."

"When you're ready to get your son, you know where he is. Otherwise delete my number." And just like that the line went dead before I even got a chance to finish what I was saying.

"Fuck!" I shouted as I rubbed my hand down my beard. I'd had enough drama for today but for some reason my gut instinct was telling me that I was about to get more.

While my phone was still in my right hand, I dialed Logan's number only to be greeted by her voicemail. "Maybe her phone is dead," I mumbled to myself as I tossed my iPhone in the passenger seat and sped the rest of the way home.

As soon as I pulled up to the front of my house, I double checked my surroundings before I got out of the car. I was no stranger to how ruthless the Gomez Cartel could be, so I'd rather be safe than sorry when it came to my life. Thankfully, nothing appeared out of the norm as I exited my car and made my way up the steps to my front door.

I wasn't even to the top of my porch yet before I spotted several items of women's clothes sprawled all out and around my front yard.

"That looks like Logan's shirt," I said out loud as I took a few steps closer to the balled up t-shirt. "Why in the...You know what? Let me go inside because something's not right."

And just like I thought, it wasn't. As soon as I stepped foot through the threshold of my house my mouth fell open and I just knew that my eyes were playing tricks on me.

My house looked like a tornado hit it. Chairs were knocked

over. There were all sorts of miscellaneous items scattered across the floor. And that was only the living room. As I walked deeper through the living room and into the kitchen, I noticed the frozen food dispersed all over the table and dried blood, that I'm assuming was from the altercation, was all over the floor.

"What the hell went on in here?" I uttered as I surveyed the damage around me. I was almost scared to go upstairs because I was unsure about what I would find. Against my better judgement, I made my way up the circular staircase and went straight to my bedroom. Upon entering, my eyes fell immediately on my hidden safe and thank God it wasn't messed with. But too bad I couldn't say that about my furniture. All the drawers to my dressers had been ransacked for what I'm assuming was money. The jewelry that sat on the top of my dresser was missing, along with a couple bottles of cologne and a few pairs of my expensive shoes.

Sierra was right! My sister is a full-fledged addict!

I was disgusted with Logan but more with myself for not recognizing the signs. They were all there right under my nose and

I failed to address them. I knew it was a possibility that she could relapse but I was too confident in the bond that we shared to think that she would do that to me. That she would do that to my son. My son loved her. And with Harlow gone, Logan was the next best thing to a mother he had. But judging from looks of things she was long gone, probably never to return.

Pulling my phone from my pocket, I sent Logan a long text because I knew that she was too much of a coward to respond.

Me: Since you're too scared to pick up the phone and face me as a woman, I'm just gonna say what I need to say to you in this text and let you know where I stand. First off, I want you to know that I'm sorry. I'm sorry that my love wasn't enough to save you from your demons. I know that you haven't always been given the long end of the stick, but I thought that you knew that I was there for you whenever you needed me. I'm sorry that you didn't feel like you could come to me for help when you felt that monkey was on your back. I know that addiction is a hard battle to fight, but like I told you,

you weren't alone. And lastly, I'm sorry that I put my trust in you. I trusted you with the most precious thing in the world to me, my son. I put way too much faith in you and instead of micromanaging like I should've, I let you be. That was my mistake though and I'll have to live with the poor decision that I made. From this point moving forward I want you to know that I've washed my hands with you. Your problem is no longer my battle. The actions that you've displayed to me I can't forgive and I hope that one day you'll be at peace with the decision you made. I'm not tripping off the things that you stole from me because they can be replaced. But what can't be replace is a sister. You chose drugs over your family and that's not cool. By the time you get this message, I'm sure that you'll be across town looking for you next high. But just know that you have 24 hours before your phone is cut off and just know that the diamonds will only get a junkie but so far. Have a blessed life Logan, and I hope that this was all worth it.

Sent!

__Tiran__

Ducked off somewhere in Prince George's county, I sat in a makeshift studio vibing to the beat. The area was small with a few chairs and a couple of computers but needless to say, I was able to make greatness. I welcomed the array of positive vibes I felt while I sat in my element and wrote what my heart spoke.

For the next hour or two I sat in the same spot, writing and recording everything that came to mind. Some songs came out dope while others needed work however it still felt good to get back to the craft that I once loved. I was tired of looking over my shoulder. And I was tired of putting my life on hold while waiting for the payback that was lurking in the shadows. I just couldn't wait anymore because whatever it was gonna be, it was gonna be. I loved my new outlook on life and thus far I had no need to change it, that is until my phone rang.

RING! RING!

"What do I owe the honor of this phone call to?" I quipped

as I pressed the green button to answer the phone.

"Tiran, I need your help!" Logan pleaded from the other end of the phone.

"You don't need anything from me, well at least what you said the last time we spoke on the phone," I reminded her.

"I know what I said and I'm sorry!" she apologized.

"No you're not. You meant every word that you said."

"I didn't, I swear!"

"Look, whatever it is Logan, I can't help. I finally have a peace of mind now and I'm not trying to jeopardize that for no one," I stated as I was about to end the call.

"Tiran please! I have no one! I'm homeless with not even a single dollar to my name. Seven left me! Jabril left me! Everybody left me! Everybody has shunned me and turned their back on me in my time of need. I begging you Tiran, hear me out please! If you don't like what I have to say afterwards than I'll accept and try to find my own way. But please just give me the chance."

"Where are you?" I questioned, shocking even myself.

"At the Starbucks cafe in Timonium Square," she revealed as she sighed in relief.

"Be there in twenty. Stay put!" I instructed as I grabbed my car keys off the digital audio workstation.

"Oh my God! Thank you so much!"

"Don't think it's that easy," I advised as locked up the room that I was in and made my out of the door. "You still have some explaining to do."

"I know, and I will as soon as you get here!"

Forty Minutes Later…

After circling the parking lot twice looking for a parking spot, I finally lucked up and found one near the entrance of the coffee shop. Skillfully, I maneuvered my car into the tight space before killing the engine and pulling out a smoke. From the time that I received her phone call to the time now, Logan has been on my mind nonstop and I just needed a moment to calm my nerves and collect my thoughts. It was crazy how she occupied a space that I thought no longer existed and the more I thought about her, the more anxious I became. I was tired of the back and forth bickering between us and honestly I hoped this conversation we were about to have left us with a clean slate. No we didn't have to be lovers. Hell we didn't even have to be friends, but the least we could be was cordial. The past was the past and I was ready to move on and let bygones be bygones.

Taking one last long pull from my cigarette, I flicked the bud on the ground and exited my car.

Just play it cool. I thought to myself as I swaggered through the front door of the establishment and scanned the room for a familiar face. "She must not be here yet," I said out loud as I bypassed the sea of patrons standing in line and took a seat at the back of the cafe.

I didn't expect to wait around all day for her to show her

face and I was almost about to say fuck it after the first ten minutes skated on by with no signs of her. It felt like she was playing games with me and I was at a time in my life where I no longer wanted to fiddle with like a controller.

"Come on, give her the benefit of the doubt," said the angel on my shoulder.

"Fuck her! Don't let her use you," the devil countered.

"Alright already!" I argued in my head. *"She has five more minutes and then I'm gone,"* I convinced.

"Idiot!" the devil scolded. *"Don't say I didn't warn you!"* And just like that, they both disappeared.

Taking a glimpse at my watch, I made note of the time before picking up the old newspaper that sat on top of my table. As soon as my eyes read the large font that was on the cover, I was immediately drawn in and almost forgot what I was waiting on.

BUZZ! BUZZ!

Logan: So you're just gonna sit over there with your newspaper and pretend that I'm not here?

Me: What are you talking about? I've been waiting on your for the past ten minutes. Where you at?

Logan: Sitting over here by the entrance. You walked right pass me when you came in.

Me: Where at? I don't see you. I texted as I stood up to get a better view.

Logan: I'm right here. This time, she waived her arm.

Zooming in with my eyes on the woman that was shaking her hand, I paused because I knew that couldn't be her.

This has to be a coincidence. I thought as I stared in the faces of those around me, trying to locate a woman that fit Logan's description. But I couldn't.

The woman was steadily waving her hand, welcoming for me to come over and I all I could do was stand there frozen.

"Tiran!" she called out and as the sound of her voice traveled, the hairs on my neck stood.

I couldn't move. A plethora of emotions hit me all at once and I couldn't stomach that, that was really her.

What happened to her? Was all that I could think about as I sat down in my chair dumbfounded.

By now Logan must have felt awkward waving across the room because she dropped her hand and took the initiative to walk in my direction.

That's really her! And all I could do was shake my head at the woman standing before me.

Logan looked horrible. I mean terrible! Her hair was in a disarray. Her clothing was torn and wrinkled. Her eye was black and blue. Her overall appearance was just a hot ass mess.

"It's rude to stare you know," Logan interrupted, breaking my chain of thought.

"I apologize," I replied as I tried to pry my eyes away. "I'm just not used to seeing you like this."

"We'll get used to it because this is what my life has come to," she expressed, sounding saddened.

"Logan…What happened? I just talked to you a few months ago and everything was good."

"You thought everything was good because that's how I presented it to be," she confessed. "My life is shambles and I think that I may have burned my last bridge with the only person who cared."

"I don't understand what you're saying. You're talking in circles right now. What's wrong?"

"I fucked up okay! I fucked up!" she revealed as she slammed her hands against the table.

"How? I can't help you Logan if you don't tell me what's wrong. I need details, not that vague shit your feeding me."

"What do you want me to say Tiran? That I'm a junkie? There I said! I get high to ease the pain of losing my son. I get high because I miss my best friend. I get high because I'm a fuck up and that's the only thing that I'm good at. Do you want me to continue?"

At the mention of hearing Harlow's name. I cringed. This was my fault. I started this domino effect and now I felt guilty. "Damn Lo, I don't even know what to say," I admitted. "I really thought that you were making it through all this. You know that you were doing good and that you didn't need a nigga for shit."

"Well I'm not!"

"Why didn't you call me? Why didn't you reach out for help?"

"Tiran don't sit there and act like you haven't been missing in action yourself. You've been ducked off who knows where, doing who knows what with your little girlfriend."

"I don't have a girlfriend," I corrected.

"I may be an addict but I'm not stupid. Someone caused you to up and leave. It may not have been the girl that Harlow told me about, but it was someone."

"Look, that doesn't matter. What matters is us getting you some help," I deflected as I began to get uncomfortable with the conversation.

"What kind of help? Because all I need right now is a place to crash until I figure out my next move."

"Therapy," I considered.

"But I don't need therapy. I know what's wrong with me!"

"Then you don't need me," I said as I stood to my feet preparing to leave.

"But Tiran that's not fair!" she whined as she reached over the table and grabbed my shirt.

"That's the only way that I'm going to agree to help. You either enroll into therapy or you're on your own."

"Tiran!"

"I gotta give you tough love Logan. Take it or leave it."

"But —"

"Take it or leave!"

"Tiran, I don't want —" I didn't give her a chance to finish her sentence before I started walking to the door.

"Fine! I'll take it! I'll take it!" she yelled as she shot up from her seat and ran after me. "I'll do it. Just don't leave me!"

It was a long road ahead of us, but if Logan put in the work then I knew we would make it. Acceptance was the first step in counseling and I accepted the role that I played in Logan's demise. Had I never left her and had her feeling insecure, she probably would have blossomed into a beautiful butterfly by now. Had I never played a hand in killing her best friend, she probably would still have her sanity right now. But most importantly, had I never pushed her into the arms of another man, I probably would not have felt this lonely. They say if you love someone so much then let them go. And if it comes back then it was meant to be. Logan was meant to come back to me because God wasn't finished with showing us how deep our love actually ran. Therapy was going to help us and with time I trusted that she would return to the woman that I fell in love with.

Chapter 6

Penelope

Seven Years Later…

DINGGGGGGGGGG!

I loved that sound!

At the sound of the bell all you could hear were pencils dropping as the students all around me gathered their things and prepared to go to their next class.

"Okay, that concludes class for today guys. Make sure you that complete the assignment that I handed out. And also study chapters seven and eight for you exam tomorrow. I trust that you guys will do well," Mr. Robinson stated while placing the dry eraser in its holder by the board.

Reaching for my backpack that sat at the bottom of my foot, I proceeded to follow the crowd of students leaving the classroom.

"Here Penny," Jayla yelled, causing me to turn on my heels. "Quan told me to give this to you," she informed while passing me a neatly folded up piece of paper.

"What's this?" I quizzed, a little skeptical of the note.

"I don't know, he just told me to give it to you. Why don't you open it and see?" she voiced with excitement. I was reluctant to read the letter in front of Jayla because I knew that she was the gossip queen; but judging by the way that she was standing over my shoulders it was obvious that she wasn't going to let me enjoy the contents of the note alone. Taking my time, I slowly unfolded the letter to see what it said. "You opening it all slow! Hurry up, I'm trying to see what he said!"

"Did Quan say this note was for me or for us?" I sassed while taking a step back and shielding the letter in my hands.

"Girl bye! Don't get cute!" Jayla chided as she rolled her neck and placed her hands on her hip. "I just wanna know what's so important that it couldn't wait until he saw you himself."

"Whatever it is, it's gonna stay between us."

Jayla must have felt offended because she screwed her face up. "Don't think you all special and stuff because he's writing you notes. Because trust me he's only doing it to get in your pants. Don't forget that you're the new girl on the block. You don't know Quan like the rest of us do. He's been known to bait em' in real good and as soon as you fall for his charm, it's a wrap. You're now a member of his team and you're doing God knows what just to satisfy him."

"Is that the reason why you passed me this note? Cause you're one of his flunkies?"

"Ewww, I don't even like Quan like that," she lied.

"Yeah okay," I didn't know who she thought she was fooling. I'm a people watcher and her body language from the jump told me that she was too invested in what Quan had to say. "Just let that hurt go Sis. You said it yourself, it's a new girl on the block."

"Ohhhh… I see where this is going," she chuckled. "You think that just because Quan wrote you a letter that means that you're the it girl now"

"You said it, I didn't."

"See this is why I hate interacting with y'all freshmen. Y'all egos always on ten and can't nobody ever tell y'all nothing."

"Jayla you don't have to tell me anything. My momma told me everything that I needed to know about boys and the hating females that come with them."

"Well since you know everything did she tell you this? The only reason why you got that note is because it's a game. Quan and the rest of the players of the football team have a bet going on to see who can snag the most freshmen and who can steal the most virginities. It's a senior thing, something that you or your old ass Momma would know nothing about."

"You just salty because yo momma face look like Esther from Sanford and Son and her hair look like Florida from Good

Times."

"And yo momma out here selling pussy like —" Jayla started to say something slick back but the look on my face said it all.

"Say it and I'll have her come down here and beat yo ass," I was dead serious too! My mother was the reason why I was forced to attend a school out of my district to begin with. She stayed fighting my battles and it was nothing for her to get a teacher or student in check and quick! My grandmother hated my mother's ghetto behavior and always said that she didn't have any class, but what Nana didn't understand was my mother was only teaching me how she was taught.

"You think that you're so big and bad ass, but we'll see how tough you are after Quan dogs you out." After that, there was nothing more that needed to be said. Jayla said her peace, threw her bag over her shoulder, and went on to her next class.

I was just about to follow her lead when Mr. Robinson

stopped me in my footsteps.

"Ms. Drew, is everything okay?" he questioned with a look of concern plastered across his face. It was apparent that he felt the tension brewing between his two students and he wanted to be sure that it was nothing serious.

"Yes, I'm fine Mr. Robinson," I replied while offering him a fake smile. "Jayla just wanted to know if I could be her study partner for the exam."

"Are you sure? Because you two seemed quite serious over there," he was still leery so he dug a little deeper, hoping that I would open up to him about what transpired between Jayla and myself.

"Yes, I'm sure and while we're at it, could you tell me if the test is multiple choice?" I deflected, hoping that he would take the bait. I was tired of talking about Jayla and in order for me to be able to read my letter in peace, I had to get Mr. Robinson out of my hair.

"Yes, but not all of it. You'll have some multiple choice, some fill in the blank, some short answer, and one essay," he disclosed while walking over and double checking the answer key that sat on top his desk. Thank God he took the bait and finally let up because I didn't feel like having to explain the issue to my guidance counselor or an administrator.

"Ugh, I hate writing essays," I groaned.

"Relax, it'll be a breeze. There are no surprise questions on here. If you study the chapters, you won't have a problem."

"I'll take your word for it then," I said while slowly backpedaling away. "I gotta go now or else I'll be late for my next class."

Scurrying off to the bathroom that was located outside of my second period class, I only had about a few seconds left to spare before class was scheduled to begin. None of that mattered though because I was way too eager to read my letter from Quan. Just the fact that he took time to acknowledge me had me cheesing all hard and I'm sure that after reading this letter that was only going to be the beginning of my butterflies. "Excuse me, Excuse me!" I yelled as I ran into the first empty stall available and sat on the toilet. I didn't care about the germs that were transferred onto my jeans from the toilet because that's what detergent was for. What I did care about though was the sweat from my hands smearing the ink. Placing the paper into my mouth, I rubbed my hands across my jeans before taking the letter out of my mouth and reading it.

Penny,

What's good with you lil mama? You got a man? Cuz I'm tryna get to know you a little better. I peeped the way you carry yourself and I'm impressed. Not to many girls around here can hold a flame to you so I'm tryna make you mine before someone else snatches you up. I'm sure that you already know who I am by now so if you liked what you saw, meet me by the stairs (by room 103) at 1pm.

And come alone because I don't need none of ya young

friends in our business.

Quan

My heart was racing and my hands were shaking as I folded the note back up and placed it in my bag. This letter was picture frame worthy and although it didn't say much, it said enough. It wasn't that often that the school's hottest jock wrote you a letter and for that very reason, I didn't want to mess it up.

Just as I expected, Quan managed to have me grinning from ear to ear just by jotting a few friendly phrases on a piece of paper. He had me feeling all giddy inside and I could barely contain my excitement as I threw my bag over my shoulder and exited the bathroom; en route to class late and all. I knew that I wouldn't be able to concentrate on nothing the teacher had to say, but I needed something to help pass my time until one' o'clock got here.

Charli

Two and a half hours later...

My stomach was in knots as I rocked back and forth on the toilet praying that that nasty cafeteria food I consumed would make a peaceful exit. It was at the tip and was almost about to come out when Sydney and her sidekick Sharay came waltzing in; interrupting my poo.

"No way! I can't believe that she fell for that," Sydney bleated as she entered the bathroom with her friend. "Even a middle schooler could tell that a girl wrote that letter."

"I'm telling you, that this is about to be the funniest senior prank ever!" Sharay cackled before entering the stall beside me. While she peed I refused to make a sound. I even held my cheeks together, preventing the poop that was threatening to fall out from hitting the water, just so I could hear what they were talking about.

"It sure is! I just hope that Ms. Baldwin's old tale stays in her classroom and doesn't ruin the prank."

"Why'd you pick those stairs anyway? You know if she catches us, we're all either gonna get detention or a suspension," Sharay advised as she stood squatting over the toilet, wiping her cooch.

"Because those steps are right at the entrance where everybody always is. I want the whole school to see this so that it can go down in the books for many years to come."

"You are so evil," she joked. "Did you get the fish guts like you said you would?"

"Not yet, but my brother just texted me and said that he's on his way with them now," Sydney informed. "He'll definitely be here by one p.m. though so we don't have to worry about that."

"I feel bad for what y'all about to do to that poor little girl," Sharay expressed while holding back a giggle. "She didn't even know that Quan was yours."

"Don't feel bad because she should have known that he

would never be interested in her. She's a freshman for goodness sake," Sydney voiced. "And besides, freshman or not, everybody knows that Quan is off limits. If the girls from our rival schools can figure out two and two, then she should be able to too."

"I guess I can't be mad because I would feel the same way if somebody was all goggley eyed over Dre. You know I don't play when it comes to my baby," Sharay admitted before flushing the toilet and walking out. "Are you sure that Quan is gonna be there though? Because if he's not, then this prank is gonna be pointless. We need him to lure her into the stairwell."

"You know he wouldn't miss this show for no one," she claimed. "Shoot, it was his idea to get the fish guts to begin with. At first, I was only gonna drop paper."

"You two crazies definitely deserve each other!" Sharay concluded while washing her hands. When she was done she reached for a paper towel to dry them off. "Come on let's go, so that we can make sure that Jayla and all the other girls know what we need them to do in order for this to go right." And then after that they left.

For a minute, I almost thought that I wasn't gonna be able to hold it that long, but I was glad that I did because I just got the inside scoop of probably one of the best senior pranks that this school has witnessed. Even though it was wrong to assert myself in someone else's business, I was kind of curious to see who Sydney and Sharay's target was. I didn't know many freshman outside of my sister Penny and this one girl named Troi, but apparently whoever this mystery girl was she must have went after Sydney's man.

After soaking up all of Sydney and Sharay's tea, I was finally ready to release the poo that had my stomach in an uproar. Giving my booty muscle one strong push, the poop dropped to the toilet and swam to the hole. "Ahhh," I sighed as I reached for the toilet paper to wipe my butt and then pulled up my pants. I felt ten pounds lighter and after today I vowed to never eat another school lunch ever again.

Peeping my head out of the stall, I looked around to see if

anyone heard me handling my business. When I saw that the coast was clear, I quickly rushed over and washed my hands before darting out of the bathroom. I didn't need anyone telling my classmates how funky I smelled. In their mind, ladies didn't poop and if they did, I'm almost positive that it didn't smell like what I just let go back there in that restroom.

Briskly walking the halls, I tried to make it back to my classroom in time before my teacher noticed that I was gone. I was one of her favorites and I didn't want her to think that I was taking advantage of the little bit of freedom that she allowed me to have.

Yes! I thought to myself when I reached my classroom door. My classmates were in groups sprawled all across the room, working on an assignment. All the groups had the same amount of members but that didn't matter to me because assigned or not, I was going to work with my best friend. After doing a quick scan of the room with my eyes, I spotted his rich waves and walked to the back of the classroom where he was seated.

"Took you long enough," Saivon complained while lifting

his head and making room for me at the table.

"Awww shut up. You know that pizza ain't right," I argued while taking a seat.

"Hard-head. I told you not to eat it."

"I didn't have a choice. It was either that or be hungry."

"What happened to the money I gave you on Tuesday from Uncle Seven?" he queried. "Don't tell me you spent it all, already."

"I did, see look," I admitted while flashing my fresh manicure in his face.

"That was $150?" he exclaimed while critiquing the colorful polish.

"I mean I got my toes done too. But yes, this was $150."

"That is too much. I pray I never have a daughter when I get older."

"You still gonna pay $150 either way. Look how much boy's tennis shoes cost. And that's only for one pair."

"But shoes lasts for a long time. How long is that polish gonna last you. A week? Two tops?"

"No smarty pants. If I let it, it can last up to a month and a half."

"That's still not enough time to be wasting $150," he reasoned. "Some of that could have went to food for the week so that you wouldn't have to be shittin your guts out in the school bathroom."

"Be quiet!" I hissed as I punched him in his arm. He was talking way too loud for my liking and he needed to shut up.

"Ouch!" he squealed while rubbing his arm. "I don't know why you hit me, they know you stink."

"I do not!" I defended as my balled my fist up to hit him again. "Keep it up and I'mma tell Sydney to get you next," I whispered.

"Who is Sydney?" he asked, confused.

"Sydney, Sydney. Quan's girl Sydney."

"Ohhhh, that Sydney," Saivon remembered. "Why would you get her on me? You know I don't like that girl."

"Me either but get this. Apparently her and Sharay have some prank planned and it's supposed to go down at one p.m. today."

"Isn't this 2017? Who still does pranks?"

I shrugged my shoulders. "I don't know. I guess they do. It's supposed to happen in the stairway by the doors."

Saivon shook his head. "The world's dumbest criminals. Who in the hell commits a crime in front of the po-po? They must be trying to get caught."

"I said the same thing to myself when I was eavesdropping on their conversation."

"I know they said when and where this was supposed to happen, but did they say what? I know it sounds bad, but wanna know what them two idiots have planned."

"They said who, but it wasn't much. All I heard was something about a freshman girl and some fish guts."

"They some whores man. They need to pick on someone their own size. I hope whoever they're after whip their ass."

"Right!" I agreed. "I wish I knew who it was so that I could warn them," I said seriously.

"You always trying to save the day," he chuckled while turning the sheet of paper over.

"No, that's not true. I just remember what it felt like to be a freshman in a new school with no friends."

"No friends?" Saivon repeated. It was clear that he was offended by my comment. "I guess I must be an associate then."

"Boy shut up! You know that you're family."

Saivon laughed, "You ain't no kin of mine."

"Yes I am." How was Saivon gonna tell me we weren't

family when my father damn near raised him. "My daddy Seven raised you so that makes us cousins."

"Okay, if it's like that, we can be kissing cousins," he said while puckering his lips up for a kiss.

"Sure! But you gotta ask my daddy first," I taunted. I wasn't Seven's daughter by blood but I was by heart, and I knew there was no way in hell that Seven would let Saivon pursue me. He was cool with us being best friends, but me having Saivon as my boyfriend? Nah, that couldn't happen. Shoot, the only reason why me and Saivon became cool in the first place was because I got tired of him following me around like a lost puppy. He used to always pop up everywhere that I was just so he could report back to Daddy Seven and eventually it got to the point where I figured if you can't beat em', join em'. And that's how we became close.

After my mother's death, my birth father Maycen was hell bent on Seven staying away from me. If you let my father Maycen tell it, Seven was a home wrecker who caused my mother to get killed by some deranged lady. But in my heart, I didn't believe that. Although I was young when my mother died, I still had vivid memories of her and half of them were with her and Seven. From what I remember they were a happy couple and Seven took great care of her, of us. He loved her and I know without a shadow of a doubt if my mother was still alive, they would still be together raising me and my brother Harlem.

"Heck no! Never mind! I'm not trying to get punched in the chest for playing like that. You know he don't play when it comes to you," Saivon surrendered.

"Scaredy cat," I teased while poking Saivon in his side.

"I'm not scared. I just have respect for the man. Uncle Seven didn't have to help me and my mom dukes out. He could have been left us for real. But he didn't. He stayed true like a real OG and helped me and my moms out of poverty."

"That's cause he like yo momma," I said while interrupting his mini speech.

"Nah, it ain't even like that. My momma and him just cool.

He make sure she good and vice versa," he explained. "They sorta like us in a way."

I smirked. I could tell that me hinting that there was more to Ms. Sierra and Seven's relationship bothered Saivon, but I kept poking anyway. "That's how it started with my momma at first."

"Yo if Seven didn't smash my mom's after all these years, then it's not gonna happen. They have too much respect for each other to ruin their friendship. And besides my momma got a boyfriend already. She just don't know that I know."

I was shocked. Saivon never mentioned Ms. Sierra having a man friend to me before. "And you better not scare him away! Ms. Sierra deserves to be happy after all that she's been through."

"I'm not. I'mma give him a chance. He just better treat her right or else I'mma shoot him with Uncle Seven's gun."

"But that sounds dumb. Why would you jeopardize your future like that? There are plenty of people that you can call on to handle that type of situation," I argued.

"So what! I don't play about my momma. That's my best friend and I'll do anything for her."

"But you just said I was your best friend."

"You are and I love you the same."

"Good, because I was about to say."

"About to say what?" he challenged.

"About to say… that I love you too," I cheesed while wrapping my arms around his body. Realizing that we'd been arguing for a minute, I broke away from Saivon's embrace and turned towards a student in a nearby group. "Sam, do you know how much longer we have in here?"

"We have like twenty minutes left," Samantha answered after checking her watch.

"And then it's one o'clock right?" I probed.

"Don't tell me you about to leave out of here to go warn that girl," Saivon quizzed while staring at me knowingly.

"You know me too well," I snickered. "I wouldn't feel right if I didn't at least try."

"And what if she doesn't believe you?"

I paused for a second to think about that. What if she didn't believe me? It's not like I had any proof. I didn't have no recording, no witness, no note. *Oh wait the letter they mentioned!* "Look, if I go out of my way to leave class and she doesn't listen then it's on her. My conscience will be clear because at least I can say that I tried."

"True," Saivon stated while nodding his head in agreeance. "Here, write your name on this assignment so that we can turn it in and leave," he instructed while passing me a pen.

"We? You coming?"

"You think I'mma let you go out there by yourself?" he countered.

"Yeah, why not?"

"What if shorty think you set her up and swing on you?"

"It's not gonna get that far because the first sign that I get that she's uninterested in what I have to say, I'm outta there. And from that point forward she'll be Sydney's problem."

"Well I'mma be there anyway, just in case you need me to DDT a nigga," he said as he stood up to mimic a WWF wrestling move.

"Honestly I don't even think it's that serious, but since you insist on being my body guard; let's go. I'mma go turn our paper in and ask to go to the nurse's office and then you can wait a few minutes after me and ask to go to the restroom."

"Man, Mrs. Walker ain't with none of that. She's gonna know we're up to something."

"That's why you have to convince her that we're not. You better do the pee-pee dance and act like you got the bubble guts."

"I'm not doing all of that in front of these people."

"Okay," I shrugged. "Guess I'll be seeing you in a few."
Bending down from my chair, I grabbed my items from off of the floor before standing to my feet and walking towards to Mrs. Walker's desk. With the most pitiful expression I could muster up, I asked if I could be excused from class so that I could go to the nurses office and just like I expected, she let me.

Clutching the nurses pass in my right hand and my bag in my left, I walked out of class and towards the stairwell in search of this mystery student at hand.

As soon as I reached the stairwell I wasted no time, climbing the steps two at a time just so that I could make it in time to stop the prank. It didn't take me long to get to the top floor but as soon as I reached the top step, I had to take a moment to get my breathing back together. Those steps were brutal and even some of our best athletes had to stop to catch their breath.

Once the tightness in my chest eased up a little, I was ready to continue on with my mission. There was still a few minutes left before class, so I didn't expect to see anybody in the main level stairway. I was prepared to wait until I saw the first questionable female come my way but imagine my surprise when I saw my little sister Penny sneaking out of the restroom and going in a direction opposite then her class.

Penelope

Hiding in the stairwell off to the side, I waited for Quan to bless my presence with his handsome face. It was 12:55p.m. and to say that I was nervous for his arrival was an understatement. While I was in class I rehearsed over and over what I would say to him, but now that it was getting close to the time for me to say it, my mind went blank. I was going to have to improvise and I prayed that I didn't get tongue-tied, sounding immature because the last thing I wanted was to be viewed as just another freshman girl.

I only had a few minutes left until the clock would strike one p.m. so I had to use my time wisely. Blowing my breath in my hand, I checked to see if it was minty fresh and thank God that it was. I was just about to pull out my small compact mirror to check my nose for any boogers when I heard a voice call my name.

"Penelope!" the voice yelled, causing me to drop my purse on the floor. I knew exactly who the voice belonged to but I refused to answer. "Penelope, I know you hear me!" she repeated.

"What do you want?" I hissed as my sister slowly walked up the stairs and came into view.

"What are you doing here? Why aren't you in class?"

"The same reason you aren't," I shot as I kneeled down to pick up my things.

"Penelope, I'm being serious right now. Why are you waiting right here? Is it to meet someone?"

Charli was worse than my mother at times, always sticking her nose in other people's business. I didn't want her to blow my spot up before I got a chance to see Quan so I lied. "I'm waiting for my friend Jayla to bring me back my homework assignment. I let her borrow it before class so that she could copy it and now I need it back so that I can turn it in."

"Penny don't lie to me because I'm trying to save you from embarrassment. I need you to tell me the truth. Are you here to meet a boy? And if so, is his name Quan?"

See this is what I meant about her being nosey! How in the French toast did she know about Quan? "Why would I be meeting Quan? I don't know him like —"

"What about Quan?" Quan quizzed as he entered the stairway unannounced.

"I...I was just saying that I didn't know you like that," I stuttered.

"Penny don't answer him! He's not your freaking daddy!" she yelled to me before turning to address him. "What do you want with my sister? Because I know you're not sincere!"

"I thought I told you to come alone Penelope," he scolded as he looked at me disapprovingly. "I don't like having to explain myself to people who aren't on my level."

"On your level? Boy please! You're not even about that

life!" Charli objected while looking him up and down and giving him menacing glare. "Penny, leave this clown alone and let's go! I'll explain to you what's going on once he leaves us alone," Charli demanded as she pulled at my arm.

"I'm not going with you, I'm staying here," I refused to let Charli get in the way of me hearing what Quan had to say.

"No you're not!" she fumed as she yanked at my arm a little harder this time.

"Get off of me!" I growled as I forcibly yanked my arm back, causing Charli to fall on the floor. I stood my ground. I wasn't about to let Charli boss me around and especially not in front of Quan. I had to let him know that her popping up wasn't my fault.

"You going with her or you staying with me?" Quan coaxed, sounding all smooth and sexy. He was curious himself to see how the situation would pan out.

"I'm staying with you," I purred as I took a step closer and allowed him to place his hand around my lower back.

"Penelope it's a set up! He doesn't want you! He has a girlfriend! And her name is Sydney! She's a senior and she knows that you like her man! Her and her friends Sharay and Jayla are upstairs somewhere waiting to throw fish guts on you!" Charli blurted out as she struggled to get up off the floor.

Wait a minute! Because Jayla was the one that gave me the letter from Quan! Is Charli telling the truth?

"Quan, what is she talking about?" I fretted while staring up at his face.

"Mannn, I don't know what your homegirl talking about. I'm as single as a dollar bill."

"She's my sister you asshole!" she corrected. "And stop lying! You and Sydney have been together since your sophomore year!"

I started to ask Quan was there truth behind the tea that Charli was spilling, but I was thrown off when I heard snickering

347

coming from somewhere inside the stairwell.

"… Three!" Was all that I could make out in between their chuckling and it was only by the grace of God that I moved out of the way in the nick of time.

"Oh my God! Ewwww, ewwww, ewwww!" I hollered as I wiped some of the residue from the splattered guts of my ankle. It felt cold and nasty and I instantly got the heebie jeebies.

My pride was wounded as the realization of what Charli said proved to be true. Just like she predicted I was embarrassed, and as I stood there plotting on my next move I could feel the tears welling up in my eyes. I wanted to cry so bad but now was not the time nor place to show any weakness. I was in beast mode and all I could see was red. Darting up the steps, my sister was hot on my heels as I moved into unfriendly territory. I didn't know what awaited me at the top of the second floor, but I was ready. And even though I could feel the steam radiating off my sister, I knew she had my back and was ready to whip some ass too.

As soon as my foot touched the top of the stairs, I swung on the first person that I saw. I didn't care if they were involved in the incident or not because in my mind, if they were standing there, they were guilty.

Sharay, the person that happened to be standing at the top of the step, must have felt me coming too because she bobbed and weaved my hard left before landing a punch of her own. I didn't even have time to stop and survey the damage done to my face because I was in attack mode, however, I was almost positive that I was going to be black and blue tomorrow. Who cared though because that was what ice was for. As long as my adrenaline continued pumping, I was good and that was enough to keep me going.

"Penny move!" I heard Charli scream and she ran up and pushed me to the side. Her big sister instincts must have went into overdrive because it seemed like she had eyes and ears everywhere.

"Don't be scared now! Run up, like you intended to and

watch me dog yo ass!" Sydney badgered as she balled up her fist. "I'mma give you everything that you're looking for."

"You talk too much!" Charli chastised as she slipped passed Jayla and punched Sydney dead in her mouth.

"Get them off of me! They're banking me!" Sydney yelled as she balled up and covered her head with hands. She was all bark and no bite and it was definitely showing big time.

"Nah baby sis! This is what you wanted! Square up!" Charli roared as she continued pounding on her like Donkey Kong.

Sydney ain't want no more smoke, but unfortunately her friends still did. Wildly swinging her hands in a fan like motion, Jayla ran towards my sister and hit her in the back of her head. "Get off of her!" she demanded as she continued swinging.

"Owwww! Fuck!" Charli grunted as paused her assault on Sydney and grabbed the back of her head. "Penny do something!" my sister needed me, but I couldn't help her because Sharay and I were too busy tussling by the steps. We were playing with fire and if we kept it up, one of us were bound to fall down the stairs but the someone wasn't gonna be me. "Ouch shit that hurt! Penny!" Charli cried out.

I tried my hardest to break away from Sharay to assist Charli and I was almost successful too. That is until the devil himself grabbed me from behind.

"Where do you think that you're going?" Quan grilled as he held me back. "She was just all big and bad a few minutes ago. Let her fight," he taunted while tightening his grip so that I couldn't move. Jerking my body around in his grasp, I tried to free myself but it was no use. Quan was at least one hundred pounds heavier than me and it was all muscle.

"Aye bruh, get up off my fam," Saivon commanded as he blind-sided Quan and placed him in a full nelson.

By this time, students and teachers began flooding the hallways, puzzled about the commotion that was going on outside of their classroom.

"Break it up! Break it!" Ms. Dickerson demanded as she pushed through the crowd. "Someone call the school police!" she instructed as she continued to make her way to the middle of the circle.

When the school police finally did arrive on the scene, we all were caught red-handed. Charli was caught delivering blow after blow to Jayla's head, while me and Saivon got caught tag-teaming Quan's big ass. Sharay was ducked off somewhere helping her friend Sydney regain her consciousness and the rest of the girls involved in the prank were dispersed in the crowd of on-lookers. They were the smart ones of the bunch because they knew if they didn't turn ghost, they were going to be up next.

<u>Maycen</u>

"Hello?" I answered as I placed the telephone in between my ear and shoulder and continued working on my client's car.

"Hello, my name is Sharon Whitfield and I'm the principal here at Mergenthaler Vocational High School. Can I speak to the parent or guardian of Charli and Penelope Drew?"

"This is he," I confirmed, while reaching for the dirty rag in my back pocket and wiping my hands.

"Hi, Mr. Drew. I'm sorry to inform you but I have both of your daughters here with me in my office right now. It has been brought to my attention that they have been involved in a physical altercation on our school's premises and we need someone to come pick them up."

"Wait a minute. Both of them were fighting? Each other?" I repeated. I had to make sure that I was hearing her right.

"No Sir, not each other, but other students," she corrected. "Are either you or," Mrs. Whitfield paused as she searched the parent contact sheet for Penelope mother's name. "Mrs. Piper Kirkland available to come get them."

"Get them for what? What, are they suspended?"

"Yes Sir, and we need the both of them off of our school's premises or else we'll have to contact Baltimore City police and have them escorted downtown for assault charges."

"Mrs. Whitfield, none of that is necessary, I'll be there shortly. Just give me a few minutes to explain what's going on to my boss and then I'll be on my way."

"Okay great! When you get on school grounds our school's police will be waiting for you at the entrance. Once they verify your identity, they'll escort you back to my office and then we'll proceed from there."

"Okay," and without giving it a second thought, I quickly ended the call and made my way across town to the girl's high school.

In all of the twelve years that Charli has been enrolled in school, this was a first for me having to leave work early to get her. To hear that she was involved in a fight had me on edge because that wasn't her normal behavior. Charli was a sweetheart. She got all A's and B's and she was the captain of the varsity volleyball team. It wasn't like her to be stirring no shit at school, so I was almost positive that this whole ordeal had to stem from something surrounding Penelope. That child was a just like her trifling ass mother so it was only right to say that the apple didn't fall far from the tree. Penny was a fire cracker who stayed in trouble, which is why I requested she live with me during the school year in the first place. I figured if she went to school with Charli, she would learn how a classy female was supposed to behave, but obviously I was wrong. I done messed around and let Penelope's rotten ass corrupt my angel, and now Charli's perfect school record was tarnished.

Pulling into Mervo's faculty and staff parking lot, I felt disappointed as I parked my car and got out. I was inquisitive to know what forced this sudden phone call and I also was dying to hear Penelope's lousy excuse as to why she dragged her sister into her bullshit.

As I walked to the entrance of my daughters' school, I was met with dozens of lustful stares from students and teachers alike. Although I was pissed, I still smirked. Back in the day I was known for talking even a nun out of her panties and judging by the smiles on these girls faces, I guess I still had it.

Stepping through the threshold of the building, I was immediately stopped by the school police, "Can I help you sir?"

"I'm looking for a principal Whitfield," I stated while looking past the officers and down the hall.

"May I ask, what for?" the big Deebo looking officer questioned.

"She called me to come down here to pick up my two daughters Penelope and Charli Drew. They were involved in an incident earlier and I'm guessing that she wanted to discuss what happened before releasing them to me."

"I.D please?" the other officer asked before retrieving a small notepad out of his shirt pocket. Reaching into my pants pocket, I pulled out my driver's license and handed it to him for him to look at. Once he looked over and saw that my credentials matched the information that was on his notepad, he handed my license back to me and instructed me to follow him to the principal's office. "Right this way."

As soon as me and the two officers rounded the corner and entered the principal office, the look on Penelope's face said it all. She looked nervous and I could tell that she dreaded what was about to come. "Daddy, it wasn't our fault," she blurted as she shot up from her seat and attempted to explain her side of the story. However, the grimace on my face that I gave her in return spoke all that I needed it to say.

"Have a seat!" I snarled before looking around for the principal. "Charli, where's Mrs. Whitfield?"

"She said she'd be right back. I think she went to go make a fax," Charli answered, afraid to look my way.

I could tell that my baby girl wanted this all to be over and I didn't blame her. "Well I'mma sit here with y'all and wait for her to come back and while I do, somebody better give me a good excuse as to why I'm here."

It was clear that Charli didn't want to snitch on her baby

sister, so she nodded her head towards Penny and let her tell the story.

"Me and Charli, We...we were only protecting ourselves Daddy. Like you taught us to," Penelope started. "Some girls were messing with me while I was in the hallway trying to go to class and when Charli saw them she said something and they got mad and tried to bank her."

"Charli, is this true?" I quizzed as I looked to her for verification. She looked like she wanted to say something and just as she was about to open her mouth to speak, Mrs. Whitfield came sashaying back into the office.

"Mr. Drew, I wish we could have met on better terms, but I still must say it's a pleasure to meet you." Mrs. Whitfield greeted as she reached in for a handshake. Mirroring her gesture, I did the same. "And now that you're here, let's get down to business," she said while taking a seat at her desk and picking up her report. "Charli Drew and Penelope Drew are both suspended for fifteen days for the brutal assault of their fellow classmates Jayla Parker,

Sydney Jordan, Sharay Batty, and TaQuan Holden. Today, around 1:20p.m., our school officers were called to the scene of a group disturbance on the second floor by room 203. It has been reported by several witnesses, including teachers, that Charli initiated the attack when she charged towards youth Sydney Jordan and swung on her with a closed fist. Charli, along with Penelope and their peer Saivon Johnson, then directed their assault towards Jayla and Sharay almost causing each of them to have a concussion."

"Daddy, she's lying! I didn't start nothing!" Charli chimed in as she objected to everything that was written in the report.

"Mr. Drew, several people have named Charli as the aggressor and judging by the marks left on the other students' bodies, I believe them."

I gave Mrs. Whitfield the once over before I cleared my throat to speak. "I'm sorry Mrs. Whitfield, but I just can't take the word of *other people*," I said while using my fingers to make air quotes. "Unless you have any real physical evidence, I'm going to have to side with my daughters on this case. You're telling me that the other kids have bruises from the incident, doesn't mean anything to me, except that I taught them well on how to defend themselves from others. At an early age I instilled in them not to place their hands on anybody, unless someone hit them first and I believed that my daughters followed that rule to a tee. You claim that your *witnesses*," Again I used air quotes. "Witnessed the altercation, but how did they catch the fight from the very beginning if they were supposed to be in class?" I probed while making a valid point. My kids knew better than to go around starting trouble with other people and as their father, it was my duty to stand up and defend them from the evil that was brought their way. I wasn't gonna let Mrs. Whitfield point the finger and play the blame game, not without her having to hear my mouth first. "And secondly, going off of hearsay for the basis of someone's suspension is foolish. My daughters' future is in jeopardy and I will not allow you destroy it. I will appeal this infraction till the very end and even hire an attorney if I have to."

"And I understand that, but if you will allow me to, I'd like to finish reading the rest of my report," she voiced, sounding unbothered. I couldn't stand a know-it-all woman and it was clear that my little speech didn't move her not one bit. "As I was saying," she emphasized before continuing, "One of the students, TaQuan Holden, wrote a tell-tale account as to what lead up to the brawl *including* the part that he played in it. In his report he stated that your daughter, Penelope Drew stopped him in the hallway while he was on his way to class and threw herself on him." Although I chose not to comment, on the inside I was fuming. All this sounded all too familiar. Penelope's infatuation with boys was on another level for someone her age, and I was constantly having to redirect her mind on her studies instead of on them. "Student T. Holden admitted that he placed his hands on Penelope to subdue her but said that was when Charli got upset and ran up and assaulted him. Student T. Holden also went on to say that students S. Batty, J. Parker, and S. Jordan were leaving the restroom when they saw Penelope and Charli Drew attacking him. All three girls attempted to break up the fight and both Charli and Penelope got mad and turned their anger towards them."

"That's enough because evidently your opinion is biased.

Just the fact that you're willing to take the word of your 'star player' says a lot about your character," I exasperated as I stood from my seat. I must have hit a nerve because her face no longer looked unbothered. In fact, she looked as if she was interested in what I had to say. "Oh, what you thought I didn't know? Because I do, it's all in the paper. TaQuan Holden is this school's all American athlete and you, Mrs. Sharon Whitfield, as his principal would like to keep it that way. I'm not stupid and neither is the lawyer that you'll be hearing from soon," I added before grabbing my copy of the suspension letter of the desk and turning to my daughters. "Come on girls, grab your things so that we can leave! I want to stop by my lawyer's office before the traffic gets bad."

Neither child said a word, they were just happy that I left them off the hook for the time being.

Larry

Two and a Half Weeks Later...

For it to be late in the year and almost October, the weather still felt like it was spring. I was convinced that we were living in our last days and for that very reason I decided to utilized my day off to do something nice for my family.

It was almost noon, and while I was downstairs in my kitchen slaving over a hot stove, my family remained upstairs in their rooms not making a sound. I was okay with that for the time, being as though I was still cooking. But once I was done, they were going to have to come downstairs and help me indulge in this delectable meal.

Twenty- five minutes and a shot of Hennessy later, I was done cooking my family's favorites. My spread consisted of fried chicken and waffles, Cajun shrimp and grits, steak and eggs, and a bowl of fruit salad. I knew I had overdone it, but it wasn't that often that I got the chance to play Top Chef in my own kitchen. Being police commissioner of the city stole the majority of my time, so I learned to appreciate the little things about life because it wasn't often that I got a chance to experience them.

As I was removing the kiss the cook apron from around my

neck, I called upstairs for my wife and daughter. "Penny! Piper! Your food is ready!" I waited a few minutes and listened for the sound of feet shuffling across our hardwood floors, and I didn't hear it. They remained quiet, like a mouse pissing on cotton so I presumed that they were still sleep. Raising my voice a little louder this time, I called out for them again. "Penny! Your food is going to get cold if you don't come downstairs! Come on, let's eat! Piper, you too! Get out of the bed, it's twelve o'clock! Come downstairs and eat your food!"

I listened closely again and still, no one made a move. I didn't make a fuss this time though, I just took matters into my own hands. One way or another, I was determined to spend some time with my family today, even it was just eating brunch.

Tossing my apron across my kitchen island, I went upstairs in search of my wife and daughter. As I ascended the stairs one at a time, I thought about which room I should bombard first. Being as though Piper was the crankiest when her sleep was disturbed, it wasn't hard for me to decide which room to choose. And furthermore, Penelope's room was the closest to the steps anyway, so I went with Penelope for win.

KNOCK! KNOCK! KNOCK! KNOCK! KNOCK!

Creeekkkkkkkk!

Opening Penelope's door slowly, I placed my head in between the threshold and spoke. "Good morning lady bug! I'm glad to see that you're up. I cooked breakfast for you and your mother and it's waiting for you downstairs on the table." I was so happy to be in the presence of my daughter that I couldn't stop cheesing. "I made your favorite too, chicken and waffles!"

At the sound of my voice, Penny didn't budge. She kept her back towards me as she laid across her bed, gripping her knees. I almost began to worry, that is until I spotted the Air Pods hidden in her ears. Taking a few steps deeper into her room, I raised my voice a little louder and repeated what I had just said. "Penny! I made you some chicken and waffles! It's downstairs!"

"Oooo! Ah! Huh?" Penny yelled as she snatched the Air

Pods from out of her ears, scared to death.

"I said that it's some food downstairs for you and your mother if you're hungry."

"Thank you, but no thank you Dad," she declined, sounding depressed. "I'm not really hungry."

"You okay Pumpkin?"

"Yes," she replied while trying to blink away her tears. It was evident that something was bothering her and it tugged at my heart not knowing what it was.

"You know that I'm here for you if you need to talk, to vent, or anything? Even if you need me to be quiet and just listen."

"I know," she said while holding back a sniffle.

"I'm serious Penny! Whatever you tell me will stay between the two of us, no matter how bad it is." I vowed as I took a seat on her bed and pulled her in for a fatherly hug. "I'm not here to judge you... I just want you to feel better. I hate seeing you all worked up like this," I expressed as I stroked her hair with one hand and patted her back with the other.

"But I'm okay," she tried to convince, but I knew otherwise.

"No you're not, don't think just because I haven't said anything that I have noticed. You've been moping around here for the last past week, not saying much to anybody and that's not like you," I protested as I stopped what I was doing and looked her in her eyes. "The only reason why I left you alone all this time is because I figured you'd come around sooner or later, but it's almost been three weeks now and nothing has changed."

"I'm good Dad, I swear," she reiterated as she climbed off her bed and walked to her dresser to get a tissue. "I'll be down in a few minutes, just let me get myself together," she said while drying her eyes.

"Alright then," I backed down, while rising from her bed. It was clear that she wasn't ready to talk and I wasn't going to badger her any further. "I'm about to go wake your mother up and then head back downstairs. I hope that you can join us for brunch but if not, I understand."

I left out of Penelope's room, in motion to the master bedroom that Piper and I shared. The loud snores that echoed off the walls in our bedroom was the only indication that I needed that she was still sound asleep. For a minute, I thought about letting her sleep in being as though it wasn't every day that I got a chance to be around peace and quiet. But then I thought against it because believe it or not, I kinda got accustomed to her hearing her loud mouth bitch and complain. It was my normal, and over the course of our marriage, I've grown to accept it.

Entering our bedroom, I quietly closed the door behind me and tip-toed over to where my wife was laying ready to surprise her with some kisses. Leaning down over our bed, I became face to face with her succulent lips and delivered a kiss to them.

"Arghhhhh," she groaned while swatting my face away. "Leave me alone, I'm trying to sleep."

"Get up girl," I instructed while slapping her on her thick thighs. Piper's thighs saved lives and that was the one thing that I couldn't get enough of. I mean that and her bomb ass pussy! It was something about the voodoo that she held in between her legs that always had me coming back for more. Hence that probably was the reason that I married her.

"Just give me a few more minutes, please!" she begged while pulling at the sheets and turning over on her side.

I knew better than to believe in Piper's five minute scheme. This was an everyday routine for us when I was home, as just like every other time, I knew what I had to do to get her up.

After roughly snatching the sheets off of her with my hands, I gawked at Piper's naked body as if this was the first time that I've seen it before. Her 5'2" frame never got old to me and as I stared at my bite sized Hershey kiss, my mouth began to salivate at the thought of tasting her. Slowly, I gripped my hands around the bottom of her ankles and gave her a gentle tug; letting her know what was up. I was ready for my daily dose of heaven and like the good girl that Piper was, she fell into compliance; seductively spreading her legs apart, allowing me access into her honeypot.

"Mmmhmm," I hummed as I placed my nose at the center of her love canal and gave it a sniff. Even after all the hours that passed, Piper still smelled fresh and that compelled me to want her juicy pearl even more. Positioning my mouth directly above her clitoris, I stuck my tongue out and gave her probing pearl a wet swirl. Piper's love canal had a mind of its own and just that one kiss, had her honey pot overflowing with sweet nectar. "You was waiting on this, huh?" I boasted, while removing my t-shirt from up over my head. "I know you was. You ain't gotta tell me. Now go ahead and open them legs up wide for Daddy so that I can finish my meal."

Instead of voicing her answer, Piper clamped her legs together around my neck and that was all the notion I needed to continue. Turning my right hand over so that my palm was facing the ceiling, I folded all of my fingers, minus my middle finger back, and placed it in her hole. As I stabbed Piper's g-spot with my finger tip, I simultaneously sucked on her clitoris, causing her body to squirm and shiver.

"Mmhhhhhhmmmm! Fuck!" Piper groaned as she slowly gyrated her hips in a circle. Judging by her actions, I could tell that her climax was near and that only motivated me to go faster. Just as Dr. Jekyll transformed into Mr. Hyde, I transformed into the king of the jungle, and I attacked my prey as if it was the last meal I would receive here on earth.

"Ooohh, I love when you eat this pussy! I love you! Mhhhhhhhmmmmmm! Fuck!" she panted while thrusting her hips in my face. "Oooooh! You the shit at this! Oooooh eat your pussy!" she cried out and it was then that she squirted all over my face.

"Damn! I think I just broke a new record," I joked as I got up from the bed to go wipe the juices off my face.

"Shut up!" she shot as she rolled over sluggishly.

"Oh no, get that ass up!" I ordered as I walked back over to the bed and tugged at her leg. "I didn't do all of that just for you to go back to sleep."

"Do all of what?" she argued. "All you did was eat my pussy! You act like you just put in hella work and fucked me into a coma or something."

"You talking like that can't happen," I challenged as I tugged at the strings of my lounging pants, exposing my dick.

"I thought that you said you wanted me to get up," she smirked while preparing to get on all fours.

"It look like you're up to me," I affirmed while stroking my shaft up and down with my right hand. "Now stop talking and bring your ass over here so I can see what that mouth do," I ordered while I continued to stroke my dick. Assuming to position on her knees, Piper enchantingly crawled over to where I stood and became face to face with the tip of my anaconda. Using her tongue ring as a toy, Piper gently stuck the metal ball in the tip and teased me a bit. "Sssssss! Ahhh!" I shivered as I tried to prevent my knees from buckling in. "Don't play with it," I accused. "Just suck it."

"Don't tell me what to do. I know what I'm doing," she sassed and without warning she opened her mouth wide and swallowed my dick whole.

"Oooooooo yeah, just like that!" I coached, while grabbing ahold of her hair.

Piper was in the middle of pleasing me when she abruptly stopped to address my hands on her head. "Uh, uh! Get off of my hair! I just got it done!"

"Girl, hush up and keep going!" I growled. Piper was making my toes curl and I didn't want her to stop. "You know I'mma get it done again."

Using both of my hands, I directed her mouth back to my penis and shoved my wood down her throat. "*Cough!* Wait a... *Cough!* ... minute damn!" she fussed, while trying to cease her coughing spell.

"Come on before you make my shit go limp!"

"What you think I care about that?" she shot before getting up off the bed and disappearing into our master bathroom.

"So what you not gonna finish?" I quizzed as I stood there with my dick sticking out, looking stupid.

"Nope!" she confirmed from the other room. "You made my throat hurt!"

"You serious?" I asked before pulling up my pants and taking a seat on the bed. Shortly after that I heard the water running from the bathroom sink followed by a brushing sound and that gave me the answer I needed.

Selfish ass! I thought to myself before I exited our bedroom. I was pissed at the thought of receiving blue balls yet again, and I almost thought about dipping off and calling my side bitch so that she could finish what my wife started.

While storming pass Penelope's room with an attitude, I noticed that her door was open and that she wasn't in there. "Piper lucky, "I mumbled under my breath as I made my way down the steps and into the kitchen. Had Penelope not have been waiting on me and her mother to come downstairs, I legit would've called Donna and had her meet somewhere for some quick sloppy toppy. But since she was seated at the table quietly eating, I decided against it.

"How's the waffles?" I queried before I grabbing a glass plate from off the table and filling it with food.

"Good," she answered, not looking up from her plate.

"Do you want some more syrup? I think we have some blueberry or maple stashed away in the cabinet?" I asked before retrieving the steak sauce from out of the refrigerator and walking over to the counter.

"No thank you, this is enough."

Very well then. I shrugged behind her back, before taking a seat at the table.

After that mini session upstairs with Penny's mother, I was ready to eat some real food. Reaching for the silverware that sat on top of the napkin, I grabbed a knife and immediately began cutting at my tender steak. As I took a bite of the juicy meat, I had to stop my eyes from rolling in the back of my head. I literally was in the middle of a foodgasm when Piper came waltzing down the stairs and into the kitchen.

"Where's my plate?" she quizzed before fastening her furry pink robe and taking a seat in the chair.

"On the island with everyone else's," I retorted before helping myself to another bite.

Rolling her eyes, Piper rose from her seat and went to go examine the spread. "Ewww, why would you make steak and chicken knowing that I don't eat meat?"

"It's shrimp and grits over there," I mouthed as I continued to munch on my food.

"But the grits look runny," she complained while using her fork to pick over the food.

"Well then don't eat then, shit!" I yelled over my shoulder.

"Nobody told your ass to be a fake vegetarian."

Piper ignored me and spoke to Penny for the first time since she entered the kitchen. "Daughter girl, what did I tell you about putting that junk up in you? It's not good for your PH balance and most importantly it's not good for your weight."

"I'm sorry Mommy, I forgot," Penelope deadpanned as she took a pause from eating.

"Ain't no you forgot," Piper chastised. "Now get up and throw it in the trash."

Penelope looked to me before slowly rising from her seat. "Don't move Penny, stay there!" I instructed.

"Don't you dare tell *my* child not to listen to me," she chided as she walked away from the spread and pointed her manicured nail in my face. With her back towards Penny she continued her verbal assault. "Penny get yo ass up and do what I said before I come over there and slap you into next week!"

Penelope didn't want problems from her mother and it

showed. She knew that Piper would make due on her threat if she didn't move fast enough and she didn't want to chance it. Quickly, she jumped up from the table and disposed her food into the trash, before scurrying off upstairs to her room.

"Penny!" I called out after her but it was no use, she was gone. Her little fast legs got out of dodge quick, fast and in a hurry and deep down, I couldn't blame her. Upset by the exchange between the two, I turned to Piper, "Why you always gotta be a bitch in the morning?"

"Because! I'm tired of you going against what I say!"

"I wouldn't go against what you say, if you wasn't a bitch!" I reiterated. "You know damn well that girl's favorite meal is chicken and waffles, but now all of a sudden since you're on this suppose it health kick, you're gonna tell her she can't eat it. Who does that?"

"I do, and?"

"And that's wrong!" I spat while leaping to my feet. Piper

found a way to deliver my second L of the day. First she deprived me from my nut and now this. I no longer had an appetite as I walked over and discarded the rest of my steak in the trash. I was over her and her bullshit already and it was only one o'clock.

Later that Night…

Buried under a stack of papers in my study room, I sat going over a few of my officer's police reports. Ever since the last run-in with the Department Internal Affairs, I decided to be proactive with my officer's cases so that I could be one step ahead of DIA.

I was almost finished with the first stack of reports when I heard a knock at the door.

KNOCK! KNOCK!

I already knew who it was and I had to admit it, I was surprised that she came down here.

"Come in," I welcomed as I kept my head down and

continued reading.

"Uh, hey...hey Dad," she greeted as she subconsciously twirled her fingers. "Do you mind if I come and talk to you for a minute?"

"Oh hey baby, sure!" I said while removing my reading glasses and placing them on top of my desk. "What's on your mind?"

"Everything," Penelope sighed as she walked in and plopped down in the chair.

"I'm listening," I urged her to continue as I folded my hands across my beer belly and sat back in my seat.

"My life sucks."

"Baby girl, you're too young to be stressing over life. These are you golden years, you should go out and enjoy them."

"How when everybody hates me?"

"Who do you think hates you?" I puzzled with a look of

concern.

"Everybody! My dad, my mom, Charli!" she rattled off one by one.

"Sweetie, we can choose our friends, but we can't choose our family. No family is perfect, we argue, we fight. We even stop talking to each other at times, but in the end, family is family. The love will always be there."

"I know that Dad, but still. Why did my Momma have to have a baby with my real daddy? Why couldn't she have it with you? Maybe if she would've, none of this would be happening."

"Penny your father loves you —" I expressed, but she cut me off.

"No he doesn't! All he cares about is my sister and that's not fair. She gets away with everything and leaves me to be the scapegoat," she bleated. "She's not even punished for getting in trouble at school, but I AM!"

"I'm sure that's not the case Penny. He's probably just

upset that you got suspended from school. That's a big deal to a parent and when you get older and have children of your own, you'll understand why."

"How is it that you treat me better than he does? You notice that something is wrong with me, but he can't."

"Because, I love you," I reassured. In no way did I want to put down Penelope's father in front of her because I knew what it felt like to have someone talk bad about mine. Thinking hard about what I was about to say next, I chose my words wisely, careful not to add salt to her wounds. "Penny not everybody is given a manual on how to be a good father. It's a learning experience and over time you grow and learn to do better than you did the day before," I lectured. "Without a shadow of a doubt, I know that your father loves you and he wants you to succeed. He's just a work in progress, so bear with him, he's human. Maybe after you cool off some, you should go and have a talk with him because he's not a mind reader. And you can't fault him for not knowing how you feel if you don't tell him."

"And what if he brushes me off, like he always does?"

"Don't think like that. You have to be optimistic if you want to see change."

"But —"

"But nothing! Give it a try first and *then* if doesn't work out, we'll discuss what to do from there."

"I thought that you said that you were gonna listen and not talk?" she sassed with a little attitude in her voice.

"I did listen and I gave you the floor to vent."

"But I wasn't done."

"You are now," I announced as I stood from my chair. "Now come on and let's get some Rita's ice cream before they close for the season."

"But Mom said —"

"She's not gonna know. It'll be gone before we get back in the house," I said as I approached my study room door. "Are you coming with me or not?"

Dwelling on her issues for a second, she thought about if she should partake in the quick outing. And after giving it much thought, she got up from her seat and decided to join me on my brief escape. "I'll come. Hopefully a gelati will make me feel better."

Closing the door behind us, we left and got us some cool treats.

Chapter 7

Omari

"Why do we have to come and see Jigsaw? You know I hate scary movies," ShyShy complained as we stood in line to place our food order.

"Jigsaw's not scary. It's funny!" I replied while looking over the menu. It was date night at the Rotunda with my love and thank God it was my turn to pick the movie.

"There is nothing funny about a midget who terrorizes people while riding a bike," she huffed while throwing a mini tantrum.

"Shidddd, that little motherfucker is funny as hell. He remind me of Deebo from *Friday* when he came through the hood and snatched Red chain. Sounding like, Da Dan Dan Dan Dan Daaaa Dann," I laughed as I mimicked the sound effects of Deebo on his bike.

"I don't care what he reminds you of, I don't want to see him, it, or his momma," she reiterated as she took a step forward in the line.

"Why you scared of my mans like that?"

"Because he's mean and ugly!"

"Well that's how you look when you put all that makeup on your face, but you don't hear me complaining. I just suck it up and love you the same," I teased.

"Don't play with me! I don't look like no damn Jigsaw!" she shot as she smacked me in the back of my head.

"Ouch damnit! That shit hurt!" I cursed, while rubbing the sore spot. "What I tell you about you and your heavy ass hands?"

"The same thing I told you about you and your slick ass mouth. To watch it!" Shaniya growled.

Although we were only horse playing with each other, all eyes were now were on us as the onlookers feared my next move.

People had their cellphones in their hands ready to record or even worse, call the police.

Using my right hand, I grabbed a chunk of Shaniya's ass and pulled her body close so that only she could hear what I was saying. "See what you did," I scolded while tightening my grip on her cheek. "Now everybody all up in our business and you know I hate that."

While plastering a phony smile on her face, Shaniya spoke through her clenched teeth. "You know I don't care about them people watching. I'm an exhibitionist, I love to put on a good show."

"You gonna fuck around and make me show you something alright. I'mma show you this dick and you gonna show me how sorry you are," I taunted before giving her ass a hard smack.

This time, Shaniya's cheese was real. "Oooooo, you know I like it when you give it to me rough," she purred. "Can we leave now? We don't even have to see the movie."

"Nah! Nice try though, your ass ain't slick. You didn't even want to see the movie to begin with," I chortled and it was then that crowd began to breathe again.

"You right, I don't," she agreed as she adjusted her long fitted skirt. "So I don't even know why we're still here."

"Because money doesn't grow on trees and the tickets are already paid for."

"And? It ain't shit but twenty dollars. Well forty since it's two tickets."

"I don't care if it was two dollars. We still watching it. You chose our last date, so this is mine."

"Grrrrrrrr! You petty as hell for this! I swear don't wanna hear shit when Xscape comes to town!"

"What Xscape got to do with me?"

"*We*," she stated while pointing back and forth between

herself and me. "Are going to be front and center stage, watching my girls do their thangggg."

"To hell if I am!" I opposed while shaking my head. "I ain't going to that shit."

"Oh yes you are! Because that's where *I'm* choosing next for *our* date," Shaniya informed before stepping up to the counter and placing her order.

"Hi, how are you doing? What you guys would like today?" The Cincbistro waiter greeted while he waited for us to tell him what we wanted.

"Hi, yes, can I get your large lump crab cake with truffle fingerling potatoes and your warm green beans?" Shy replied while I continued to read over their menu. "Oohh, and I wanna try y'all red velvet lava cake too. My homegirl Neek told me it was good," she added while handing the waiter the laminated cuisine list.

"Damn girl, you hungry ain't you?" I teased, after returning my menu to the waiter as well.

"I am! You know I ain't eat all day," she lied.

"Will that be all for you ma'am?" the waiter asked as he punched Shy's order into the monitor in front of him.

"Yeah, that's it for me," she announced while reaching in her purse and grabbing her MAC lipstick. "You can ask this big head nigga what he want."

The young male waiter stifled a laugh before redirecting his attention towards me. "And for you sir? What would you like?"

"I'll take your steak and cake with the potatoes and green beans as well."

"How would you like you steak cooked?"

"Well-done. I don't want no cows moving on my plate."

"Will that be all Sir?"

"Hell no, I'mma fat boy," I joked as I patted my stomach. "You also give me an order of your Maryland Old Bay wings. I

390

want all flats too," I added.

"That'll be two dollars extra."

"That's fine," I answered as I pulled out my wallet and handed him a hundred dollar bill.

"See, I was gonna pay too," ShyShy announced before rubbing her lips together and placing her lipstick back in her bag. "But since you making me watch this movie, I ain't doing shit. I'm about to go in this here theater, wait till my food is done, and when it is, I'mma stay up just long enough for me to eat it. After that, I'm counting sheep and then you can wake me up at the end."

"You can go to sleep if you want to, I'mma leave your ass right here as soon as the credits hit," I quipped

"Picture that," she dared. "You know better than to leave me anywhere unattended. I'll come back home with two new baes and a pocket fully of money."

"Bet. But before you do all of that, just let me know what song you want me to sing at your funeral," I responded sinisterly.

Shaniya knew I was dead serious too because the only way she was leaving me for another nigga was in a body bag.

"Ooohh that's easy, it's only right that I go out with a bang. I want you and all my bitches to sing Trina, 'The Baddest Bitch. And at my recession I want y'all to get Money Bagg Yo and them to perform Gang Gang," she laughed as she stuck out her tongue and hit the infamous Baltimore two step. My baby wasn't much of a dancer so that was all that she could do. I preferred it that way too because I'll be damned if I let her shake her ass all around at a club.

"Here you go Sir," the waiter interrupted as he handed me my change and along with a buzzer. "The buzzer will light up when your food is ready."

"Okay, thanks," I said as I grabbed the change from his hands and headed towards our theater. Shaniya followed me but stopped when she realized that we didn't even know the theater location.

"Where are you going? You don't even know which theater we're in," ShyShy voiced as she retrieved the tickets from her bag. I kept walking anyway. We were already missing the previews for the next up incoming movies and that was my favorite part. "Omari! Where are you going? Our tickets say theater three! You're going the wrong way!" she shouted.

"I am not!" I yelled over my shoulder. "Now bring your ass on, it's this way!"

Shaniya checked the tickets once again before blowing out her breath. "That's stupid! Why would theater three be all the way up there and not near the entrance?" she grumbled while walking hastily so that she could catch up.

Finally! I thought to myself when I looked up and noticed that we were in front of theater three. Walking in, I could hear the cinema movie instructions playing and immediately I got happy. The previews were usually set to begin after this, so I had about five minutes max to find our seats and to get our food. "What seats we in?" I quizzed as I stood at the bottom of the stairs and looked

393

up.

"Seat F6 and F5. They're in the back and in the middle," she stated, while pointing to the top.

BUZZ! BUZZ!

Just as I was about to begin walking up the steps, my buzzer lit up. "Just in time," I mumbled under my breath before turning to Shaniya to speak. "Go up there and get our seats for us," I instructed while backpedaling towards the entrance. "I'm about to go get our food, I'll be back."

Scurrying down the short, dark hallway, I was in a rush and didn't even notice the patrons walking through the theater door until it was too late.

"Oh my God, no! I wanted that!" the stranger cried as her plate came crashing down to the ground.

"I told you let me carry it, clumsy ass!" the guy, who I assuming was her date, fussed.

The floor was covered with steak and potatoes, and me being the fat boy that I was, I felt her pain. "Damn! I am so sorry," I apologized, not once lifting my eyes up from off the ground. Upset, the stranger bent down to pick up her meal and I followed her. "Here, let me help you with that," I offered while kneeling down and picking up the soiled food.

"Thank you, but I got ..." she started to say, but paused when she noticed my face. "Omari?"

Snapping my head in her direction, I zcroed in on the figure before me. For a second, I hesitated because it's been a while since I've seen her face. "Logan?"

"Um, h-hey. How have you been?" she wondered, while soaring to her feet and patting at her clothing. "Tiran, it's Omari, Seven's brother. You remember him don't you?" She explained while her eyes remained glued to me. They say that the eyes held the depths of our souls and it was apparent that she was studying mine. I understood why though because the last time that we crossed paths, it wasn't so merry. And although that incident was well over six years ago, that betrayal was still fresh in my heart. I still remember the phone call I received from my brother that day and everything. And had it not been for the sake of my sister, I probably would have been sent this crackhead on to meet her maker.

"Yeah, I remember him," Tiran deadpanned as he eyed me closely. There once was a time where Tiran would have greeted me with open arms, but I guess times have changed. Furthermore, I was even more shocked to see these two were back dealing with each other because the last time I heard, Tiran had moved to another state for his rap career and got himself a new bitch. Come to find out his new bitch is actually his old bitch, which actually is a crackhead bitch, but that's neither here nor there.

"Damn bruh, you don't look happy to see me," I chuckled, mischievously

"Nah, I'm good off you," he tossed, and I actually found it funny. I mean I legit, laughed in this man's face because he knew better to crack slick with me. I wasn't playing with a full deck upstairs in my head, and I was more than positive that he knew that.

BUZZ! BUZZ!

Looking down at the buzzer that was on the floor, it reminded me why I came out of the theater in the first place. *My food!* I thought to myself as I bent down to pick up the flashing remote. I knew I had to miss some of the movie already but fuck it, that's what they made the Firestick for.

Remembering who I had sitting in the theater waiting on me, made me not want to even start any trouble because without a shadow of a doubt, I knew that Shaniya would surely give Logan the business, no questions asked. ShyShy was reckless and she was the Harley Quinn to my Joker. Throwing my deuces up, I backpedaled to the pick-up counter, but not before shouting, "Y'all be good out here. I'll see y'all around."

Had it been somebody else's food that I knocked on the floor, I probably would have paid for their replacement meal, but it since it was Logan's thieving ass, I decided against it. That was only a small price to pay for the large lump sum of money she stole from my brother so in my mind, she could take that money for her meal out of the money she owed Seven.

<u>Logan</u>

Three Days Later...

Tuesdays and Thursdays were the most essential days of the week for me. They were my therapy days and without them, I wouldn't know how much of my life I would be able to tolerate sober. It has been a long time coming, but after five and a half long years, I was glad to say that I was finally drug free.

That encounter with Tiran in the coffee shop seven years ago, saved my life and as much as I hated to admit it, I would forever be indebted to him for forcing me to get my shit together. He could have left me like everyone else had, but he didn't. He took a chance on me and I beat the odds of addiction. I scared my demons away with the power of God, something that no force could withstand and now I was free to be normal. My shackles were removed and I was free to live a regular life without having to deal with that monkey on my back. And overall I must say, it felt great!

My journey hasn't always been easy, in fact I've had more bad days than good, but in my heart I was a fighter and I refused to give up. Between the power of my Holy Father and the strong word and advice from my therapist, I was good and I had faith that I could handle anything that was thrown my way. I knew that nothing could have been any worse than what I've already endured and that alone caused me to have an optimistic outlook on life. I had already hit rock bottom once in my lifetime so there was no way to go other than up!

"So Logan, how was your weekend? Were you able to get any rest like we talked about? Did you do anything exciting? Tell me what's new," Dr. Hawkins inquired as she fired off question after question.

Dr. Patricia Hawkins was pretty much my lifeline and she

was the person responsible for helping me achieve my breakthrough. Even though she was only technically my therapist, I considered her to be so much more. She was my fairy godmother who helped me organize my mental and she was also my voice of reason when I got off of track. Her wisdom was unmatched and although sometimes her delivery seemed brutal, her heart was always behind it; and that always remained pure.

"My weekend was okay for the most part. I didn't have any major complaints. Surprisingly, Tiran didn't make me workout with him Saturday morning, so I was able to sleep in. I only slept for about an extra three hours though because by 9:30a.m my body was like *nope, it's time to get up*," I recalled before sitting back on the comfy couch and popping a piece of chocolate in my mouth.

"Well I'm happy that you were able to get some rest." Dr. Hawkins smiled while jotting down some short notes in my file. "Did you and your fiancé do anything? I know you were saying that he was planning something special to help take your mind of the anniversary of your son's death. Did he fill you in on his plans yet?"

"Soooo, I was getting around to telling you about that. So this weekend Tiran planned an amazing date for us. I'm talking bout he pulled out alllll his tricks, just to see me smile," I cheesed, while showing all thirty-two teeth.

"Okay! I'm listening. Tell me more," she urged.

"Okay, so on Friday he sent me to the Four Seasons for a spa day. I got a mani and pedi, a two-hour massage, and a facial. Which all felt amazing! You should go one day! They were super sweet and professional! And they took great care of me! To the point that I'm thinking about making that monthly thing," I avowed rather gleefully.

"I know my daughters took me there for Mother's Day last year, aren't they bomb?"

"Oh my God, yes!" I exclaimed. "Prior to this weekend, I have never been there before and I was surprised that they even had mimosas for their guests while we wait."

"I don't drink alcohol, but my daughters said the drinks were tasty when we went."

"They were!" I confirmed before getting back to my story. "So anyway, Tiran planned this relaxing day for me at the spa and I honestly felt 100% better after everything was all complete."

"That was nice of him," she applauded before placing my folder in her lap. "I remember a time when he refused to do nice things for you, because he thought that you wouldn't be appreciative."

I nodded my head in agreement to her statement. "I know right! It's crazy how things can change over the course of time."

"Chile, that ain't nothing but God. When you submit to him, he will show you favor and plead the blood over your life."

"Amen to that!" I praised as I closed my eyes and took a minute to reflect on my past. Mrs. Hawkins was right. Once I stopped running and addressed where the pain was coming from, I was able to let go, but that was only with the help of the

Magnificent One.

"Amen," she repeated as she moved the file from her lap, to her desk. "So other than your amazing date was there anything else that you would like to discuss today?"

"Yes, there is! I almost forgot to finish telling you," I said and Dr. Hawkins instantly picked up her pen back up, ready to write. "So not only did Tiran plan a spa day for me, but he also took me to this exclusive movie theater to see my favorite movie, *Saw*. The date was going wonderful too! I ordered a nice five star meal and I was gonna enjoy it once I sat down in the theater. It didn't make it that far though because someone bumped into me on purpose and caused me to waste it all over my clothes before I even had a chance to make it inside."

"Oh my God, no! I know you were upset! Did you practice the breathing technique we worked on to help you cool off?"

"Nope!"

"Come on Logan, we've gotten too far for you to revert

back to your old ways. Don't tell me you went off."

"I didn't, but I should have."

"Well I'm glad that you didn't."

"But you don't understand."

"What am I not understanding? You should be proud that you were able to move on from the situation without getting out of character."

"Let me finish telling you the story so that you can get the full scoop," I advised before continuing. "So as I was walking into the theater with my food in hand, this man comes up and bum rushes me to the floor. Normally, I would have been upset, but this time I wasn't because Tiran had already put me in a good mood earlier that day."

"Where was Tiran when this happened? Was he there?"

"Yeah, he was there," I answered. "He was right behind me."

"Okay. I'm following you. So you said that you and Tiran were walking in the theater and a man bum rushed you. But you didn't get upset. Right?"

"Right," I verified.

"Did the man say sorry for making you drop your food? Was it an accident?"

"No because it was on purpose."

"What is this world coming to? Why would a stranger push someone he didn't know? And a woman at that."

"Because I think it was payback. I knew the man that pushed me," I revealed. "And once upon a time a long time ago, I did some bad things to his brother, that I'm ashamed of."

"Wait a minute, how did I miss this? So the guy that you're saying pushed you, have we ever had a discussion about him? Because I don't remember ever talking about him."

"Sorta kinda," I answered truthfully. "When I first came to

you, we had a conversation about him and his brother Seven. They were my best friend's family which in turn became mine as well."

"Refresh my memory then. What happened between you and him that would make him cause bodily harm to you?"

Although I was passed this stage in my life, it still bothered me to talk about it. Nobody liked to point out there faults to other people and this was no different. Thankfully I knew that Dr. Patricia would never judge me, so I divulged an old secret.

"Back when I was getting high," I hesitated for a minute so that I could find a way to sugarcoat what I needed to say. "I…I stole some big money from him and his brother. Omari and Seven were taking care of me after my child's father put me out and I stole from them. I'm not proud of what I did and if I could, I would take it back. Seven and Omari were the only real family that I had besides Harlow at the time and I let them down. I almost caused Seven's friend, whatever her name is, to lose her child. And… it just was bad," I finished. I didn't feel the need to go into specific detail because like I said that part of my life was over.

"So Tiran just stood right there and let this happen? He didn't say anything? I mean he must not have because you would have said something about it by now."

"I was stuck myself when it happened, so I'm guessing that Tiran felt the same way," I defended. "Tiran and Omari used to be cool years ago, but something happened that caused them to have a falling out."

"Was it cause of the drugs you stole?" she fished.

"No. I don't think so because their falling out happened way before that. I started to notice it around the time my best friend died in the car accident."

"Do you have any reason to believe that this Omari character is after you or Tiran? And when I say after you, I mean do you think he would cause more harm to you if he ever saw you again?"

"I —"

"Wait a minute, before you answer my question, remember

that by law I have a duty to warn the authorities if you disclose any type of information about yourself and others that may appear violent or impose a danger."

"I don't know," was the best answer I could think of. I felt like it was too premature for me to fear that my life was in danger because after all, if Omari and Seven really wanted to get me after all these years, they knew where to find me. Baltimore, or should I say PG county, was too small for me not to be on their radar.

"I feel like you should report this to the authorities to cover your tail and Tiran's. Omari and his brother sound like some very dangerous men and I'd rather you be safe than sorry," she voiced, while expressing her concern.

"How about this? As soon as I get the feeling that something is wrong, I promise to report it."

"Okay, that's all that I can ask from you," she said, sounding worried. "Since you don't want to intervene just yet, how about you tell me where you want me to meet you at? Do you want advice on the matter? Do you want me to give you options as to what you can do? Do you want me to leave it alone? You tell me."

"I want a little bit of all of that," I answered. "I want you to tell me what you'd do if you were in the same situation and I also want you to give me other alternative just in case I don't like that answer."

"I already told you what I would do. I would call the police and file a report. But since you're obviously against that, I would save my money and get out of town. I would either go somewhere down south like Georgia or North Carolina or I would go somewhere north like Jersey," she suggested.

"I don't think I'm ready to leave Maryland all together yet," I bleated.

"Well then you're gonna have to be ready for whatever Omari and his brother Seven throw your way."

Shifting my position on the couch, I marinated on my unspoken truth. Realizing that I didn't have any other options to choose from, I took Dr. Hawkins' suggestion into consideration. A change of scenery didn't seem like *that* bad of an idea. I mean if you think about it, it wasn't like I would be leaving behind any friends. Leaving Baltimore could be the fresh start that I dreamed of. Nobody would know me or the past life that I lived. And I would be surrounded by new beginnings. *You know what? Moving didn't so bad after all. Now all I gotta do is get Tiran on board and we're outta here for good!*

Chapter 8

Inez

Three Weeks Later…

"Mommy does our new house have a backyard?" Christopher asked as he gathered all of the clothing from out of his closet and placed it on his race car bed.

"Of course," I affirmed while helping him with his things. "And once we're all settled into our new place, we can build a mini playground back there with some swings and a maybe even a treehouse."

"Coolllllll!" he gushed as he balled up the shirts and pants and threw them into the plastic bin.

My kids and I were set to move into our very first house in a couple of weeks and we all were excited for this new milestone in our lives. As a single mother, I was proud of myself for finally getting it done and I'm sure that my kids couldn't be any happier.

This was the first time around where everyone would have their own rooms, and that right there was enough to make me wanna do cartwheels around our new place. Aside from the bedrooms, we also had several bathrooms, a few walk in closets, and all the necessary amenities needed to run a modern day household. To say I was blessed for this new venture, was an understatement and I looked forward to making memories with my kids.

"Christopher, fold your clothes up so that you'll have more space in there," I instructed as I walked over to the container and removed the previously thrown items.

"But it sooooo much clothes," he exaggerated while acting as if he was about to faint. "My hands hurt Mommy, look!"

"Oh okay! Not a problem," I calmly stated as I paused from folding his clothes. "I guess I better give away your X-Box system to one of the little boys down the street whose fingers still work."

"Nooooooo wait! Don't give it away! I was only playing Mommy!" Christopher cried out as he dropped down to his knees and grabbed my leg. It was sad that I had to coerce my kids into doing what I needed them to do, but I guess that's how motherhood went when you were the mother of two hard-headed boys.

"Then stop playing and fix it," my voice boomed as I shoved the balled up clothing into his face. I hated to be harsh with him, but today and tomorrow were the only days that I could squeeze in for packing, so we had to get it done.

Pouting like the spoiled brat he was, Christopher reached for the clothing out of my hands and started folding his clothing the correct way. "That a boy," I praised while patting him on his back. "That's the way that you do it. Now finish up in here so that I can get Christian to carry your boxes downstairs for you," I added before leaving out of their bedroom door and heading for my room. "I'm about to get a start on things in my room, if you need me," I shouted behind me as I continued walking down the hallway.

As I made my way down the hall and into my room, I

413

dreaded the labor that I was about to put in. I was what you called a pack rat, and I harbored everything from unnecessary papers to *as seen on TV* gadgets. It was bad, and I knew if I wanted to start off on a clean slate at my new household, I had to throw all this mess away.

Surveying the cluttered area around me with my eyes, I tried to find the easiest place to start my mission. But the more I scanned the room with my frowned up face, I realized that there wasn't really an "easy" place to begin. There was shit everywhere to the point that it made me want to just throw the whole room away. Nothing was in its right place and I was already frustrated. As I continued to analyze the hard work ahead of me, my eyes fell on my dresser drawers. *The dresser!* I thought to myself as I kicked the scattered shoes out of my way and made a makeshift path on the floor. Being careful not to stub my toe, I tip-toed over to the fully covered furniture and began the task at hand.

It was a shame that I had so much junk strewed across dresser that I could no longer see the cherry-wood coating at the top. Locating the black trash bag that sat hidden on the floor, I immediately snatched it up and began disposing the useless nick-knacks that sat on top of the surface.

"This is old...I don't need this anymore... Why would I still have this?" I mumbled as I tossed the items in the trash. "This ain't nothing but junk, junk, and more junk," I sighed out loud. It seemed as if the more papers I threw away, the more that reappeared and judging by the little progress that I made, I could already tell that it was gonna be a long night. "What in the world! Why do I have a cable bill from three years ago in here?" I grumbled as I ripped up the envelope and its contents and threw it in the black hefty bag.

"This don't make no damn sense. Somebody is gonna fuck around and nominate me for that Hoarders show," I chuckled as I continued throwing the miscellaneous things away. "More bills...more bills," I huffed as I blew out a breath and shuffled threw the nine million envelopes sitting in a pile at the back of my dresser. I started to just throw them all away without going through them, but I decided against it because who knows what else was in that pile. I knew that Imani's social security envelope was somewhere around here, along Christian's birth certificate. So I played it safe and went through each envelope individually.

"Ooooh, what's this?" I wondered as I came across an envelope with no logo or lettering on it. "I hope it's a check that I forgot about," I prayed as I dropped the trash bag and anxiously opened the sealed document. As soon as my eyes skimmed across the first line, I choked. "Oh my God! I forgot! I forgot!" I shrilled as I took a step back to sit on my bed. It had been a long time since I last spoke her name, so it pained me to find this. Wiping away the tears that nearly blinded my eyes, I held my breath as I read my late friend Khia's final will and testament.

My last dying breath...

It took a lot for me to sit down and write this letter because deep down that meant that I had to come to terms and accept that someone was going to kill me. I, Khia Rochelle Caldwell, born November 19, 1987 am writing this letter to inform you that person

416

responsible for my untimely demise was Seven Freeman, of Baltimore, Maryland.

On June 1st, sometime around 8:30 p.m., Seven Freeman entered the Hunt Valley dealership where I worked and requested an all-white Mercedes-Benz 350 SUV. I informed Mr. Freeman that we had the car in stock and after allowing him to conduct the appropriate tests (a test drive and showing him a copy of the car's history) Mr. Seven Freeman purchased the car the same night and drove off of our lot with it. The following day, due to things out of my control, Mr. Freeman's fiancé Harlow Stevenson was found dead in a car crash with that exact same car.

Please understand, that in no way shape or form was I responsible for the death of his beloved fiancé. As stated above, the Mercedes Benz 350 vin number 1BNCG35Z3M0152612, issued to him on June 1st was in perfect working condition prior to his purchase and although I explained that to Mr. Freeman numerous times, he still was irate.

On June 7, exactly one week after the accident, Seven

Freeman returned to my place of business on a mission. After speaking with my boss, Thomas Gronkowski, about my whereabouts, Mr. Freeman waited for me to return from my lunch break and approached me at my desk about a faulty car that I sold him. I offered to show him the car's history report once again, but he declined and that's when he flashed a gun and demanded that I give him some answers. From afar, my boss saw the whole interaction and that's when with great courage, he intervened. Seven Freeman fled from the dealership that day but he threatened to return if I didn't produce him the answers that he needed.

As you read this letter, you're probably wondering why I didn't go to the police about this matter, but the answer is ... I was scared. I am no stranger to the amount influence Mr. Freeman has in the police department, thus why I didn't report him.

I pray that this letter is enough to begin an investigation on the above man and bring him to justice for the malicious act that he's done. I know that it's not a lot to work with, but hopefully it's a start.

From Heaven's Angel,

Khia Rochelle Caldwell.

As I was reading the letter, it felt like an eternity had went by and I didn't release my breath until I was finished. *What type of friend was I? How could I forget about something so serious as this?*

To hell with packing! I thought to myself as I quickly leaped to my feet. Clutching the letter tightly in my hands, I bolted out of my bedroom and into my daughter Imani's.

"Imani, I need you to watch your brothers for me while I go run and take care of something real quick!" I babbled as my heart raced rapidly. It was better late than never and I was determined to bring Seven to justice for my friend.

"But Ma!" she whined. "I was about to go out with Stacey and Katrina."

"What did I just say!" I growled as spit flew from out my mouth. I didn't mean to growl at her but she had to understand that this was serious.

"But can't it wait until tomorrow? I really wanna go to Sarah's party," she pleaded

"No it can't because this is important! Now watch your brothers like I asked and stop giving me backtalk."

"This isn't fair," she quavered as she fell back on her bed and crossed her arms. "I always have to suffer because of them! Why couldn't I just have been the only child?" she cried.

"Get your ass up before I make you stay in the house your whole winter break!"

Imani changed her tune real quick too. Climbing off the bed, Imani submissively rose to her feet and went to go check on her brothers. She knew better than to buck back because I sure as hell was a gonna make due on my threat.

Backtracking into my bedroom, I grabbed my keys and wallet from under the rubbish and then I jetted out of the door, en route to handle something I shoulda did a long time ago.

Maycen

One Week Later…

RING! RING! RING! RING!

After staying up until the wee hours in the morning helping Charli arrange together her science project, I was spent and I wanted nothing more than to lay down and make love to my pillow.

RING! RING! RING!

"Damn it," I groaned. I thought that the caller would take the hint the first time that I ignored the phone, but apparently not. Keeping my eyes glued shut, I reached across the nightstand and patted around for my phone. "Hello," I croaked, my voice dry and in a whisper.

"Hello, Maycen Drew?"

"Yes," I sighed, already annoyed at the upbeat caller.

"This is Detective Wade from the Baltimore County Police

Department."

"Okay," I responded, confused of the random call.

"I have a few questions that I would like to ask you and I wanted to know would you mind coming down to our station a little later on today?" the officer queried as I sat up in my bed, alarmed.

"Questions about what? Is something wrong?" I probed. I haven't did anything to my knowledge, so I was clueless as to what this officer could possibly want.

"Would you happen to know a Khia Caldwell?" he quizzed and it was then that my forehead began to sweat and he caught my interest.

"Yeah," I gulped. "What about her?" Khia was a memory of the past that care not to discuss with either police nor anyone else.

"I need you to come down to the station so that you can answer a few questions for me about her character," he informed.

"We were given an anonymous letter earlier last week, and we need help validating if it's true."

"A letter about what?" I urged him to continue. Khia had been gone for a minute so I was curious and also nervous to hear what she left behind.

"I'm sorry Sir, but I can't say over the phone. If you like, I could go into it with a little more detail in person. But that's if you agree to come down here."

What was up with this officer trying to get me to come down to the station? Did he know something that I didn't? Was he trying to lock me up? Either way I wasn't about to let him throw me in a trick bag. I knew my rights and until they came knocking on my door to get me, I wasn't going to them. "I'm sorry Detective, but I'm going to have to take a raincheck on that. You have a good day," I finished as I rushed him off the phone and then dialed up Tiran.

It was still early in the morning and I felt bad that I was

about to disturb him, but this was urgent and it couldn't wait.

"Yo this better be an emergency," he yawned while glancing over at the clock. The time read 7:00 a.m. and even the birds were still sleep.

"It is," I responded while getting up from out of my bed. I didn't wanna say too much over the phone for the fear that they might have been tapped, so I was selective over my word choice. "You by yourself?"

"Nah," he answered. "Logan laying right here next to me."

"Get up and go to the bathroom," I whispered. "I don't want her to overhear what I'm about to tell you."

Doing as he was told, Tiran slowly slid out of the bed with Logan and crept out into the hall and inside of the bathroom.

"Okay... now what?" he pressed as he held the phone close to his ear and waited for me to continue.

"I'mma say a name and just say yes if you're following

where I'm going with it."

"Okay."

"Khia?"

"What about her —"

"I said say yes or no," I scolded a litter louder than I intended to.

"Okay then. No!" he hollered back.

"Lower your voice dumb ass, before Logan hears you."

"And if she hears me, it's gonna be your fault!" he accused. "Stop beating around the bush with these little guessing games and tell me what's going on." It was evident that Tiran was running out of patience, the agitation in his voice showed.

"Shut up and listen then," I demanded, while peeking out of my room for my kids. "I got a phone call not too long ago from BCPD demanding that I come down for the questioning of Khia's death."

"What the fuck?" he cursed as he bit down on his inner cheek. Tiran tended to do that when he was either guilty or upset so I was glad that I was able to give him a heads up so that he wouldn't incriminate himself. "Why they digging up old shit?"

"Apparently the police found a letter and I'm almost positive that our names were somewhere in there misconstrued."

"We already know about the letter idiot! I wrote it!"

"Not that letter smart ass! It's another one and apparently somebody gave it to them last week."

"How could they get a letter from a dead person Maycen? That doesn't make any sense."

"I don't know. Why don't you go and ask the detective and then come back and tell me," I sarcastically replied. "Of course that doesn't make sense. That's what we're trying to figure out."

"Do you think that they could be pulling your leg?" he asked, trying his best to sound optimistic.

"They could be, but why would they mention Khia? Or a note? That's too much of a coincidence to ignore," I considered. "Somebody has to know something."

"Fuckkkk!" he hissed. "We gotta find out what that letter says and then get rid of it."

"They already have it, genius."

"Can't you get one of you police contacts to make it disappear?"

"I'mma try to, but until then we gotta act normal. We don't need anybody sniffing their nose into the past because the last thing we need is for someone to find out about Harlow's accident."

"Shit! I forgot all about that! Fuck them finding out about Khia! We can't let them find out about Harlow! That nigga Seven is still around and he still can have us touched."

"Ain't nobody scared of that pussy ass nigga Seven!" I barked. Hearing that nigga's name caused my pressure to rise. "He bleeds just like I do!"

"Yeah aight! You say that now, but when he put that chrome to ya dome, we'll see if you're still screaming fuck Seven then."

"Nigga get off of that nigga's nut sack! You the same nigga that was just plotting on him but now all of a sudden you scared," I was amped at this point and my common sense went out the window as I pressed my point. "Seven ain't gonna do shit to us because we're gonna always gonna be one step ahead of him. Just like we got the heads up when he brought that car, we got the heads up about this letter," I pointed out. "We know what to expect of him which is why we're going to be ready., I voiced. "Seven can be froggy and leap if he want to, but I promise you this time, I'll do more than just cut the break line."

"Bet!" Tiran agreed as prepared to return back into his bedroom. "We just gotta stay ten toes down and get this shit done this time."

"Agreed."

"So what's the plan? Do you think they gonna call me too?"

"More than likely. You're the only one with a real connection to her so I'm sure they're gonna come at you next."

"And when they do?"

"Answer all their questions and play it cool."

"This shit is gonna make a nigga start smoking again," Tiran announced before approaching his bedroom door. "Aight bro, tell Charli if she has any more problems outta him, that I'll come up her school to address it," Tiran lied and I caught on to what he was doing. He didn't know if Logan was still sleep so he played it safe just in case she wasn't.

Chuckling at his wit, I took that as my cue and hung up the phone.

Charli

One hour ago...

"Aaaaaaahh," I yawned as I climbed out of my bed and stretched my bones. It was before the time that I was supposed to get up for school, but I couldn't sleep last night so I figured why not get a move on my day.

Last night took everything out of me, and I was just happy to say that I only had one more day until Thanksgiving break.

Careful not to wake anybody else up in the house, I tip-toped down the steps and into the kitchen to pour myself a bowl of cereal.

"Brrrrr! It's cold down here," I shivered as I crept over to the refrigerator to retrieve a gallon of milk. My feet were frozen against the cool marble floor and I hated the fact that I misplaced my slippers.

Pouring the iced milk in my bowl, I placed the galloon beside my oversized dish and took a seat at the table.

Munch! Munch! Munch! Was all I could hear as the sound of the cereal crunching echoed inside of my head.

Should I turn the television on? I thought as stood up and looked around the kitchen for the cable remote. The fact that I couldn't find told me that I didn't need it, so I gave it up. "I didn't feel like hearing him complain anyway," I mumbled as I quietly resumed eating my cereal.

After a few minutes of sitting alone, I heard my father's voice and immediately thought that I was in trouble. Grabbing my bowl and milk from off the table, I hurriedly scurried off into the other room so that he wouldn't see me.

"Ain't nobody scared of that pussy ass nigga Seven! He bleeds just like I do!" My father's voice traveled down to where I was in the living room and just hearing him mention my stepfather's name made me want to know more. Softly placing my food on the carpet floor, I crept over to the steps so that I could finish listening to the rest of his conversation.

"Nigga get off of that nigga's nut sack! You the same nigga that was just plotting on him but now all of a sudden you scared. Seven ain't gonna do shit to us because we're gonna always gonna be one step ahead of him. Just like we got the heads up when he brought that car, we got the heads up about this letter. We know what to expect of him which is why we're going to be ready. Seven can be froggy and leap if he want to, but I promise you this time, I'll do more than just cut the break line."

I had heard enough! Just that little bit of information was enough to make me throw up my breakfast and if I'd still been holding the glass bowl I probably would've dropped that too.

My life was based off of a lie and after all these years the truth was finally out! How could my father do my mother so dirty? He preached to Penny and I all the time about black love and how it could stand the test of time but finding out that he was the one behind my mother's death proved that he was nothing but a hypocrite. This was a tough pill to swallow and I desperately needed to vent because right about now, I felt like the room was closing in on me and I couldn't breathe.

What do I do? What do I do? I panicked and wracked my brain for what to do next. Glancing at the clock on the wall, I realized that it was nearing the time that I usually got up for school and that was when it hit me. *Saivon!* Saivon knew what to do in situations like this and for once since I found out, I was able to breathe.

Thinking hard of a way to get back to my room undetected, I came up with nothing. My father's room was right by the steps so there was no use in creeping back up the steps because he was up now and nine times outta ten, he was gonna see me. Coming to grips that I just was gonna have to walk up the steps, I retracted my footsteps back into the living room, retrieved my stuff and went on with my day as if everything was normal.

Placing my bowl in the sink, I made sure that I made noise going up the steps as I passed my father's room.

"Charli? Is that you?" My father called out from inside his

room and it disgusted me to have to respond.

"Yeah Dad, it's me," I answered. "I'm just getting ready for school," I advised before returning to my bedroom and locking the door behind me. As soon as I crossed the threshold, I located my phone on my nightstand and sent Saivon an emergency text.

Me: When you get to school, don't go inside. Meet me at our spot.

Saivon: Aight cool! You good?

Me: Long story & it's too much to text. I'll tell you about it when I see you.

Saivon: Ok cool. I'm gettin ready now!

Me: Me too! See you soon!

Casting my phone aside on my bed. I got up and rushed through my hygiene so that I could meet Saivon in time before class.

Sliding my toned legs into my Joe's Jeans, I wiggled my

slim frame into them and buttoned them up. Usually I would have paid more attention to my appearance in the mirror, but now was not the time to worry about being cute. Grabbing a *Pink* sweatshirt from my dresser drawer, I threw it over my head and sprinted down the stairs to the door.

I was ready like hell to get the heck out of the devil's kitchen, and I'm sure my body language showed. Reaching for the door knob, I almost made it out of the door unbothered, but leave it to my father to find a way to make his presence known.

"Aren't you forgetting something?" he quizzed as he paused in the living room and stared at me.

I was terrified and for some reason. I felt as if he could tell that I knew. "N-no. I got everything," I stammered, while going through the mental checklist in my head.

"Your project," he reminded.

I was so worried about getting to Saivon that I completely forgot about my science project. "Ohh yeah! Thanks Dad!" I replied while jogging over to retrieve it from off the dining room table.

"Have a good day at school baby girl!" he stated before reaching in for a hug from his seat.

I hesitated. *Hug him Charli. Hug him.* I convinced myself as I bent down and allowed my father to shower me in love. It took everything in me not to vomit as I literally could feel the chunks of waste rising. *Breathe baby. Breathe.* I coached as patted his back and pulled away.

"See you later," I waved as I dashed out the door.

The entire ride on the MTA bus, my mind raced. I couldn't get to Saivon fast enough and as the bus slowly creeped to a stop in front of my school. I got off and raced to our spot over by the construction site.

Yes! I exclaimed when my eyes fell on Saivon waiting on me. I was happy that Saivon beat me there because honestly my nerves were too bad to keep this in any longer.

"What's up best friend? Why your face look like that?" he greeted as soon as he saw me.

Saivon and I were in sync with each other so I knew that he would pick up on my strange behavior. "I just found out the worse news of my life," I glumly replied while tugging at my North Face coat. The hawk was out and although my insides burned like fire, my outer body was still cold.

"You okay? What happened?" he asked genuinely concerned.

"I don't know if I'll ever be able to recover from this," I responded doubtfully while shaking my head "This is too much for my young heart to handle.."

"What happened?" he stressed for the second time.

"I'mma tell you, but you have to promise me that this is gonna stay between us," I said with all seriousness. "I can't let anyone find out about this until I figure out what to do next."

"When do I ever run my mouth?" he asked, offended.

"Never!" I admitted while locking eyes with him. "But this is serious."

"Aight then, so tell me!"

There was no easy way to come out and say this, so I blurted it out. "Today I found out who killed my mother," I revealed while studying his expression for a reaction.

"But you already knew that," he replied unfazed and that threw me off guard. I expected him to upset like I was but instead I got a shoulder shrug, something that he knew I hated.

"No you don't understand," I was persistent to get a reaction out of him and until I got the shock I was looking for I was gonna continue to bait him in. "All this time, we were wrong about who killed my mother. It's not the psyhco lady that we thought it was."

Saivon still wasn't catching on and it frustrated me. "Ok," he said sounding confused. "So then who was it?"

"My father...Maycen," I conceded as I finally uncovered

the truth. "Promise me that you won't say anything to Seven. I don't want him to know," I beseeched as I expressed my wishes.

"Nah. That ain't sitting too good with me. I'm not sure that I can do that," Saivon objected and I should have known that he would because at the end of the day his loyalty was with Seven.

"But you just swore that you wouldn't tell!" I shrieked. "That's going against everything that you just said."

"I know, but I didn't think that it would be this serious," he reasoned. "You know that I can't keep nothing like this away from that man. He would kill me."

"Sai, I need you to not think about yourself right now and consider what I'm saying. I just found out that the man that created me had something to do with the death of my mother. The woman who's ground that I worship. That's too much for even the toughest person to bear. All I need from you right now is to lend a listening ear and help me find a leg to stand on. Is that too much to ask? Can you just be unselfish for a minute and be a friend?"

"Yo, you tripping. Like for real, what you call me out here for if you not gonna do nothing about it?" he scoffed. "You can't let your father get away with that Charli. On God you can't! He murdered your mother in cold blood! Don't you want him to pay for what he did?"

"I do!" I paused. "And he is!" I was reserved for a minute. I was uncertain if what I was about to say next came from me being high off of my emotions or if it the God's honest truth. Either way, I knew at this very exact moment, the hatred in my heart made me believe that the words that I spoke were real. "I just want to be the one to kill himself."

Saivon's eyes widened. Never had he heard me sound so... so evil before. It was if the devil himself came over me and forced me to carry out his dirty deed. "Charli you a good girl, you ain't no killer! You don't even know the first thing about shooting a gun," he tried to convince me, but I wasn't listening.

"That's what I have you for. To teach me."

"How you expect for me to teach you something that I barely even know? I don't know how to shoot a gun like that."

"Well I guess that we're gonna learn together because on my dead momma, I'mma get my revenge on my father!"

For the first time since that conversation in our class, I knew how Saivon felt when he said that he would do anything for his Momma. Maycen Alexander Drew was on borrowed time and he was gonna have to see me soon for what he did to my angel. And when he did... I was gonna make him suffer a very painful death!

To Be Continued...

Be on the lookout for The Wright

Life's Hottest Up-and-coming

Authoress

A'me Reigns

Coming October 2018

For more information visit

www.thewrightlifepresents.com

Facebook: The Wright Life Presents Authoress

Hershe Wrights

Instagram: TheWright_Life

www.ingramcontent.com/pod-product-compliance
Lightning Source LLC
Chambersburg PA
CBHW060807030726
47503CB00002B/368